BLOODLINE

BLOODLINE

KATY MORAN

CANDLEWICK PRESS

Copyright © 2008 by Katy Moran

First U.S. edition 2009

Library of Congress Cataloging-in-Publication Data

Moran, Katy (Katy Jane).
Bloodline / Katy Moran. — 1st U.S. ed.
p. cm.
Summary: When traveling through early seventh-century Britain trying to stop an impending war, Essa, who bears the blood of native British tribes and of the invading Anglish, discovers that his mother is alive and he, himself, is a prince of the northern kingdom, but he has loyalties and loved ones in the south to whom he is compelled to return.
ISBN 978-0-7636-4083-5
[1. Adventure and adventurers — Fiction. 2. War — Fiction. 3. Identity — Fiction. 4. Great Britain — History — Anglo-Saxon period, 449–1066 — Fiction.] I. Title.
PZ7.M788196Blo 2009
[Fic] — dc22   2008021413

2 4 6 8 10 9 7 5 3 1

Printed in the United States of America

This book was typeset in Giovanni.

Candlewick Press
99 Dover Street
Somerville, Massachusetts 02144

visit us at www.candlewick.com

*This book is dedicated to
Andy and Julie Moran, for finding the brooch;
David Hill, Suzannah Dunn, and Ron Berry, for being
excellent teachers; Steph Hinde, for coming with me
to the British Museum; and Jude Evans and
Will Llewellyn, for the rest.*

And now my spirit twists
out of my breast,
my spirit
out in the waterways,
over the whale's path
it soars widely
through all the corners of the world —
it comes back to me
eager and unsated

From "The Seafarer," an Anglo-Saxon
poem translated by Sean Miller

Essa's Britain c. AD 630

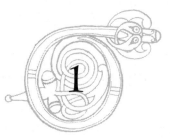

*Middle Anglia, eastern Britain,
late summer, AD 631*

Tbe Sun rose above the flatlands, spreading a
bloody glow across the mere. Shafts of brilliance
swept into the hall through a side door left ajar
the previous night. A streak of pale light swung across the
floorboards to touch the head of a sleeping boy with hair
like a lick of fire in the dark. His name was Essa, he was
nine summers old, and when he opened his eyes, the first
thing he saw was the red dawn waiting.

Red sky in the morning, Essa thought. *If Da wants to ride
out today, we'll get wet.* And ride out they would, he was sure.
Essa sometimes wished they might stay in a place long
enough for him to make friends, but they never did.

He stretched out an arm, working it free of the blue blanket drawn too close around his neck and chin. The blanket
had been given to them in exchange for a song only a few
days before.

"And not a moment too soon." Cai had held up their old

rug so that Essa could see sunlight streaming through the holes. Cai had quick black eyes, like the pieces of obsidian he'd once sold to the High King in Northumbria. He was dark and light-boned like a bird. Nobody could tell what he was thinking, not even his son, who knew him better than anyone.

Essa sat up, shrugging the blanket away from his shoulders. Next to him a fat man lay on his back, snoring gently. On his other side a small child was curled up next to her mother. The entire hall was filled with sleeping people. Cai preferred to sleep outside with their horse, Melyor, when the weather was warm enough, choosing the mare's company over the closeness of strangers. This village was a rich place with two grassy, hollow mounds behind the weaving hall, where big clay jars of barley and wheat were stored in the earthy coolness. They had a stable full of horses too, although Essa had noticed last night that two were old wrecks and one was lame. Maybe Cai was in the stable.

He squinted in the half-light at a small bundle lying at his feet, unwound himself from the blanket, and snatched the tooled leather bag to his chest. Cai must have been very drunk last night. They had so few things that everything was guarded like a dragon's hoard, especially this. Without it they'd starve, because Cai was British and proud. He was of the Iceni, whose great queen Boudicca had almost driven the Romans back into the sea, long ago. Cai used to say that more generations had come and gone since the high days of the Iceni than Essa could count on the fingers and thumbs of both his hands, and if anyone knew, Cai did, for he was a song man and a keeper of the past. But this was an Anglish village, and Essa knew Cai would never beg a meal from these people, who knew nothing of Christ the Redeemer and sang of their grand-fathers crossing the eastern water in long ships with sea serpents snarling at the prows.

The night before last, Essa and Cai had been given a linen package containing dried yellow saffron and a lump of amber that had delighted Essa because it looked like the head of a dog: a rich haul. He loosened the drawstring and dug his fingers inside the bag, reassured by the smoothness of the amber in his hand. The linen packet of saffron heads was there too, rustling against his fingertips. He buckled his belt around his waist, pushed the bag inside his tunic, and ran to the door, leaping over sleeping bodies. He'd managed to get a place near the fire, and there were a lot of people between the hearth and the nearest door.

The yard was quiet and peaceful in the dawn light. Opposite the hall, a row of scythes lay against the barn wall under the low, thatched roof. He ran for the stables, where the air was quiet and thick with the warm, sweet smell of horses. When he got to the stall where he'd left Melyor the night before, Cai was not there, and neither was the horse. It was always Essa's job to bed her down whenever they arrived at a new place, whether it was a clearing in a wood or the golden-banded hall of a king. For the first time since waking, he was afraid. Had he not bolted the stable door behind him? He should have left her tethered. Without Melyor, they would be beggars. Men of song did not travel on foot. He would have to catch Melyor and bring her in quick before anyone noticed she had got out. Cai was already angry with him, and it would do no good to remind Cai of his own mistake in leaving the tooled leather bag lying around for anyone to take.

The argument had started in a hall across the border, in the kingdom of Mercia, when Cai sent a messenger to summon Essa away from a game of Fox and Geese.

"Tell him I'll come soon." Essa watched his opponent move a goose piece across the board. He was a tall, wiry boy with stooping shoulders, and he was about to get beaten. Two more moves and Essa would be the owner of a knife with a bone handle.

"He says come now."

"Tell him to be patient," Essa said, earning a burst of laughter from his opponent and the small gathering of onlookers. He watched the board, pretending to think over his next move, although he knew exactly what he was going to do: in two moves, the game would be his. He was the fox and he had captured nearly all the geese. How would it be to slink like a real fox through the night, he wondered. Cupping the small wooden figure in his hand, he could almost feel the thrill of running slick and silent in the darkness, and the thirst for hot blood.

Cai could wait. Anyway, these Mercians would probably

give him another drink. He had played well the night before. The women cried when he sang of the dying bear king who was taken away in a boat by nine maidens, leaving his warriors asleep in a green cave. They could not understand a word Cai was singing, of course, but the notes he reached were so mournful and beautiful and his lyre sang so sweetly that they cried anyway. Maybe they'd be asked back to sing at a feast, and then they would get a garnet brooch, or a barrel of Frankish wine, or some green glass bottles. The messenger left, and after a short while Cai himself arrived, riding Melyor across the courtyard.

"Come up." Cai sat as still as a hawk, wrapped in his worn cloak with the ragged bear pelt around his shoulders. The long sword hung from the saddle in a scabbard that glittered with silver dragon-snakes artfully inlaid into the oiled leather. The Silver Serpent, she was called. Essa had never seen Cai use her, nor had he ever seen him go anywhere without her. She would have fetched a good price, too.

"Hadn't you better go?" said the boy who was losing. He had narrow green eyes the color of ivy leaves. For someone who looked clever, he was really bad at Fox and Geese.

Essa grinned. "You just don't want to lose your knife." He turned to Cai and spoke in British. "I've nearly beaten him, the fool."

Cai dismounted in a dark swirl of bear pelt and pulled Essa sharply to his feet, so that he dropped the little wooden goose pieces he'd captured. His opponent and the onlookers scattered in all directions, the wooden figures bounced off across the dusty courtyard, and the bone-handled knife was gone forever.

"You come when I call you," Cai said. "Get up in the saddle."

"I'm not a dog," said Essa. "Why don't you just whistle at me and be done with it? You've ruined everything. I nearly won a knife."

"I do not care. Get up." Cai's face was impassive and his eyes shone like dark water, seamy around the edges from staring too long into the sun. There was no sense in arguing. Essa shoved past him and swung himself up into the saddle.

Essa expressed his disdain with silence. Cai would not usually have suffered this childishness, but he was brooding on something, and their routine was so deeply ingrained that they were able to ride across open marshland, while the sun moved over their heads, without saying a word. Essa sat before his father in the saddle; usually, Essa practiced playing the lyre while they rode, but this time the beautiful cherrywood instrument remained folded in its leather bag. He would not give Cai the satisfaction of pointing out his mistakes. At any rate, it was a fast ride with plumes of marsh water spraying up around their legs and Melyor's mane flying in Essa's face. Together, Cai and Melyor seemed to sense where the ground was true; although sometimes Melyor was up to her fetlocks, they never got stuck. Cai's thin brown hands held the reins with loose ease, but Essa could feel the muscles taut in his arms. The wind rushing past his face made the blood surge at his heart, and it felt as if they were no longer tied to the earth as a man and a boy but flying like the curlews circling above.

The silence persisted until they dismounted at the gates of a hall across the marshes from the Mercian fort. They were now in Middle Anglia—a land of marsh and wild white horses and sweeping skies, harried without mercy by Mercian cattle raiders. The hall was heavily fortified, surrounded by high earthen walls. On the horizon, Essa could see another such wall, huge and stretching across the rim of the marsh.

"Look," Cai said. "That wall's the East Anglian border; beyond that lie the marches of the Wolf Folk. The Wolves have all East Anglia in their power, and they rule parts of Mid Anglia too, like this place. They fight with Mercia for the rest of it, and more men have given their lives in that cause than there are birds in the sky." Cai glanced up at the great village walls, shaking his head. "These people are the Wixna tribe. Years ago, before you were born, Redwald the Wolf King sent one of his nieces out here to marry the Wixnan chief, with a gold ring for him to wear so that he'd always be loyal to East Anglia and not lend his sword to the Mercians instead. So they're bound to the Wolf Folk now, like it or not."

Cai paused, and Essa knew he was waiting for a question. Essa, son of no tribe, child of no kingdom, was usually fascinated by the knotted, gory pattern of loyalty and betrayal linking the different realms of Britain. He loved bloody tales of girls sent to marry their fathers' worst enemies, and he especially loved songs of men bound by gold rings to their lords, promising to fight till death took them.

But we're bound to no man, Cai would say. *And you must not forget that's the best of all. Because being bound by a ring is the same as being shackled by an iron chain. They're drunk on the power of gold, these Anglish people; fire of the sea, they call it, and it makes them think of the sunlight burning on the waves when they came here in their ships. It turns their minds, sends them mad. And if they give you a ring of gold, you're as good as a slave. Better you follow the hawk's path, free under the sky.*

Suddenly, Essa wanted to ask a stream of questions about the Wixna and the battles they fought, and if there were British people in their village too, or just Anglish. In some villages there were people like Cai, dark and slight, who had stayed when the Anglish and the Saxons and the Jutes came from across the sea, and taught them how to grow barley and where the deer ran. But in other places, the only British were just ghosts of the long dead.

Yet it was Cai's fault Essa had lost the knife, so he kept quiet, staring at the ground instead.

Cai glanced at him, his dark eyes narrowing with laughter. "All right. Sulk, then. But you should know this; you should know how things work. They call King Penda the Mad Dog of Mercia. He wants to be High King over all Britain, and he won't stop till he is or till he's dead. So always he presses east, trying to snatch land off the Wolf Folk and get not only Mid Anglia but all East Anglia for himself. Then he'd have more land than any other king in Britain, and he'd be more powerful than the High King in Northumbria. The Wixna are stuck in the middle, right between Penda and the Wolf Folk, more fool them." Cai banged on the gate with the hilt of his sword.

Essa shrugged, trying to look as if he were not interested. If he'd gotten that knife, he would have been able to skin a hare all by himself. He could have carved faces into sticks. Or dug for worms. But he could not help thinking the Wixna had gotten the worst end of the bargain — everyone knew that Mercia was the most powerful kingdom in the whole of Britain after Northumbria, where the palace of the High King sat, windblown on the wild moors. And now the Wixna had Mercia as their enemy. It could not have been much fun for Redwald's niece either, getting sent to live in the middle of a bog. What a place. He wanted to ask his father what they were doing here, but he didn't.

"Suit yourself," said Cai, and struck the gate again.

A woman with a flaming torch came out to meet them. Essa saw her first in shadow: a tall, slender figure wrapped in a cloak against the night air. She had come out to the gate followed by a huge female hunting dog fat with unborn pups.

"We're always pleased to see a scop," she said, glancing at the cherrywood lyre in Cai's hands. "Who are you?"

Cai stepped forward into the torchlight. "Hild," he said.

The woman cried out, and threw her arms around him, laughing. "Oh, Cai! Oh, it's been such a long time. I can't—

And who is this?" Another expression flickered across her face as she looked down at Essa—what was it? He could not tell. Surprise? Fear? Maybe both. But why would anyone be afraid of him? The woman looked across at Cai questioningly. "Is it—?"

"My son, Aesc," said Cai.

The woman smiled down at him. "Ah, a little ash tree, are you? That's not a British name. Oh, Cai, I can't believe it's been this long since I've seen you."

"His mother was one of your people—Anglish. Elfgift gave him the name before she died, God rest her soul. I call him Essa."

The woman flinched, as if Cai had struck her face, and Essa looked up at his father in surprise. "*Tasik,*" he said, speaking in British, "why do you talk of my mother to this woman, when you never mention her name to me?"

Cai ignored him, and the woman smiled brightly, saying, "I am pleased to meet you, Essa. Well, do you both come in out of this fearful mist." She stood back, allowing them through the gateway. Essa decided he liked her. Her hair was coming undone from its braid and hanging loose in curly strands around her face. But he did not reply to her: he was still too annoyed with Cai to be polite. Essa thirsted for talk of his mother, but hers was the one tale Cai would not tell. Essa knew only her name, Elfgift, and that she was called elf-shining: fairer than any earthly woman. And that she was dead. So why was Cai speaking of her now, to this stranger?

"I was sorry to hear your husband died," said Cai, and

another look passed between them both that Essa did not understand. Cai did not really look sorry, and she did not really look sad.

"Yes," said Hild. "Fighting the Mercians, last year. So I'm the chief here now."

She must be the niece of King Redwald, then. Essa squinted at Hild in the wobbling torchlight. She looked just like a normal person (well, a normal Anglish one, anyway): tall and bright-haired with a scattering of freckles across her cheekbones and nose, wearing a plain robe hitched up into her belt. In the shadowy gloom, he could just make out the bottom hem was dark with ash, as though she had been lifting pots out of the fire.

Cai had told him stories about the British kings and queens of the west, with their black hair oiled into shining snakes, the swirling blue clan tattoos on their faces and the gold torcs around their necks: twisted ropes of shining metal. That was how a royal person should look. But these Anglish were different. Hild was chief of a whole village, yet she came to open the gate herself, and her robe was dusty.

"I hope you look to your safety, then," said Cai. He tightened his grip on Essa's shoulder and spoke in British. "You had better be more gracious to my foster sister than you have been to me. Take Melyor to the stable and stay there with her until you recall your manners."

Foster sister? So King Redwald's niece, the girl that had been sent out here to marry the Wixnan chief, was Cai's foster sister?

The words were out before Essa could swallow them. *"I hate you."*

He turned around to give Cai the look that said, *I didn't mean it*, but Cai was already walking across the yard with Hild.

Essa stayed behind in the stable for as long as he could, cleaning the fine bronze stirrups that his father had won by beating a braggart in a horse race. Why did Cai never tell him anything about his past life? Essa knew his father had lived with a foster family by the sea, the only child of Iceni nobles who'd thrown in their lot with King Redwald once they'd seen how the power of the Anglish settlers was rising. They had both died when Cai was young, leaving him to the care of Redwald's court.

That was why Cai looked different from other pure-blooded Britons—he had no swirling blue clan tattoos on his face to tell the story of his people. Yet he told Essa they had the blood of kings and queens in their veins: of how the Iceni had once been the most powerful tribe in Britain.

But that was all generations ago. The Iceni ruled the east coast no more, and Cai had never mentioned a foster sister before. That was not really surprising, since he hardly talked about his childhood, only of long-dead queens and forgotten heroes.

Essa polished ferociously at the stirrups with a scrap of thin, floppy leather until they glowed like firebrands and he was so hungry that he felt sick, and so cold in his damp clothes that his teeth started to chatter. Then he hung the

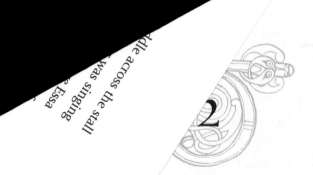

bridle on a nail in the wall, laid the saddle across the stall door, and went into the hall where his father was singing by the fire, the lyre propped in his lap. A woman gave Essa a bowl of chicken stewed with white grapes, and a wedge of bread. He took his food and went to sit at his father's feet. Sometimes he sang with Cai, but on this night he just sat and listened until he fell asleep.

And in the long years afterward, Essa often wished he had at least said good night, and that the last words he'd spoken to Cai had not been *I hate you*.

Alone with the Wixna

ESSA stood in the stable. It was all gone: bridle, stirrups, even the carefully coiled leading rein and the heavy brown rug that went underneath the saddle on Melyor's back. Perhaps somebody had moved it all in the night. He knew nobody had. It was taboo. Nobody would touch Melyor without asking. It was the leather bag resting safe inside his tunic that told the truth. No matter how drunk, Cai was never careless. He was gone.

Essa closed his eyes. When he opened them, Melyor would be tugging hay from the old fishing net nailed to the wall. She would turn her great roan head and nibble gently at his fingers when he held out his hand. He stood for a moment in darkness, breathing quickly.

They'll be somewhere. He opened his eyes. *Think on it. The trough is dry now. He's taken her to the pond for a drink. They'll be back any moment.* He stared at the trough. There was something inside it: a long dark shape. Cai's sword lay in the bottom, carefully placed right in the middle. The Silver Serpent, asleep in the dark. He could see the silver dragon-snakes glittering against the black scabbard, the thick leather peace bands binding the scabbard to the hilt, so that the blade could not be drawn in drunkenness or anger. The Silver Serpent had been given to Cai by a great king in exchange for a service, or so the tale went. Some folk believed it, others not.

Cai never rode hard in the morning. If Essa ran fast he might catch them. But when he reached the gate, it was bolted shut.

"What are you doing, thief?"

Essa turned. Two boys stood watching. Both were bigger than him; one had milk-white hair, the other was darker, his face spattered with brown freckles.

"Where'd you steal that from, then?"

Essa looked down at the sword in his hands. "It's mine — I mean, it's my father's." He struggled to form the Anglish words — they fell from his mouth like gobbets of thick spittle.

"Listen, Red, he can't hardly speak!" said the white-haired boy. They both laughed.

Red reached out, snatched the sword, and held it high up above Essa's head. Did these marsh villagers really think he was of a mind to play games? He punched Red as hard as he could in the stomach. Red coughed and choked, and his fist cracked into Essa's face. Dull pain burst across his right cheekbone, and he went down, grazing his elbows on the dusty ground.

"Easy!" said the white-haired boy. "He's just a little brat."

Essa felt a flash of annoyance—they were a year older than him at the most.

"He comes in here, thieving stuff off us, starting fights—"

"*You* started it!" Essa scrambled to his feet. "She's *my* sword! Give her back."

"Oh, save it for someone who cares." Red grabbed Essa's arm and dragged him toward the hall. The white-haired boy followed, telling Red to leave him be: he was just a traveler's brat, not worth it.

Maybe Cai was inside. He would be angry with Essa for breaking the taboo and fighting in a village where they were guests, but at least he would be there. Essa pulled away from Red's grasp, waiting for Cai to come toward him, saying, "What's this, little cub? Tell me you have not been waging war on the Wixna boys."

He saw nothing but a jumble of unfamiliar faces.

Women were rolling up blankets and sheepskins from the floor and taking them outside to air in the yard. A group of men carrying weeding baskets pushed by on their way out to the fields: strange, exotic creatures with long bright hair and freckled skin. A woman sat on one of the benches, combing out the silvery pale braids of a twisting, wriggling girl who stood wedged between her legs.

"You'll get lice if you don't watch out, Lark."

"I don't care. I like lice." The girl grinned at Essa, her eyes slanted with mischief, as if they were sharing a secret. For a moment, he felt as if she were on his side, somehow. But then her mother rapped her on the top of the head with the comb, and she looked away, saying, "Ma, I'm just going to cut it all off one day. I mean it!"

Staring desperately around the hall for his father, Essa's eyes were drawn to an old man sitting by the fire, wrapped in a cloak. Essa had never seen anyone so ancient. Time had drained the brightness from the man: his long hair and beard were the color of snow in the western mountains, and the skin sagged from his cheekbones as though he were melting. He was sharpening a knife against a whetstone resting in his lap. It was a strange way to hone a knife, and Essa stared, drawn in, until he saw that the old man had only one arm. But then he looked up, his gaze lingering on Essa's face in a way that made him feel as though his thoughts, his secrets, and his dreams had been laid bare. It felt as if his outer self had been stripped away, like skin torn from flesh by a whip, and that the man knew everything about him.

Essa looked away, sucking in a deep, wounded breath, wondering if he had just been put under a curse, and the old man had sent the elvish kind to plague his every step. *Where is Cai?* Essa did not want to stay in this place anymore, but Cai was nowhere to be seen.

Essa turned to Red, hissing, "Give me back my sword."

Red smirked. "How does it work? Does your father leave you to root out the good stuff so he can come back in a few days and steal it all? Well, you came to the wrong village this time! Hild! Hild!"

"It's not true, she's my sword and my father hasn't left me here. He hasn't!" Even as he spoke, Essa knew Cai had gone. He was alone.

"Red, what's this fuss?" Hild came toward them, holding a copper basin filled with oats and etched with round whorls. She had clear, wide gray eyes, and Essa wanted to tell her everything. She turned to Red's white-haired friend. "Cole? What have you been doing?"

"We caught him trying to run away with this." Red butted in, holding up the sword by the shoulder strap. "He's thieved it."

"Oh, use your head!" said the girl who was having her hair combed. "When've *you* ever seen a sword as fine as that, Red? He might've thieved it, but not from here."

Red flushed, saying, "Stow your gab, Lark—what do you know?"

Hild set her bowl carefully on the long table that ran down one whole side of the hall, striking a soft, low note of copper against old wood. Essa tried to concentrate on the carved antler comb as it swept through Lark's hair. Her mother was staring at him too, combing the same hank of silvery pale hair again and again. His eyes would not stop burning. Ragged black wings of panic beat inside his chest.

"We found him trying to get out of the gate," said Cole. "As if he could open it!"

"Neither could you!" said the girl.

"Shut your mouth, Lark!"

"You shut yours."

Hild ignored them both. "Have you seen your father this morning, Essa?"

He shook his head, unable to speak in his own tongue or any other. Everyone was watching him.

"Go on, take it." Essa reached inside his tunic for the packet of saffron heads and the knot of amber. He threw them on the floor at Hild's feet. The linen packet burst, and dark orange saffron stalks bounced on the floorboards. "That's your payment, and when you've spent it then you can do what you like with me. That's what he meant."

Hild took a step closer. She was smiling, but her eyes looked sad. "I'm sorry, Essa. I hardly know how to tell you this. Cai must have thought it would be easier for you not to say good-bye."

"What do you mean?" Essa spat out the words. He could feel tears snaking down his face like drops of molten iron. "He wouldn't just leave me here."

"I'm sorry, Essa, but he's gone." She reached out and put her hand on his arm.

"Get off me!" He snatched himself away from her and ran out of the hall back to the gate. He clawed at the heavy iron bolt with both hands, but it would not move. He called out, hoping Cai was still within hearing distance. Cai had ears like a dog: he could hear a mouse sneezing. But Essa knew Cai would not hear him this time. He was gone. Blinded by tears, Essa heaved at the bolt, but he might as well have tried pulling the great ash tree in the courtyard up by the roots.

He felt someone put their hands on his shoulders, gently pulling him away from the gate, and he heard Hild behind him, saying, "No, Essa. This won't do, will it?" He tried to wrench out of her grasp, but she steered him toward the big ash tree and made him sit with her at its roots. He was glad to sit, really, because his legs had lost all their strength and his fingers were shaking like the little leaves at the top of the tree, stirred by the wind. A fat raindrop landed on the hard-packed earth at his feet; another hit his arm. Cai would be getting wet, out there in the marsh.

She took off her shawl and wrapped it around his shoulders. "Listen to me, Essa. I don't know how much Cai's told you about his life, but there was a time when every king in Britain would have paid his own weight in gold for your father's advice — well, for the secrets he'd sell them, at any rate. But the king of East Anglia, old Redwald's nephew, he's dead, he's been murdered, and Cai was loyal to that family before anyone else. He heard it across the border, when you were in Mercia."

"I don't see what that's got to do with me," Essa said.

Hild shrugged. "The Mercians know we're weak now that the king's dead, and they want to come across the border and try to grab as much of our land as they can. Your father has gone riding to the coast, to the king's hall, to raise the alarm. That's why you're going to stay here, with me."

"But when's he coming back?" said Essa, hope leaping in his chest. "Will he come back when he's told them?"

"I don't know," said Hild. "I don't think so. Look, Essa.

It's just how it works: until the Wolf Folk choose another king, we're wide open to attack from Mercia. And picking a king isn't easy. I don't think Cai will be able to come back for a long while. Now, do you come inside and we'll get you something to eat. You must be hungry."

Essa stared across the courtyard at the hall. He could hear voices, people talking inside, and someone laughed. If he went in there, it would be final. He'd belong to them, and Cai would never return.

"I'm staying out here." He expected her to be angry. Cai had no patience with this sort of thing—he just expected his word to be followed. But Hild did not look angry. She got up, flicking her heavy braid over her shoulder, briskly brushing the dust off her skirt.

"Well enough," she said. "But if you won't come into the hall, I've a job for you. Come."

For a moment, Essa considered staying where he was, sitting under the tree whose name he bore: Aesc, an ash tree, buffeted by the wind, rooted to one spot forever. But Hild was already making her way across the courtyard toward the stables. He scrambled to his feet and followed her, running to catch up. The hall crouched on the other side of the yard, waiting to swallow him up into a new life. There was someone watching him from one of the side doors—the white-haired girl, Lark. She lifted her fingers in a little wave and disappeared suddenly, as if someone had just whisked her away from the door.

Feeling even more alone, he followed Hild into the

stables, past the empty stall where he had taken Melyor the night before. Hild was in the next stall, crouching on the floor.

"Come you in and look," she said.

He went in, and she smiled up at him. "See, Meadowsweet has had her pups." It was the hunting hound who had come with Hild to the gate the night before. Hild stroked Meadowsweet's brindled gray ears as she lay on her side, eyes half closed, suckling three writhing dog cubs: one brindled gray like its mother, the other two black as charcoal. He crouched down beside Hild and held out his hand for Meadowsweet to sniff. She showed her teeth and he drew back, but Hild said, "No, Meadowsweet, it's all right, it's Essa," and scratched the dog between her ears. This time, Meadowsweet licked his fingers, her tongue hot and damp against his skin.

"Now, do you stay here and watch them for me," said Hild. "I know they'll be safe then. One of them has already died, poor thing, and she's afraid."

Essa nodded, feeling tears prickle at his eyes again. Meadowsweet pushed her bony head against his hand as he stroked her, as if she knew his sadness and understood.

Three years later:
The rising of the Wixna bees

E SSA climbed up into the pear tree where the bees lived and sat cradled in its branches, breathing in wood smoke and the hot, dry smells of lavender and thyme rising from the herb garden. Someone was cooking in the hall, too — eel stew again, by the stink of it. Essa was not fond of eel, but there was little choice at this time of year, weeks before harvest. He could hear the others talking and laughing in the shade of the trees, and then Lark scrambled up beside him. They leaned comfortably together watching swallows looping in the sky above the hall.

It was Litha time, and the smoke from the solstice fire the Wixna had lit at the far end of the orchard drifted lazily on the air. It was the third time the flames of midsummer had licked up at the sky since Cai had left, and the silvery music of Essa's own language played only in his dreams. He thought and spoke like the Wixna now. He was becoming more Anglish with every season that passed, growing tall, his red hair curling around his shoulders. Only their eyes were clear and gray, green, or blue, like shards of colored glass, and Essa knew that his were dark like his father's.

Don't think about him.

"I hate midsummer," Lark said. "Everyone's so hungry, and they snap the head off you for nothing. I got wrong of Hild this morning just for breaking that old cracked cup. As if it matters!"

"It'll be the horse hunt soon," Essa said. "I'll race you."

"Maybe there'll be a horse hunt for you," Lark said. "I bet my knife with the black handle they won't let me go."

The old stallion had died last winter, so the men were going to race the wild horses of the flatlands. The Wixna knew the marsh; they understood where it was safe to ride and where bottomless pools awaited like doors to the underworld. Together, the men would bring back a strong young male and perhaps a new mare to break in. It would take days and days, and they would sit around fires at night, drinking and boasting and singing to scare away the marsh wights that waited for the unwary to miss their footing.

"It'll be a good ride," Essa said. "It's not fair you'll miss it."

"I might go anyhow," Lark replied. "I could follow you all. I don't want to stay here with the girls. All they talk about is their hair and when they'll get the curse." Peering down through the branches of the tree, they watched disdainfully as Red's little sister Helith played a clapping game with Freo, who was Lark's cousin.

Lulled by the soft murmuring of the bees, Essa dozed, leaning into Lark's warm body. He was tired from pulling up weeds in the barley field all day, and there was a warm smell of lavender about her that made him feel even sleepier.

Then, just as his eyes were closing, Essa felt a strange tugging in the pit of his belly, and a powerful sense of anger and fear swept through him.

What's this? Had he been dreaming? His eyes snapped open. The bees were no longer murmuring but buzzing ferociously.

"Red, don't!" Helith was saying.

"What?" Lark sat up, letting her bare feet dangle off the branch. "Ow! I've just been stung!"

Essa looked down. Red was leaning against the crab-apple tree, arm raised to throw another stone.

"Oh, do you stop, Red! We'll all be stung to bits!" cried Helith. Red made to throw the stone at her instead and, squealing like piglets, Helith and Freo jumped to their feet and ran to the other end of the orchard.

"Cole, stop him!" shouted Lark.

Cole shrugged. "Leave it, Red," he said. "There'll be a fuss if you raise up all the bees."

"You like that half-breed sitting up there with your sister, then?" Red said, and threw another stone.

The buzzing grew louder, and Essa said, "I might be a half-breed, but at least I'm not a fool." A flash of white-hot anger shot through him — he wanted to leap down from the tree and drive his fist into Red's sneering face. But he could not move. It was as if he were no longer in his own body, but part of the bee folk: scores of them all thinking with the same mind so that really they were one creature.

Go for him.

The bee folk rose up in a cloud. They hung there for a moment, a dark smear against the summer sky. No one spoke. Then, as if obeying a command, the bees drifted toward Red. He got up and started running, but the bees only followed him, as if he were on fire and they were the smoke. Helith and Freo went after him, shrieking with laughter. Lark climbed down from the tree and followed them.

Did I do that? Essa thought, heart hammering, then told himself not to be silly. It was Red's fault, throwing stones at a bees' nest.

Cole turned to Essa. "Now you've done it," he said. "Come on, we'd better go after them. I don't want my sister getting in a fight with Red."

"But I didn't do anything!"

"You don't normally lie; I know that," Cole said.

"I *didn't*!"

But Cole was already sprinting toward the yard, so Essa went after him, flooded with a strange, hot panic.

They found some of the older villagers slouching against the weaving-shed wall, flushed with the day's work out in the fields, sharing a cup of cider. A couple of the girls had spindles and were idly twiddling gray wool into threads. Most of them did not even deign to look up at Essa and Cole.

"If you're looking for my brother, he went into the smithy, chased by a gaggle of screaming girls and scores of bees," said Starling, smiling. She was merry and kind, and Essa often found it hard to believe she was Red's sister. Starling was pregnant. They said the baby would come before midsummer but it hadn't yet. She leaned back into the arms of Ariulf, who had put the child in her, and he rested both hands on the rounded lump of her belly.

"What did you do to the bees?" Ariulf took a swig of cider and passed the cup to one of the others. He was fifteen summers old and bright faced, and he wore the ring of the Wolf Folk on his finger. Essa longed to be like him.

"Nothing," Essa said.

"You know what bees are like, Uncle." Cole grabbed Essa's arm, hissing, "Come *on!*"

Inside the smithy, they found Red climbing up the woodpile after Helith and Freo, who were now weeping and laughing at the same time, and Lark swiping at his legs, yelling, "Leave them alone! It's not their fault you made yourself look like a chicken head!"

Essa slammed the door behind them, and Red, kicking Lark away, came barreling across the smithy toward him.

"You half-bred elvish dog son!" Red shouted, shoving Essa to the floor. "You think you're so sly, don't you, but I saw what you did!"

Breathless with the fall, Essa grabbed his legs and brought him crashing down, but Red just rolled over and drove his fist hard into Essa's face, so that the wet-iron taste of blood burst in his mouth.

"Let that teach you, half-breed," said Red, scrabbling to his feet.

Essa sprang up and shoved him so hard that Red went sprawling, missing the forge fire by a finger's width. Suddenly, all went quiet. Why was Red smiling? Someone grabbed the back of Essa's tunic and yanked him around.

It was Ariulf. "What do you think you are doing?" he shouted. He turned to the others. "Get outside! This is the smithy — it's not for you to tear about in." They fled, and Ariulf shook Essa's shoulder. "If you must fight with Red, do you stay away from the forge fire. Go and find him and make your peace. There's times I wonder if you even want to fit in here, Essa."

Essa glared up at him, hissing, "Why should I fit in? My father's going to come soon and take me away."

Ariulf shook his head. "You'd do better to forget all about your father," he said, and the sudden kindness in his voice made Essa even more angry and miserable, because he knew Ariulf really meant it.

He left, letting the big door swing shut behind him, and Essa sat down on the ground, heavy with sorrow. *Tasik*, he thought, *when are you coming back?* Only a few short months after Cai had left him here with the Wixna, word had come from the east that there was a new Wolf King—

Seobert the Christian—and Essa had been sure that Cai would come riding back on Melyor, play his lyre one night in the hall of the Wixna, and rise early the next morning, saying, *Come, little cub, it is time we were away.* But three years later, he still had not come.

Essa would never be one of the Wixna. How would it feel to be like Ariulf, wearing a gold ring for Hild and the Wolf Folk, sitting around the fire with the men and women, *belonging*? Maybe soon it would be Cole's and Red's turn to get gold rings from Hild, leaving Essa behind as a boy when they turned into men. What would he do then?

Essa felt that a wild, leaping fire burned within him, and he longed to ride tearing across the marshes to dampen its touch. The barn, the weaving hall, and the smithy crowded in on him, always the same. Nothing ever changed here. Everyone got older and that was all. One of the girls would have a baby, or someone would die, like Red, Helith, and Starling's mother had done that winter, with a great swelling throbbing on her neck. But the Wixna were happy to live and die in their fortress with the sky sweeping above, and the rich, dark fields, and the marshes glittering all around.

Essa was not like them; he would never be like them.

Tasik, he thought, *where are you?*

He was trapped here, as though he were rolled up in a sheepskin, stuffed into some forgotten corner of the barn, and no matter how loud he shouted to be let free, no one would come.

I could leave this place. Essa pushed the thought away. What would he do, out in the wide wilderness by himself, away from the brightness of the hall? And what if Cai came back, and he was not here?

He would just have to wait. There was no other choice.

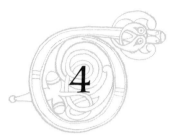

Two days later:
A killing in Wixna-land

ESSA lay on his belly in the grass, the sun warm on his bare back as he watched Lark run down the meadow with her bow bouncing against her shoulders.

He had been forbidden to go on the horse hunt.

Cole and Red had ridden out that morning alongside Ariulf, and they would come back laden with boastful stories and glory while Essa stayed behind with the women and children.

"Is it because of what happened with the bees?" Essa had asked Hild the night before. "I told you it wasn't my fault!"

Hild had sighed, shaking her head. "I'm sorry, but really, my honey, you're too young to go riding out in the marshes, and I've a misgiving about it." She shivered, pulling the cloak tighter around her shoulders, even though it was a warm evening. "You don't mind it, do you, dear heart?"

"No!" Essa said. "But I know it'll take them twice as long

without me, that's all. They'll be sorry you didn't let me."
And he stalked off across the yard to the stables. Essa had
spent the first nine years of his life in the saddle, and he
often felt more at home out here with the horse folk than
he did in the hall. The horses sensed his coming, and they
all stepped forward in their stalls so they could nose his
face with their soft, warm muzzles. Moving from one to
another, he blew down his nose into their nostrils, just as
Cai had taught him long ago, and he felt their warm breath
on his face.

Tomorrow you'll have a gallop in the marshlands, he thought,
and a new herd leader will come from there to put foals in you.
And the mares tossed their heads and put back their ears as
if they'd heard what he had been thinking.

Kept behind in the village, Essa was meant to be in the
yard, throwing his spear at a sack of hay hanging outside the
smithy. Hild would not even let him go beyond the village
walls to pull up weeds in the barley field. Lark should have
been in the weaving shed — everyone's clothes seemed to
have worn through at once, and there was only a scrap of
linen left in the great lavender-scented wooden chest in the
hall. Usually the Wixna girls practiced spear throwing and
swordplay with the boys, but not when there were clothes
to be made.

A woman can die with a spear in her belly just as easily as a
man, Hild would say. *So there's no reason you girls should not*
know how to defend yourselves.

But the sky was wide and blue; it was the wrong sort of

day for throwing spears at sacks, and it was the wrong sort of day for being shut inside with the women and the looms. So when Hild was in the orchard feeding the pigs and talking to the bees, Essa whistled for his dog, Fenrir, and ran with Lark out of the village gate.

It was good being out here, with Fenrir lying by his side, guarding the two ducks Essa had shot, but he could not shake an uneasy sense that something out of the ordinary was going to happen. The feeling had been with him all day. Did he feel guilty for disobeying Hild? he asked himself. No — in a way, it was her fault he'd sneaked out of the village. Had she let him go with the men, he would not have needed to disobey anyone. There would be trouble when he got back, but that was hardly out of the ordinary.

So what was the cause of this unease, this creeping feeling that spread across his shoulders and down his spine, chilling his skin, even under the midday sun? What did it remind him of?

It's like being watched, he thought. *It's like when you think you're alone, and suddenly you feel it in the back of your neck — and when you look up, someone's watching you.*

He told himself not to be silly; there was no one in the meadow but him and Lark. He watched as she reached the far end of the meadow, white-blond hair flying out behind her as she ran. When she got to the coppice, she stopped and turned around, pacing out thirty long steps. Lark was a good archer — even Ariulf grudgingly admitted she was better than him — but it was a long shot.

The jay had no idea what was coming, perched in the green shade of the beech leaves. Beside him, Essa felt Fenrir tense, her hard body quivering with excitement. He dug his fingers into the thick, brindled fur under her ears, watching Lark fit an arrow to her bow.

Calm, girl, calm. He could feel Fenrir's need to run, to chase; she had seen the girl with the flying claw that plucked birds from the sky; she knew there would soon be a trail to follow. The jay's blue tail feathers flashed, jewel-like, and it darted from its perch, wings spread, rising, rising. Essa closed his eyes, and for a breath he was the jay, or the jay was him, and he saw the dry meadow dropping far below. He felt the thrill as wings spread, catching a warm shelf of air that rose and rose.

It was as if his spirit had somehow slipped the ties holding it close to his body and, wandering, had briefly occupied the jay.

Essa saw what the jay saw: the meadow a golden-green blur far below, the sheep and cattle grazing Long Acre, the marshes spreading out to the east. He saw the mere, a flat shining coin of water. Then the coppice, and something else: a dark, crouching shape, down beneath the feathery green canopy of beech leaves. It was a man, and he was hiding.

A stranger.

In a breath, Essa was back in his own body, rigid with fear.

What just happened? he thought. *It's just like with the bees.* Suddenly, Cai was at the front of his mind again, his black

34

eyes mocking but full of knowledge, and Essa wished he were there to explain.

At that moment, Essa heard Lark suck in a breath, the soft twang of the bowstring relaxing, her arrow hissing through the air. Fenrir let out a whine, hungry for the chase. Essa watched the arrow shoot up, a slender claw, dark against the blue sky, and then it was gone, out of sight. The jay banked and wheeled back toward the coppice, seeking shelter among the trees. Lark's arrow struck, plucking the bird from its sky path. For a moment, Essa felt a flash of darkness, of nothing, and he knew what it was like to be a jay, free under the sky, and then dead.

Lark was running back toward the trees.

The dark figure crouching among the beeches sprang into Essa's mind, and in that instant, he knew that his spirit really had left his body, flown with the jay, and shown him a stranger hiding in the coppice. "No!" Essa yelled. "Lark, come back!" With Fenrir at his side, he broke into a sprint, still shouting at Lark to stop. But she did not seem to hear, and in a moment, she had melted away into the trees.

Fenrir was howling now, sensing a chase, and Essa crashed through the whip-thin beech saplings, hardly feeling it when they lashed his skin. "Lark!" he shouted. "I think there's someone —"

Then, there she was, running toward him, screaming, "Essa, there's a —"

And someone grabbed him from behind, squeezing the breath from his throat. Choking, wild with fright, Essa looked down—he could see a man's arm around his neck, thickly muscled, grained with coarse brown hairs, freckled by the sun. He heard Fenrir's frenzied barking and wished there was something he could do to ease her fear.

Essa snatched the dagger from his belt and plunged it backward, hard into the soft belly of the man holding him. There was a gasping, bubbling noise, and Essa's sight darkened as the man's grip tightened around his neck. He could still hear Lark screaming and wanted to tell her to run, but he could not breathe. He felt a hand grab his, hot and slippery with blood, trying to wrest the knife from his grasp. Without thinking, Essa tightened his grip on the handle and plunged the knife backward again. This time, he was dragged over as the man stumbled and fell, and Essa landed on his body.

Shouting out in horror, Essa scrambled up, whipping around. Lark grabbed him, sobbing, and they stared down at the man on the floor. His tunic was dark and wet with blood. Essa dropped to his knees, saying, "Who are you? *Who are you?*"

"It's in tha face." The man gasped, coughing up dark blood. "Anyone can see—"

And then he died.

"Run!" Essa grabbed Lark's arm, hauling her to her feet. Her brown legs were splashed with blood, her linen tunic creased and smeared.

They tore out of the coppice and back across the meadow, hand in hand.

The gate had been shut and bolted again, and they had to bang on it with their fists, yelling to be let in. It was Starling who came, dropping her spindle as they rushed past her. At first, she didn't even seem to notice anything amiss, saying, "Where have you been? Hild and your ma are spitting fire, Lark!" But then she looked at them, and saw them both covered in blood, and her eyes were full of suspicion.

Lark threw herself into Starling's arms, and Starling stared at Essa, her dark freckles standing out vividly as the color drained from her cheeks. "What have you done?" she cried. "What did you do to her?"

"It wasn't him; it wasn't!" Lark sobbed. Burning under Starling's accusation, Essa ran for the stables, hardly knowing where he was going, just wishing more than anything that the last three years could be peeled away, and he would find his father waiting for him there with Melyor.

Essa sat alone in the stable, shivering. His neck ached where the strangler's fingers had pressed, trying to squeeze the life out of him.

He was taboo.

He stared at the circle Onela White-beard had drawn around him on the dusty ground with the end of his stick. Essa knew that if he stepped outside it, even for a moment, the dead man would find him. He was not even allowed to see Fenrir, lest the spirit wreak mischief with her.

He was alone with the ghost, and he sensed its cold presence all around him. He could not stop shaking.

He flinched when he heard soft footsteps behind him, in the weed-tangled patch between the back of the stable and the foot of the village wall. Someone was coming by stealth. Was it the spirit? he wondered. Did spirits leave footsteps?

There was a loose board in the back wall of the stable where one of the horse folk had kicked through the planks when she had colic. Essa could hear something scrabbling at the board, its breath coming in panicky starts. Not a spirit, then. Spirits did not panic. Not a spirit, but Lark.

"Shhh," she said, pushing the board up and easing herself through the space as if she were a cat. She was wearing a clean tunic, and her eyes were red with spent tears. She crept quietly across the floor until she sat right by him in the circle, her arms around his shoulders, her hair warm against his face.

"Get out," Essa said, trying not to look at her. "His spirit will find you if you're near me."

"I'm not afraid of the spirit," she answered, and Essa knew she was lying.

"Who was he?" Lark whispered.

Essa shrugged, heavy with misery. "I don't know."

"Everyone's saying he must have been a Mercian scout sent to see where we run the cattle," Lark said. "But *he knew your face*—" She broke off, staring at Essa as though she had never seen him before. "Essa—"

"Listen, swear you won't tell anyone what he said." Hild was careful enough of him as it was. If she heard about this, he'd not be let out alone again. The thought of being trapped within the village walls scared Essa more than the chance that there was someone else out there wanting to take his life.

He knows me. But how? Essa was certain he'd never laid eyes on the man before. *It's in tha face,* he'd said. Essa pictured the blurry reflection he had seen on the surface of the mere when the wind was quiet and there were no ripples. What had the man seen there? Sin? Did that man think Essa had done something so terrible that it showed in his face and meant he had to die? Essa had almost forgotten about sin: they never spoke of it in the village, and their gods, the Aesir, were just as prone to lying, killing, and theft as ordinary men and women. But Essa felt sure that he had sinned now.

I killed him! he thought. *He's dead. Because of me, he'll never see his woman again, his children, his home. He'll never drink beer again, or sit up late by the fire.*

He felt cold inside.

Lark put her hand on his arm. "Don't think on it too much," she said. "If you'd not killed him, it would've been us lying cold out there, waiting to be put in the ground. He almost throttled you. But don't you think we should tell Hild what he said? I —"

"No. Just swear you won't say anything, not ever."

"All right, I swear," said Lark.

Essa fiddled with a piece of dry hay, unable to look at her. "Is Hild still angry with me?" That had been the worst of it all. *Get out of my sight!* she had shouted. *How could you disobey me like this? I don't want to look at you.*

Lark let out an empty laugh. "Not as much as Ma," she said. "I wish my father was still alive. He always said he'd take me out to the marsh and we'd get a mare for me and break her in together. I hate those Mercians that killed him — may their spirits wander forever. I hate Ma, too."

"No, you don't," said Essa. He could not even remember his own mother. If she were not dead, Cai would never have left him here with the Wixna. She would not have let him.

"I do hate her. I'm not allowed to be with you anymore." The words came out in a rush, and Lark held him tighter, so that he could smell the warmth of her skin. Essa wound his fingers around hers, their hands clasped. "She said we're not to be friends, that I should be with Starling and Helith and the other girls instead of running about with you."

"What does Hild say?" Essa asked. He felt hollow, like an old skull.

"That Ma is right — I should be more with the girls, and you with Cole and the others."

"She was wrong not to let me go on the horse chase, then—"

"Maybe she was, but Hild does nothing but in care of you." Onela White-beard stood in the doorway, leaning on his stick.

Essa and Lark looked up as one, holding each other tighter. Essa felt a jolt of fear. Like his father, he could hear like a dog. How, then, had Onela approached without him knowing?

"Granfer!" Lark said. "Don't tell Ma I was here."

Onela smiled down at them both. "I wouldn't be such a fool, my dear heart," he said. "You had better be gone, though. Essa is taboo, and I do not want the dead man's spirit to find you."

Lark got up, her face turned away, and Essa knew it was because she was crying and did not want him to see. He watched her run out into the yard, his best friend, feeling sure he now knew how Onela had felt when he lost his right arm at the battle of the River Idle, years before.

"Do you listen to me, Essa," said Onela. "Tell me how you knew there was someone in the coppice. You say you ran after Lark, afraid she'd be hurt. But where did you think she'd find the hurt? How did you know the man was there?"

Essa found he could hardly frame the words. He would not have admitted it to anyone, but Essa was afraid of the old man and had been ever since he had first laid eyes on him the morning Cai left. Onela did not speak much, because he had to save his breath for conversing with the elvish on his journeys into the spirit world, and this only made him seem more mysterious.

"Tell me how it came about, Aesc, little ash tree," he said. "And do not you leave anything out."

So Essa took a deep breath and told him.

"What does it mean, though?" he said. "Has someone laid a curse on me?"

Onela sighed and sat slowly down on the floor next to him. "Before he left, your father warned me of this. He said he sensed a streak of brightness in you that would break out when you got older. And when I saw you that morning he went, I knew it, too."

"Brightness?" Essa said, and in his mind, he was inside the jay again, watching the meadow rise and dip far beneath him as he flew.

"I was told about the bees in the orchard," Onela said. "Are you sure you did not wish them to fly after Red? It is a great gift you have, if used well." Suddenly Essa felt that the old man was no longer truly in the stable with him: that his inner self had gone elsewhere. He spoke again. "I, like most spirit men, must drink strong herbs, boil roots and mushrooms to loosen the ties that hold my spirit to my body. I slip between the worlds to treat with the elvish; I fly with hawks and gulls, run with the deer, and so I can tell the best places to hunt and fish.

"Sometimes, Essa, not very often, there is one whose spirit can wander without such help. These men and women are able to bend the will of any bird or animal — they can get inside the body of a wolf lord and make it lead the pack far from any village. They can cause eagles to fly over our enemies' camps, or swim with the whale folk and learn where the mackerel go. It is a great gift you have, little ash tree, and I wish I could teach you the skill of it."

Essa stared at him, his entire body tingling. "But where does it come from? Why can I do it?"

"From what I saw that night before he left you, your father's skills lie elsewhere — in song, and in the trickery of his speech. But both your father's kind and ours know of people whose spirits can leave their bodies. Only I'll wager the British tried to forget it once their Lord Jesus came to this island—they call it witchery now. And our kind? We Anglish are farmers and have been since time out of mind, but the songs tell us that once we lived by hunting alone. And now we are forgetting these skills too. We have less need to know where the deer run."

"But can you not teach me how to do it properly—whenever I want?" asked Essa, the dead man forgotten for a moment. He felt hot and breathless with the thrill of it. "I couldn't have made that jay fly off the other way—and I think the bees only went after Red because he threw stones at them. It wasn't like riding a horse when I was in the jay. I was more like a flea on a goat, just carried along."

Onela shook his head. "I cannot teach you how to master this skill, no matter how dearly I wish otherwise." He smiled, his eyes slanting, and Essa saw how like him Lark was. "Look on it as a gift from your mother and father. They are not with you now, but they have left you this. You must learn to manage it yourself."

"But I don't know what to do," Essa said.

"Listen. You have a dog. Let her teach you. And do you go out into the woods and catch a hunting bird, and learn to call it to your side. Learn from the beasts themselves what you can do."

The old man got awkwardly to his feet and, leaning on his stick, walked back to the hall. Watching him go, Essa knew that he was different now, like pig iron forged into an iron blade, sharp and true. He had killed a man, and he had flown with a blue jay above the meadow. Even if Cai came back tomorrow, Essa knew that he could not ride away with him on Melyor like a little child.

He was changed.

5

Two years later:
The atheling

The mind of a goshawk is fierce and red. Through her eyes, Essa saw the marshes spread out like a sheet of beaten metal pricked through by reeds, a dark smear of woodland off to the west. Beyond the woods King Penda's camp lay crouched in the night, lit with fires. Essa willed the goshawk to fly closer, but she knew only hunger. The trees were full of prey, and she longed to burst down through the tree cover and swoop close to the ground, down where the small creatures hid. She saw the man on horseback coming from the east, but he was nothing to her, for there was prey, and she wanted meat.

And then Essa was back in his own body.

"He's coming, Cole!" he said. "She saw him." They were up on the great mound of earth that surrounded the hall like a necklace, watching the fields and then the wetlands stretching out toward the dark trees marking the wood shore. Every time Essa came up here, he remembered that long-ago game of Fox and Geese: playing for a knife in a Mercian hall. He remembered Cai riding across the courtyard, saying, *Come up*. How strange to think he'd said that, knowing what he was about to do. *He should've let me finish my game*, Essa thought.

"It makes my skin creep, the way you do this," Cole said. "Where's Myfanwy now?"

"In the woods. She's hungry. I wanted her to fly over the Mercian camp, but she wouldn't. I saw *him*, though. It's got to be him — no one else comes here." Essa's fingers ached with cold, and he blew on his cupped hands, sending a dragon's puff of warm air into the night. One moon had come and gone since Yule: it was Sun-cake month, when they buried yellow saffron cakes in the mud to tempt back the sun and coax the barley to push its green tips up out of the soil. Winter was only just releasing its grip on the land.

"If I go out to meet him, do you take Myfanwy back to the barn?" Essa reached down to stroke Fenrir's ears. She lay beside him, radiating warmth, dozing with her heavy brindled head on her front paws. She was five years old now, long-legged and strong, and he loved her.

Cole shrugged. "I can try — Myfanwy never comes to anyone but you."

So Essa whistled, long and low. *Come on, my dear one. Time to come home.*

And then there she was, his goshawk, a shrew dangling from her claws. Essa whistled again, and she dropped it. Circling once more, Myfanwy came down to rest on his

46

leather-gloved hand — surprisingly heavy, as always, for one who flew so fast and graceful. Her yellow eyes were burning, full of fire, and Essa could feel the terrible strength of her claws, even through the glove. Essa had caught Myfanwy when she was just a chick, but she would never be like Fenrir, who loved him.

Cole picked up the shrew, holding it out to her, and she snatched it with her beak. He winced and jumped back. "I'm sure she'll have out your eyes one day."

Essa laughed. "Not this one. And she keeps the mice down in the barn, so don't complain."

Cole opened his mouth to speak again, but Essa laid a hand on his arm. He could hear a distant rumbling that boomed up from below ground as if something sleeping under the green mantle of earth were stirring, ready to wake. "Listen!" Beside him, Fenrir's ears were twitching. He rested his hand on her head.

"What? I can't hear anything." Cole's voice seemed to ring out louder than before. "You're a strange one, Essa — the way you hear what others don't and let your spirit run with the beasts. You know what the women say? *Regard his unearthly beauty, such bright hair, and dark, mysterious eyes. Mark you, his father lay with the elvish, like all the British do.*"

"Oh, do you be quiet!" Essa said, laughing. Cole meant no harm, but Essa had long grown tired of people making little protective signs against the spirits whenever he passed by, and of the girls whistling at him, and whispering, and giggling. The only girl who left him alone was Lark, but it would not do to think of her, now. She was silent and cold, as if she froze into iron whenever he was near.

"Listen," he said. "I can hear it now—a horse, on the old road."

"If you say so," said Cole, grinning, and they fell into an easy silence. Essa had been sent up here to wait for a messenger from the palace of the king of East Anglia, the Wolf King, but, even after five years, the sound of a rider coming closer still lit a quick, hot flame in Essa's belly.

What if it's him? Essa thought. *What if it's Cai? I will say nothing to him. It will be as if he has been gone only a morning.* But it would not be Cai; he knew that, really. They were waiting for a messenger.

"There!" Cole said. "I can hear it now. Do you let me take Myfanwy to the barn, and I'll go in and tell Hild."

Gently, Essa eased his hand out of the glove, Myfanwy still gripping the leather, staring at them with her cold, golden eyes. Cole put it on, holding out the bloody remains of the shrew for her to eat.

Essa ran down the mound while Cole shouted, "Bring them in quick—it's enough to freeze the blood out here."

Hild and the men were waiting for news from the east, and it was not likely to be good. A few months earlier, just before midsummer, Hild had been summoned by a messenger to her old home, the royal palace of the Wolf Folk at Rendlesham. She had ridden out, taking Ariulf and Onela White-beard as her escorts. Wishing he had been allowed to accompany them, Essa counted the days until they returned, cutting notches in the stable door. Seventeen notches later, they had come back with the news that King Seobert had left his hall and retreated into a monastery, leaving East Anglia in the hands of his royal kinsmen, the athelings. Once again, the Wolf Folk were kingless, helpless like a boat with no rudder.

"But they're refusing to pick another king," Hild had said, brushing the road dust from her dress. "The court's entirely Christian now, and they think Seobert's been chosen by their God."

"I knew the Christians would bring nothing but trouble," Onela White-beard said, allowing Red and Essa to help him from the saddle. "I remember when that witless fool came with news of it from Rome, all the way across the sea he came, back before the time of Redwald, and word spread up from Kent that there was this one new God that could do the job of all ours, and better, too. I said it was a lot of mazy talk then, and now I know it is. It's made wise men blind to what stares them in the face. Seobert's no king, nor ever was. Why else did Redwald send him out of the way to Francia? He knew the lad was no good."

And now, months later, a messenger was due from the east, bringing more news. Hopefully, Essa thought, there'd be another king chosen, Seobert would be left in peace in his monastery, and the throne of the Wolf Folk would be secure against the Mercians again.

Essa stopped just outside the hall door, listening to the hum of voices inside. He squeezed his eyes shut and felt the trembling of the earth beneath his feet again, a low rumble that sounded like a drumbeat. Sound traveled quicker on clear nights like this, when the new moon hung in the blackness like a sliver of polished silver. It had been a long winter.

They were coming down the old road, all right, coming hard and fast. He turned his back on the hall and the smell of smoked pig meat being fried, and fish stew, and ran up the dirt track toward the village gate. There was nobody guarding it: someone would get wrong of Hild and the old men for that. He felt a shiver of unease. He could hear hoofbeats clearly now, drumming down the old road across the fields. It was dangerous to be riding this fast in the dark, he reflected. He lifted the great bar bolting the gateway and slipped outside: now he was easy prey for any Mercian scouting party.

Everyone in the village, including Hild, told Essa that the man whose life he had taken two years ago had surely been a Mercian scout. *Coming to see how many cattle we've got,* they used to say. *Plotting another raid, I shouldn't wonder. That was a good day's work when you killed the Mercian, little halfling.*

The Wixna had chosen to believe that Essa had killed a Mercian spy. But only Essa and Lark had heard the words the man spoke before dying.

It's in tha face. Anyone can see —

He was no Mercian, Essa was sure. The accent was wrong, for one thing: more northern than anything else. Essa had recognized it from a long-ago trip to Elmet, where he and

Cai once met a gang of Northumbrian traders traveling south from Ad Gefrin, the seat of the High King.

And what had the man seen in his face?

He was looking for me, Essa thought as he drew near the coppice. *He was seeking me out.*

Even now, years later, each time he came near these trees, he felt a chill down his back. He had escaped death here once—would he be so lucky a second time? He remembered the morning after the killing, waking up in the stable, and Onela by his side, saying, "His spirit is gone, and you are safe now."

But Essa had not felt safe. The man had wanted to kill him, and Essa did not know why. *Don't think on it,* he told himself. *Maybe he was just mazed in the head, crazy after wandering too long from other men. Maybe he was just a cattle thief.* But Essa could not make himself believe it.

Shivering slightly, he cut through the alder coppice and skirted the mere, a flat, dark swath of shining metal under the thin moonlight. It had not rained for several weeks, and the ground beneath his feet was hard. His own breathing sounded so loud that Essa was convinced anyone riding toward the hall would be able to hear it. There was no wind, and despite the cold, his whole body felt damp with sweat. The grass came to an end, and he was standing on the edge of the narrow, muddy road.

Then they came. The thundering of hooves grew louder. He held his breath tight inside his chest and watched a man on horseback rounding the corner. He was riding hard with his cloak flapping out behind him like wings. Essa wished he had slipped into the hall or the forge to grab a flaming torch and cursed himself for not doing so. If he ran out into the road without being seen, the horse would take fright. The man raised an arm high above his head as if he were trying to snatch a handful of the night sky. He let out a wild yell that echoed up into the stillness.

This was no messenger. Essa felt a quick thrill of fear. The moon was just bright enough to catch the fine gold pin that held the rider's heavy plaid cloak. At first it looked as if he were draped in gold the way the night was speckled with stars, and then Essa saw that he wore a great sword belt with gold strap ends and a gold buckle. The horse slowed down and stopped. He heard ragged breathing as it snorted and stamped in the cold air. An ungelded male: a stallion. *That'll be fresh riding,* Essa thought, remembering how many times they had all been thrown breaking in the milk-white marsh stallion the men had captured on that long-ago horse hunt: everyone except Essa, of course. He had never been thrown from a horse.

"You! Come out, whoever you are!" The voice was rich, as if it dripped with gold like the man it belonged to.

Essa stepped into the road. This was his hall, and Hild had sent him out here. "Who are you, and where do you come from?" he said.

A pair of eyes stared back at him, hard and bright and gray like the inside of an oyster shell, partially drained of color by the moonlight. They held on to him for so long that Essa noticed barely anything else about the rest of the man except that he was big without running to fat, with fair hair swept back from his face by the ride. The flanks of his horse heaved up and down, glistening with sweat.

"You ride like a berserker," Essa said.

The man laughed and swung himself out of the saddle. "My name is Egric the Atheling. I've been sent here by my cousin." The gold tips on his sword belt and buckle clinked slightly as he moved, as if somebody were playing music for him at every step.

"Who's your cousin?" Essa said, although he had a feeling that he already knew the answer and had been much too rude.

"Seobert the Wolf King." Egric laughed. "Do you show me where to stable my horse — we've had a long ride through this cursed marsh of yours. And what of you, boy? There aren't many like you so far east, with red hair and such dark eyes. You are a half-breed, am I right? How came you to be in this East Anglian hall?"

Essa turned to him, taking the horse's bridle. They were almost the same height. "We are the Wixna," he said. "We are not East Anglian. When we go in, a woman will greet you. Do not ask her the name of the man who is chief. He is dead, and she sits at the top of the table here now."

Egric raised an eyebrow. He looked as if he were struggling not to laugh again. "Really? I heard her mate was killed, oh, eight winters back it must have been, but I thought some ambitious young man would have supplanted her by now."

"Well, no one has," said Essa. "I just thought you should know."

Once the black stallion was stabled, fed, and watered, Essa took Egric to the hall, shoving open the door as he led the atheling forward into the light. The babble of chat and laughter died, and silence washed across the hall like a wave as it became clear that King Seobert had sent no ordinary messenger. Hild was at the fireplace with Cole and Lark's mother, peering into the copper pot.

"It just needs a little while longer." Hild turned around and stood up straight; she was still holding the spoon and set it on the table, laughing. She was growing fuller this past year, Essa thought, and he wondered if she'd ever look like Cole's mother, who was round and red-faced and ran out of breath when she chased across the yard after one of the chickens. Yet Hild was very fair still, standing in her hall wearing a gown the color of blood, held up at the shoulders with a pair of gold brooches. The bones of her face were fine and strong, and she looked equal to anything.

But when she glanced past Essa and her eyes settled on Egric, her mouth set in a straight line as though something had angered her. *It must be that she's fretting about the news from the court*, Essa thought. *The news from the Wolf King.* And he wondered what Egric was going to tell her.

"Pike stewed in cream and tarragon," Hild said. "I am so sorry, my lord, but we are rough around the edges this evening. I was not expecting Egric the Atheling."

He loosed the scabbard from his belt and bowed low,

laying his sword at her feet. "My lady. I am honored to be your guest."

Hild dropped to her knees and took up the sword. She stood up straight again, stopping to rest with her hands pressed to her thighs as though she had hurt her back, and returned the sword to the prince. "The pleasure is all ours," she said in a thin, colorless voice. "I see you have met Essa, my fosterling. Now, do you come and meet the rest of my men." She turned to Essa. "Take the drinking horn and fill it, my honey. Don't forget the stand—the silver one." There was a strange yearning look to her face that Essa didn't like: it made him think of when he was younger and she hated to let him out of her sight. What was wrong with Hild tonight? Maybe it was her time of the month, and she wanted a hot stone from the fire to wrap in a blanket and hold against her back. Maybe her head ached and she was tired. Either way, Essa hoped she wouldn't treat him like a little child in front of the atheling.

She turned away, and Essa was about to move when he felt a hand on his arm.

"I thank you for the warning," Egric said softly into Essa's ear. "But be warned yourself, Aesc, son of Cai, that I do not take kindly to impertinence."

It had been so long since anyone had spoken to Essa in his own language that at first the rushing, songlike words were like nothing but the sound of water tumbling over rock. And then he saw their meaning.

Aesc, son of Cai.

For a moment Essa stood still, unable to move. Then he ran outside and stood in the yard, letting the air chill his burning face. He knew he should go back in and pour the mead as Hild had asked, but he could not.

He ran up to the top of the earthworks on the Mercian side, where the flatlands stretched out toward their camp, and lay flat on his back in the long grass, staring up at the night. Out in Long Acre the cattle were restless, lowing up at the night. It sounded like the calling of lost spirits.

How does he know who I am? Essa thought. *And how dare he? How dare he come here and say such things to me, as if Father is still alive? It's as if he knows something about me I don't know myself.*

Egric the Wolf Prince was playing games with him.

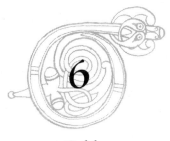

6

Gold

COLE came next, scrambling breathless up the earthen wall. "Why did you run off like that?"

Essa sat up. "Nothing. I just — never mind it. What's the atheling's news, then?"

"Well, you know Seobert's a Christian?" said Cole. "They're saying he's given up violence for good; he won't strike another man ever again. He won't go back to the Wolf Hall at Rendlesham; he says he's going to stay in Bedricsworth monastery till the day he dies. And all the court of the Wolf Folk believe it. But they still won't pick another king, because they reckon Seobert was chosen by their God. Egric and a few of the other athelings are the only ones left with any sense, so they're riding out to all the border people, like us, to make sure we're still swearing allegiance to the Wolves and not about to throw in our lot with the Mercians.

"Anyway, I don't understand these Christians. Isn't the

High King Christian too? King Godsrule, the one who took over after Penda killed Edwin. Is he going to go off into one of these monastery places?"

"Not every Christian does it," said Essa, and then added uncomfortably, "I'm one, aren't I?" He had only formless memories of kneeling with his father in little wooden god houses, and threads of dreams about fiery angels, and a brave young lord dying in sorrow to save his people. "But you can't be a king without having to kill a few folk. If Seobert won't lead an army, we'll be overrun by Mercia before the year's done. There'll have to be another king."

"Huh," said Cole. "Do you know what they say about Mercians? They say they've got heads like dogs and eat children."

"I suppose they can fly like birds and breathe fire as well," said Essa, remembering his opponent at Fox and Geese in that Mercian hall across the border, his clever green eyes and rounded shoulders, the way he moved with the loose grace of a hound or a wolf. "Don't be such a half-wit. They're just the same as us."

"Maybe they are and maybe they're not," Cole said. "But they killed our father seven summers back, Lark's and mine, and if we have a fight on our hands, I hope I'll send a few of them after him—"

"Hild says come in." It was Lark, standing framed in the firelit doorway of the hall. In the glow, the braided coils of her hair looked like shining metal. Essa flinched at the sound of her voice. What gave her the right to stare right through him the way she did, as if he were nothing more than the mud out in the yard?

Cole rolled his eyes. "We should get back." Essa followed him down the mound and across the yard, brushing past Lark on his way through the hall door. She stepped back, holding herself away from him as though his touch disgusted her. He felt a flash of anger, and he did not meet her eye.

Inside the hall, the benches were crammed with people, and Hild stood at the end of the table with the big copper pot before her, holding the drinking horn with both hands. The atheling was seated to her right. The only other person standing was Red, who grinned when he saw Essa come in.

What was happening? The whole hall was wreathed in silence. It was as if they had walked into the aftermath of an argument. People glanced over their shoulders at them and looked away, staring back at the table. Lark did not look away so quickly, though. She turned in her place on the bench, and as her eyes rested on Essa he felt the blood rush to his face. She was looking at him. For the first time in years, she was looking at him. Something had changed, changed in the time it had taken him to step into the hall. It was only a moment, but when she turned away, Essa felt a crushing hollowness inside.

"I've a bad feeling about this." He hadn't realized he was speaking aloud until he felt Cole's hand on his arm.

"Shhh, it's—" Cole said.

"Thank you for coming in," said Hild. She raised the

great ivory horn, and Egric held out a cup, ready for her to pour. Essa felt as if they were speaking in a language he had never heard before. The drinking horn and Egric's cup must mean something to bring such a deep quiet over the benches, like the damp sods of earth they laid over the fire at night.

Cole nodded. He had gone very pale. "She's got the mead cup," he said. "It must be rings — Egric's going to give rings to Hild, and she'll give them to us, and she'll be our lady."

"Not you, Essa," said Hild.

Everybody stared at Essa, and then Cole and Red walked around the table to Egric and Hild, watched by the whole hall.

Every muscle in Essa's body tensed as he sat down, shouldering aside his neighbors. Had they all known this would happen? Somehow, he found himself next to Lark, her body warm against his. Why did she not draw away? It had been so long since they had touched. What was it — two, three years since that morning when she had left him in the stable? The heat of her drew the breath from his lungs, making him feel dizzy. He stared straight ahead.

Egric waited while Hild poured a stream of straw-gold mead into his cup. He got to his feet, raised the silver cup to his lips, and drank. Essa felt his chest tighten as all around him people started to cheer. It was as if the silence had never been. A huge bubble of noise rose to the rafters and broke against the roof. Hild let the horn rest in its stand on the table and unhooked a small pouch from her belt. She laid it next to the copper pot and unwrapped it. Even from this distance, he caught the glimmer of gold within the leather folds.

"Honorable ring bearers of the Wolf Folk," Egric said to the hall. "You now have two more fighting men." The cheering grew louder; people shouted Red's name and Cole's name and drummed their cups and knife handles on the table, their eyes bright and shining. Egric held up one hand for quiet. "The Mercian dogs may be howling at our gates," he yelled. "But we shall fight to the death to defend our borders, for we are the Wolves, and by God, we shall run once more." Egric turned to face Hild, bowing his head in a show of deference. Tonight, she was chieftain of this hall as if she were a man, a war leader.

"Once again, the Wixna pledge their loyalty to East Anglia and the Wolf Folk," she said quietly. Not everyone was joining in the cheering and clapping: at the back of the hall, Essa saw some of the older men shaking their heads, grim faced. But they had no choice: the Wixna were buffeted on one side by the might of the Wolf Folk, and threatened on the other by the Mercian hordes. Their old chief had worn the ring of the Wolves and taken a Wolf Princess into his hall. So the Wixna were bound by gold and by Hild, whom they all loved, and they had no choice.

Essa forced himself to watch Cole receive a golden ring from Hild, then Red. He imagined the feel of the cold metal slipping around his own finger, binding him forever to his lord.

Everybody raised their cups, drinking to the young men who would now be fighting for their lady and their king the next time Penda of the Mercians chose to send his men across the border. Then Egric spoke again.

"Aesc."

Essa flinched at the use of his proper name; the sound of it pulled him back down into the hall next to Lark, who sat so still beside him. He was Aesc, ash, an ash tree swaying in the wind.

"Get up!" Lark said, her voice low. It was the first time she had spoken directly to him in years, since the day he had killed the man in the woods and they had been forbidden each other's company.

A different kind of silence had settled on the hall now. There was an air of unease. He could feel every single person in the village watching him. Their eyes were like needles in his back.

"Hold out your hand," said Egric.

Essa obeyed, feeling as if somebody else were directing his movements. Surely he couldn't lift his arm when it was heavier than the whetstone by the hearth? But he did, and he felt cool metal slipping down the middle finger of his right hand.

"I have a feeling you might come in useful to me," said Egric, his voice low and quiet against the tumult that had broken out on the mead benches. People were clapping and cheering. "Wear my ring, Aesc. I'm going to need your keen ears and your sharp eyes soon. But you'll need to learn absolute obedience, and I can tell you're going to find that more difficult than most." He laughed. "But you must learn, all the same."

Essa hardly heard. He looked down at his hand and saw the band of gold. He was bound now. He belonged to Egric; he had been chosen. Why then, instead of being wild with joy, did he feel as if a heavy weight were pressing on his chest, squeezing the life out of him?

In his mind, Essa heard his father's voice: *Being bound by a ring is the same as being shackled by an iron chain.* For one moment, he thought of ripping the ring from his finger and hurling it across the room: he would be bound to no man. But then what would he be in this Wixna village with no ring? Neither a man nor a child, bound in honor to no one. He would be nothing.

He dropped to his knees before the atheling.

When he looked up, Egric was standing behind Hild with one hand resting on her shoulder, and she leaned back against him, wearing a smile that was like a fine gown covering a body mangled by the pox. The smile was for everybody else in the hall, not for Essa and his ring. He had never seen Hild touched by a man. She was always carrying some child, and he'd seen plenty of women braiding her hair, touching her arm in passing, but never a man anywhere near her. It must have been lonely for Hild in those long years since Penda's men had killed her husband: lonely and rather cold at night.

To the spirit world,
and then to Mercia

ESSA lay on his back, watching the stars through the gently shifting branches of the ash tree, stirred by the wind. He could still taste the bitterness of the herbs he'd been given to drink: herbs he had never tasted before. Cole and Red were breathing quietly beside him: they were all forbidden to speak. They had worn their rings for a night and a day now, and they were going on a spirit journey. A little distance away, Onela and a few of the other older men were talking quietly, but it was impossible to make out what they were saying — the words seemed to melt into one another.

As Essa lay there, the stars began to move, blurring and spinning, and he found he could hear the ash tree growing, her great roots creaking as they crept through the ground beneath him. He was no longer lying beneath the ash tree in the courtyard, but soaring through the branches of Yggdrasil, the World Tree, the great ash whose trunk contained the world of men, her branches the marches of the gods — the Aesir — where dead warriors feasted and whose roots cradled other, more mysterious realms.

Essa knew he had once thought of the world in a different way, of earth, heaven, and hell, all watched over by the Holy Father. But that had been long ago. In the village, they sang of the Aesir, and Yggdrasil, and the battle of the world's end that would come when mankind's time was done. And now Essa was soaring up to the realm of the Aesir, hovering between the world of the living and somewhere else.

Then, suddenly, he felt he was circling above the village, looking down on the wisps of smoke rising from the thatched roof of the hall.

Burning with the thrill of it, Essa realized his spirit had left his body, but not to fly with the swallows that lived under the eaves, or run with the horses or the red roe deer. This was different. He was no longer tied to flesh and blood in any form. He was flying free.

He saw the great earthen wall coiled around the village. Dark woods stretched off to the west and faded out toward marshland that reached all the way to the great Mercian forest. Caught between the woods and the marsh, he saw Penda's camp, a dark hump on the landscape: a fort built by people long forgotten.

Beyond the old fortress, the Mercian forest spread even farther west, for miles and miles. It seemed almost endless. Soaring in the sky like a bird, as if he were flying with Myfanwy again, Essa looked to the east and saw the long line of the Wolf Folk's western defenses: a huge earthen wall lying there like a sleeping snake. The flatlands stretched toward the coast, vast skeins of fenny water and boggy islands. Beyond that was the sea—and then he was no longer flying high above the earth but was in a boat, crouching below the prow, soaked with seawater, listening to the song of the oarsmen. That was how his ancestors had come here, in the time of his grandfathers. His mother's people, come from across the eastern water.

Then he was soaring again, up, up toward the stars, and he ached with the joy of it, because he was free.

Essa was the first to wake the next morning, opening his eyes to a clear dawn sky. Someone had been out in the night and laid blankets over them. His had slipped off in the night, and his linen tunic was damp with dew. Off to his right he could see Cole and Red: humped, sleeping shapes. His head felt strangely clear—he had expected the herb drink to leave him feeling sick at least. He was tempted to lean over and shake Cole awake. *Only that wouldn't help, would it?* he told himself. They were forbidden to ever speak of what had happened last night, of what they'd seen, and the places they had gone to. It was a journey you could only take alone. It was a journey that led to your secret self.

He sat up, the blanket bunched around his legs, leaning against the ridged, knobbly trunk of the ash tree. Spreading the fingers of his right hand out in his lap, he gazed at Egric's ring, bright metal shining against his skin, burning golden light — the fire of the sea. He wore the ring of the Wolf Folk. So why had he dreamed of flying like a bird instead of running with wolves?

Later that morning, after the rugs and sheepskins had been taken out to air in the yard and everyone had scattered to the day's tasks, Hild called Essa into the hall. Egric stood by the hearth; it was very quiet. Smoke from last night's fire still hung in the air, not quite drawn up through the thatch. The doors had been thrown open, though, and a fresh breeze disturbed the ashes. Red's sister Starling was nursing the smallest of her children and sat on the wooden linen trunk crooning to it, but apart from that, everyone had gone to lay hedges and spread muck on the fields, or into the weaving shed.

Egric looked up and smiled. "So," he said. "I'm glad to see you're not looking too mazed after last night's sport. Forgive me, but I don't hold with these unchristian rites — drinking mysterious herbs and leaping about."

Leaping about? Essa thought. He did not remember doing that.

"Look around, Egric," Hild said. "Do you see one Christian but yourself in this village? We keep the old ways here, and the spirit journey has power. It turns boys into men."

"They're men now that they wear rings for us. And you seem to have forgotten that Essa is a Christian. You know my views on brewing these old beliefs, my lady."

"And you know mine. Yes, Essa is a Christian born, but

he has been here with us five years and come to no harm. You might be Christian, you and your good lady wife, but as soon as the harvest fails you'll be leaving little presents for the Aesir, back to the old ways, just in case." Hild turned and scraped leftover porridge from the pan into the pig bucket.

"Well, Essa," said Egric. "I hope you found your journey useful, all the same."

Essa suddenly felt cold: what if Egric found out where it had taken him? Every clan had its own sacred spirit animal — the Mercians had the wild boar, and the East Anglians had their wolves. That was why they were called the Wolf Folk. He was bound to them by gold, but instead of taking him running through the night like a wolf, Essa's spirit journey had taken him flying high above the earth, and he had no sense of what that meant.

"You must kneel before the atheling, my honey." Hild's voice broke into his thoughts, bringing him back to the everyday world. "Now you are his to command, and I no longer have any say." She turned to leave, then said to him, "Essa, come to me in the weaving hall when my lord has finished with you. There's something I wish to speak to you of." He watched her go and then dropped to his knees, sinking down so low that his forehead touched the floorboards. What could Hild want to talk to him about, he wondered, staring at the grain in the old wood. Egric had most likely complained to her of Essa's rudeness the night he arrived. *He knows my father*, he thought. *I wonder —* But what Egric said next drove all thoughts of Cai from Essa's mind.

"I want you to get into Penda's camp," said the atheling. "The one across the marsh, and see if he's garrisoned it or not. He must know of Seobert's retreat by now — it's been months. I need to find out if he's gathering his men to the border, ready to attack us. And if he has, I want to know when he plans to do it. You will be my eyes and ears, right in the guts of Penda's camp, Essa, so do not fail me."

Essa remained kneeling, excitement burning in his belly, waiting for permission to sit up. They stored provisions in the dark, cool foundations of the hall, beneath the ancient floorboards. He could smell the old oiled wood, the earthy reek of last harvest's carrots packed in sand, and the sharp stink of garlic bulbs and onions hanging to dry from nails banged into the floorboards from the undercroft below. The point of one of the nails had worked its way up through the wood and was poking into his knee, but he knew he must not move till Egric gave him leave.

So Essa knelt, trying to ignore the jabbing nail till, at last, he felt Egric lay a hand on the back of his head, saying, "Rise. You'll leave tomorrow night at dusk. I want you back here by dawn."

Essa got to his feet, murmuring, "Thank you, my lord."

Egric laughed. "You make a good show of it, Aesc, son of Cai, but you do not deceive me. I know your kind — you think you can do whatever you like. But you will do well to remember what happens to a man who does not follow the word of his lord."

Essa nodded. He had heard all the stories. He would be

cast out, banished to the wildwood, never to know the warmth of a hall again. "I understand, my lord," he said. "But — there is one thing I want to ask: how do you know who I am? Who my father is? Do you know him? You can speak our language. Is he still alive?"

Egric held up his hand and Essa fell silent.

"That is not one thing," Egric said. "And it is not your place to ask questions of me. Your place is to do exactly as I tell you, saying nothing. Now go; you must have work to do."

Essa swallowed his anger, bowing his head. He could feel the gold ring, cold and unfamiliar around the middle finger of his right hand.

Cai had been right all those years ago. It was as good as a shackle.

And when Essa went out into the chilly spring light in the yard, Red and Cole came up to him, Cole saying, "Come on, we've been waiting. Ariulf's just told us we're to go out and help them spread muck on the bottom field."

Red handed Essa a flask of cider. "Do you still join in the lowly tasks now you wear a ring for Egric, halfling?" Essa shoved him in the arm, laughing; they all went out of the village gate, and Essa forgot all about Hild wanting to speak to him.

Essa went quietly and at an even pace through the trees; he could smell the night drawing in before the light started to fade. It was a good night for being outside.

A hundred paces beyond the village walls, once he was well into the woods, he dropped to his knees and whistled a long, low note, hardly audible to a man's ear. He grinned, wanting to laugh out loud. This was his first act of disobedience, but no one would ever know. As if he would go without her, anyway.

He waited, feeling his mind drift, his spirit leave his body. Suddenly, everything grew sharper, every smell and every sound. He was inside Fenrir. The wood shore rang with the hum of heartbeats; he could hear small creatures crackling through dead bracken, the creak of an owl's wing. His heart soared with the desire to chase, to run, to seek hot-blooded creatures in the night. Then he was back inside himself, and he knew she was coming. She came loping through the trees toward him, and he held out his hands for her to lick.

Come on, girl, let's go. Get across the marsh. Over the wall. Watch. Listen. Wait.

He had to keep running through his task. It was the only way of shutting out the echo of Cai's voice at the back of his mind.

Being bound by a ring is the same as being shackled by an iron chain. Better you follow the hawk's path, free under the sky. They call it fire of the sea, but gold's just a trap, and it'll lure you into slavery.

"That's well enough for him to say," Essa said, digging his fingers into the thick fur at Fenrir's neck as she paced along beside him. "He left me here with these folk. What else can

I do but follow their ways?" But Fenrir had no answers.

The cold air chilled his skin. Crows shrieked mournfully as they soared up to their high nests, clustered in the trees at the edge of the wood. He heard the coughing bark of a roe deer in the distance, and Fenrir tensed, torn by the longing to chase it. *Not now, not yet. There'll be time for that, girl.* By the time he was through the woods to the marshes, darkness had settled over the land like a heavy blanket.

The night had turned overcast. The stars were obscured by skeins of cloud, stained silver by the narrow, sickle-shaped moon. The ground started feeling boggy beneath his feet and the trees were thinning out. There were more willows here, their great thirsty roots inching down through the marshy soil. Weak moonlight shone silver off the wetlands, filtered through long, stretching fingers of cloud. A long-dead oak stood skeletal against the horizon, and Essa's breath caught in his chest. The marshes had a strange beauty about them, even though a lot of people refused to even go there after dark. He'd last been here in autumn, reed cutting with Cole, Red, Fenrir, and some of the other hall dogs. They had poled their way across the flatlands in the flat-bottomed coracle, edging into the reedbeds, surprising a family of coots swimming briskly away in a neat line, their white foreheads bobbing haughtily.

Even at night the marshes pulsed with life, rich and bubbling beneath the surface. Essa knelt down, took off his sheepskin boots, and rolled up his trousers to his knees. He tied the boots together by their leather straps and hung them over his shoulders. Flat fish nestled in the mud, feeling tremors rippling through their dark, warm world as he waded through it, carefully testing with each footfall, knowing that with one misstep he could be sucked into the dark heart of the marsh, never to be seen again. Fenrir followed an arm's length behind him, her paws kicking up soft mounds of water, leaving a wake behind her. She knew how to move quietly. He could feel the marsh mud between his toes. There was always the chance he would step on something that moved.

The Mercian camp rose up out of the flat skyline like the crooked knee of a sleeping giant. As a child, Essa had always imagined the earth in this way: a dreaming giant under a blanket of green, speckled with mountains and marshes and forests. The earthworks loomed before him as he edged closer through the great reedbed at the Mercian end of the marsh, trying to suppress the desire to shudder as his bare toes were tugged and tangled by invisible roots and drowned fronds of reed. Alders clawed up at the moon with branches like gnarled fingers, pointing him toward the Mercian mound that Hild said had been there since before the men from Rome came and went, leaving their strange buildings of stone for folk to marvel at in songs by the fire.

Essa walked around the outside of it, reluctant to leave the sheltering trees. Everything was more or less how he remembered from his visit with Cai long ago, but now the ring of piled earth surrounding the fort looked higher, the ditch below it deeper. There were probably guards stationed at the top of the mound, a circle of watchful eyes, looking east across the marshes toward the border and out west, where the great woods stretched all the way to Powys. It would be impossible to get past them. He'd have to move like smoke. He smiled to himself in the dark: this was madness. But the thought of going back to the hall with nothing to report to Egric was worse. He crept away from the reeds at the edge of the marsh and slid around the hump of the mound. From this angle it looked even more like a sleeping giant, the crook of an enormous elbow curving around under a blanket of grass and mud. Here, there was the dark scar of a gateway carved into the side of the mound, just like at the hall. Outside the gates a long, dark finger pointed up at the night sky, drawing a line through the moon. The flag mast. Essa squinted into the gloom. There it was. Penda's standard flapped like a crow's wing against the night, a white boar on scarlet.

The Mercian king was at the fortress, then. It made sense: now that Seobert was refusing to come out of Bedricsworth monastery, Penda must have all eyes on the border — just as Egric did. Essa wondered briefly if there was another boy who came to spy on their village under the orders of his Mercian lord. He would have seen Egric's royal standard flapping on the flag mast by the village gate: the running wolf. He would have known the atheling had come to rouse the border people for a fight.

Now that Essa was closer, he could see the palisade fence running in a ring around the flattened top of the mound.

That was where the fighting men would be, if there were any, cooped up behind the fence like dogs before the hunt. He remembered Cai riding Melyor across the yard, saying, *Come up*. He remembered the smooth wooden goose pieces cupped in his palm as he laughed, not knowing Cai was about to leave him forever. He stood still for a moment, and the smell of wood smoke hit the back of his throat. If those guards caught him, they would kill him. Essa breathed out slowly, knelt by Fenrir, pushing his face close to hers, twining his fingers about her ears. *Stay here, in the shadows. Wait for me to come. By the rising of the sun, I'll be back.* She whined, a soft growl that made her ribs quiver. He knew she would wait for him. It meant she could be free to hunt alone for a night, and he whispered a silent apology that she would have no pack, no swift brothers and sisters at her side, no two-legs waiting with words of praise when she returned with a kill.

But if he did not do it now, he never would. Drawing in a long breath, Essa sprang across the ditch, landing in a crouch an arm's length above the water. He ran lightly and quickly up the mound and stood by the fence for a while, listening. After a few moments of hearing nothing but voices muffled by distance, he loosened the rope knotted around his waist and took the iron grappling hook from his belt. His fingers fumbled over the knot and for a moment Essa thought he would have to give up and go back because his hands were shaking too much. Then the hook was fixed to the rope, and in one swift movement he threw it over the fence and heard the iron prongs catch into the wooden fence on the other side. He smiled to himself in the dark. This was almost too easy.

He was nearly at the top of the fence when somebody on the other side dropped a cup and swore. Essa heard it clearly: a metal cup, bouncing on beaten earth with a hollow ring. There were sentries walking around the inside of the palisade. Well, he would have come across them sooner or later.

"There goes my ale. I'll get another. Will you have one?"

There was a muttered reply from an unseen companion.

Essa's arms were beginning to ache. He waited until the sound of their footfalls faded into the distance, and he could feel the muscles in his shoulders wanting to tear. He swung one leg over the top of the fence, still holding on to the rope. Soon the tension would give and the hook would come loose. He managed the other leg and lay, for a moment, facedown, balanced on the top edge of the palisade. In the distance, somebody belched. The ordinariness of the sound seemed wildly out of place. He landed quietly in a crouch in a tangle of hawthorn, still holding the rope, and managed to catch the hook before it hit the ground. Coiling the rope, Essa knelt and pushed it with the hook into the undergrowth, marking his place in relation to the flag mast. It would do no good to lose them if he had to leave in a hurry.

Now he could see the shadowed bulk of the hall, surrounded by more tents than he could count on two hands, pale shapes clustering under the night. He stared for a moment, remembering his place by the fire in there, leaning against Cai's knees as he sang of the bear king from the old days who went across the lake with nine maidens and would return at the hour of his people's direst need. *Well,* Essa thought, *where is he? He hasn't shown his face yet, and his people have been overrun by Anglish.* He could smell the tanned skins used to make the tents: leather and old sailcloth that still stank of rotting seaweed. (When was the last time he'd seen the sea? Seven summers ago?) So there *were* fighting men here with their king, whose standard flapped against the flag mast outside the gate.

Where are you, king of the Mercians?

And then Essa heard the sound of footfalls on the beaten earth: the guard, King Penda's guard. Every fiber in his body urged him to move, get away as fast as he could. A man with a torch emerged from the shadowy jumble of tents, coming closer — a tall, rangy figure with slightly stooped shoulders, moving with the same sense of restrained speed as one of Hild's hunting dogs.

There was nowhere to run.

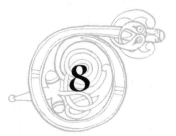

Mercia:
Inside King Penda's fortress

The GUARD stared at Essa for a moment, then let out a loud, sharp crack of laughter. He drew a knife from his belt, and Essa stepped back, heart hammering. "Oh, no," said the guard. "I think it's time I paid out my debt, don't you?" He held the knife by the blade, proffering the bone handle.

Essa laughed, unable to believe his luck, feeling the weight of fear lift. "No, you keep it," he said. "It's been too long."

Of all the people in this camp who could have found him, here was the boy he had once beaten at Fox and Geese.

"Really. You should have it." The boy held out the knife again. Essa took it, buckling the leather scabbard to his belt, nodding his thanks, and sending a silent prayer of gratitude to Jesus Christ and the entire host of the Aesir.

The boy laughed in a friendly way. "I remember your father dragging you off, last time you were here. I was glad to keep my knife, but I always felt bad about it—you'd won fairly."

"That was a long while ago," said Essa, fighting the urge to scramble back over the fence and run for the village as if wild dogs were at his heels. He noticed a brooch in the shape of a boar glittering gold at the boy's throat, holding the thick folds of his cloak together. *Who is he? And why hasn't he asked what I'm doing here?* A prickling feeling slid down his back, and looking down at his arm, Essa saw that every tiny hair was standing on end.

"I don't think I ever learned your name!" said the boy. "I'm Wulf." He held out his hand, and Essa took it.

"I'm Essa." He paid no heed to what he had said at first—his mind was racing through all the possible ways of getting out of the fortress with his skin intact. Back over the wall, once this Wulf had gone? Or out through the gate, even? He had to get back to the village somehow. There was already plenty to tell Egric—it was bad enough that the Mercians had sent fighting men to the border again, with King Penda himself among their number. How much worse could it get? Egric needed to know so that he could ride to the king and lure him out of that monastery to fight.

Then, with a sick jolt, Essa realized he had just given his name.

Wulf looked at him curiously. "Is something wrong? If you're looking for your father, I can show you where they are. So easy to get lost among all these tents, isn't it?"

Essa's insides turned to ice.

"Yes," he said at last. "Please show me — I did get lost; I'm such a gapeseed."

"Come you on." Wulf grabbed Essa's arm, steering him through the camp toward one large tent just by the old hall. "This way," he said. "The hall roof fell in when it snowed last winter, so we're in here." He pulled aside a flap of stitched-together deerskins, pushing Essa through.

Inside the tent, a small group of men sat around a fire that sent a thick column of smoke up through a hole at the top, where the long poles met overhead. They had been talking but fell silent when Wulf and Essa came in.

Essa's eyes were drawn to a man sitting slightly apart from the others. He was dark, hunched in a cloak of ragged bearskin, and his eyes were blacker than well water.

Essa felt as if a fire had been started in his belly that would burn him to ash. Their eyes locked for a moment, and then Cai looked away, speaking to the person next to him: a gray-haired man with thin lips twisted into a faint smile and heavy-lidded eyes that made him look half asleep.

"This is my son, dear lord," Cai said. "He has been here before, when he was a child. I beg you, forgive his low manners. As his father, the blame is all mine."

For years, Essa had pictured this moment, and what he would say: just a cool greeting, as if Cai had been gone only a morning. He knew he should speak, if only to honor the king, but finally faced with his father, he found he could do nothing but stare. Essa heard Wulf laugh quietly behind him. "You have to kneel, Essa," he said. "Even I do, and I'm his son."

It was like being in a dream where he ran and ran but never moved. Trapped, Essa bowed his head and then kneeled before the king of the Mercians, swallowing the desire to rush at Cai and shake answers from him.

"Stand, boy, stand." The king looked Essa up and down as he scrambled to his feet. His eyes narrowed, and Essa's skin prickled. It felt as if Penda could see his thoughts. "He does not resemble you much, Cai. But he does look a bit native, especially around the eyes. Where's your mother, boy? You didn't get red hair like that with a native mother."

"She's dead. And my name is Essa."

A hiss of surprise rose up from the small group of men Cai was sitting with. The king raised his eyebrows; Wulf looked stricken. Clearly this was not the way to speak in front of the king of Mercia.

"My lord," Cai said lightly, "allow me a moment with the boy. It would seem I must remind him of the proper way to speak before a king."

Looking amused, Penda inclined his head in assent.

Outside, Essa turned on his father, but no words would come. He felt as if he were in the spirit world, and that if he touched his father now, Cai would be gone like smoke on the wind.

"Come away." Cai's fingers closed around Essa's forearm, leading him to the shadowed eaves of the hall, and Essa noticed with a jolt that they were now the same height. If anything, Essa was a shade taller.

Cai caught his hand, holding it up so that the gold ring glittered faintly. "What is the meaning of this? How did you come to be here? Answer me."

Essa snatched his hand away. "It is none of your concern!" he hissed, the British words flying to his lips. "You're the last person on earth I must answer to. How could you just *leave*? How could you—"

"Whatever I have done, there has been good reason for," Cai said. "Now tell me why you are here, and who has seen fit to bind you with this ring."

"*Good reason?*" shouted Essa. "I wish you may tell me what these *reasons* were—I've spent many a long night wondering."

He flinched as Cai reached out and laid a hand on his face. Cai's touch was dry and warm as he pushed the hair away from Essa's eyes.

"Jesu, child, you look so much like your mother that I want to weep," Cai said, his voice gentle. Essa felt himself grow sleepy, as if his father had breathed some kind of elf magic on him. "Now, tell me, where did you get this ring? Are you bound to Penda—how did you come to be here? Let me help you."

And Essa heard the words leave his mouth, even though every instinct was telling him to remain silent. "Egric the Atheling gave it me, and he sent me to see if this camp was full of fighting men."

As soon as he spoke, Essa felt sure he had been tricked. He had not meant to say anything, but somehow Cai had drawn the words from his lips.

Cai raised an eyebrow, then smiled and said, "A sly move, Egric. I had not known you were so cunning. Essa, take off the ring."

"*What?*" Essa felt a flash of anger. "How dare you trick me with your elf talk and my mother's name, and then give me orders? I'll not tell you anything more, and the ring stays. I'm bound to Egric now, not you."

Cai's eyes narrowed into dark slits, and he reached out and turned Essa's face to his. This time, his touch seemed to burn, and Essa had to stifle a gasp of pain. "I see a streak of the elvish in you, too," Cai said softly. "It's there, at the back of your eyes, burning away like marshfire. What manner of craft have you been dabbling in, away at that village?"

"Nothing," Essa said breathlessly, and it seemed that his spirit felt Fenrir's calling out to him as she hunted the marsh and that Cai saw this and knew about his skill. He had warned Onela of it; he had known.

"You are lying," Cai said. "But that is for another time. Now listen to me. If anyone here sees that ring, they will cut your throat and probably mine too. What did you think you were going to say when they asked who your lord was? Get rid of it and do it quickly — let us pray that no one has already seen it. How did you get into this place?"

Riled, Essa saw that Cai was right about the ring — there would be no way of explaining it. He slipped it off his finger and strung it up with the blue glass beads that hung around his neck on a leather thong. "There," he said. "But I have answered enough of your questions now. I thought you were loyal to the Wolf Folk — why are you here with Penda, while Egric is rousing the Wolves to defend themselves against him? Tell me!"

Cai smiled, mocking. "You have grown so commanding, little cub. I am here to spy on Penda. Egric's cousin, Anno, sent me. And Penda thinks I am working for him, spying on the Wolf Folk. Lucky for you, I have only just got here; otherwise you'd be dead — although they might have asked a few questions before they killed you, about how many fighting men Hild has got, useful things like that. I thought Egric had more sense."

Essa stared at him, sickened, as he remembered what Hild had said in the yard long ago. I *don't know how much Cai's told you about his life, but there was a time when every king in Britain would have paid their own weight in gold for his advice — well, for the secrets he'd sell them, at any rate.*

"And do you sell tales of the Wolf Folk back to Penda for double the cost?" Essa asked. "Well, even if you are a traitor, I am not. I must go back."

"I do not think so." The laughing edge had left Cai's voice. "I have heard enough from you for now. Come, it is time we returned to Penda."

"You've no command over me," Essa said. "I'm going."

"You will not get far."

"Would you betray me, then?" asked Essa. "I know my

life means no more to you than a fly's, but this is low, even for you, *Father*."

"Do not try me," Cai said. "Now come — and do your best to be respectful to the king. He is a proud fool, and he'll have your throat cut if you cross him."

And for the first time in years, Essa sensed he was in the presence of one who could bend his will just as he was able to do with Fenrir or Myfanwy. No one in the village had managed that, not even Hild, and he loved her more than anyone. Cai laughed, as if he had sensed the color of Essa's thoughts, then turned, walking back to the tent. And Essa followed him.

9

An order from the king of Mercia

BACK in the tent, Essa dropped to his knees and sank down so his forehead rested on the sheepskin at Penda's feet. "I am sorry for my ill conduct, my lord," he said, inhaling the smoky, sheep-oil stink of the wool, and waited there. "My father has taught me better, and the lapse was all mine."

He knew now what these men liked: people on their knees before them. It was so much easier that way to see who was in command.

"You may rise," Penda said, and Essa sat up, his head still bowed. He felt his skin prickle with hatred. "Boys are like dogs, Cai," Penda continued. "If they do not learn absolute obedience, they are not of the smallest use. Now, I own I was not expecting your father to bring you, Essa, but since you are here, it chances that I have a use for you. Next sunrise but one, you will ride with my son to Powys."

"*Powys?*" said Essa, before he could stop himself.

"Father—" Wulf began.

Cai was staring off into the middle distance, as if he had not heard a thing.

Penda held up one thin, blue-veined hand. "We've gone over this matter enough times, Wulfhere. You'll ride to King Eiludd of Powys, and when he's given you his daughter, who I have no doubt will be both fair and wise and bear you many fine sons, you'll return here." He smiled. "And then, if Eiludd wants to come creeping across from the west while I'm taking Anglia off the Christian, I'll cut his daughter's throat, and he knows it. She's his youngest, too. Let us hope he's a fond father."

Wulf shrugged, looking furious. "I know about all that, Father," he said in a tight, angry voice. "But maybe Essa has got other things to do. We cannot just—"

"Of course we can," said Penda. "I can spare no one else, and it will not do for you to go alone. It will look shabby enough with just the two of you. What you need is a lot of pious Christian women as an escort—that would be really proper." He snorted irritably. "You've enough sisters— where are they when I need them? That's the trouble with daughters. Once they're married, that's it—useless. Next sunrise but one, you leave. Cai?"

Cai glanced up and lifted his fingers in a languid gesture of dismissal. "It's about time the boy did something but follow me around," he said. "It makes my teeth hurt when he plays the lyre, so he'll not be earning his keep that way.

87

Let him go with Wulf—and maybe your lordship will have other uses for the boy later."

Penda showed his teeth. It could hardly be described as a smile. "Maybe I will, Cai, maybe I will."

"I am indebted to you, my lord." Cai inclined his head in a slight bow. "No father has been so honored."

"Much you care!" said Essa, in British. "What if I can't go? What if I've got something else to do? And anyway, they're expecting me back in the morning."

"Your manners are filthy," Cai replied, in the same tongue. His voice was like a whipcrack. "Pull yourself together, boy, or you'll be dead by morning. If he finds out where you've come from, there'll be nothing I can do. The man's a savage brute." Then he switched languages so everyone could understand. "What have you to do, anyway, apart from what I tell you?"

Essa bowed his head again. "Of course, Father," he said. "Forgive me."

Penda laughed. "I wager you will be glad to get rid of the unruly brat, Cai. Now, come you all with me—we have sport tonight."

Penda led them through a maze of tents, Wulf holding a torch to light the way, until they came to a small clearing just outside the old hall. Everywhere Essa looked there were fighting men: leaning against the walls, standing around in groups, sleeping by sputtering, fitful campfires outside the tents. But they were all silent—the air was thick with tension.

Essa was walking behind his father, hardly trusting his own eyes — everything about Cai was so familiar, even the way he walked along with one thumb hitched into his belt, his fingers teasing the hilt of his dagger. Had he missed the Silver Serpent all those years? *Did he miss me?*

Then Cai turned, placing his hand on Essa's arm. "We stop here," he said quietly, in British. "We're honored: this little show is in part for our benefit."

Tethered in the clearing before them was a boy, hardly older than Essa. He was dark haired, British, his head bowed, face hidden. Next to him, also tethered, was a woman with thin, hollow cheeks and a tangle of loose black hair. Essa could just make out the faint outlines of the clan tattoos on her cheekbones. She was looking up, staring blankly at the gathering crowd.

They're going to die.

He realized with a prickle of horror that Penda was standing right next to him, so close that Essa could detect the faint scent of garlic and stale wine on his breath.

"Such a waste," Penda said conversationally. "Dai and his sister have been with me for years; he was doing well and would have been a good man to hold a boar shield. You natives aren't short on courage, and I've had more than a few fine fighting men out of your tribes. But it turns out that all along I've not been their master at all: they've been selling Mercian secrets along my northern border.

"Ah well, I'd been wondering why the king of Elmet

stopped paying me his taxes. He sent word saying he'd pay no pagan a single sceatta. He'd pay only the true High King, a Christian man, he says. So the fool wouldn't stop sending his tribute to that witless sap Godsrule in Northumbria. Utter folly, of course. But every time I sent men to collect what was rightfully mine, his camp was gone, like smoke on a spring breeze."

As Penda spoke, the boy, Dai, continued to stare at the ground, but his sister sat back on her heels, staring at the crowd, her eyes dark holes of hatred.

"So they must go," said Penda, almost cheerfully. "Although I do hate a waste. Wulfhere, kill them."

Essa watched, horrified, as Wulf drew a long knife from his belt and walked over to the clearing. People stepped quickly out of the way to let him by. Some made little protective signs above their breasts, silent pleas to the Aesir.

Essa badly wanted to close his eyes, but he knew Penda was watching him. He wanted to shove his way into the clearing and untie the British boy and his sister, run for the gates with them, set them free. But he could not. He had to pretend that this was right and just, the only possible reply to an outright betrayal, otherwise he and Cai would be there in the clearing with them, waiting to die.

Wulf tried to make it quick. He moved swiftly, surely, and the boy died without a sound, slumping forward into the dirt, his throat slit. But the girl's curse was cut off by the knife — a scream that tore into the night. A roar went up from the crowd; Essa could not tell if they were in sympathy with her or just stirred up by the sight of it. Wulf let her body fall to the ground and wiped the knife on his leg as if he had just killed a pig.

"Such a pity," muttered Penda, then raised his voice. "Wulf, take their heads, we'll have them as a warning to anyone else who might be thinking of crossing me. Their bodies we shall give to Lady Frigya — drag them to the bog and throw them in, and give Our Lady the knife as well, that she might lick the blood. You see, Cai — Wulf is a good son. He does everything I ask of him, without question. Essa — assist him. You may as well be useful."

Essa felt faint with horror. For a moment, he thought he was going to have to sit down until his head stopped spinning. He had never seen anyone put to death before. Once, a traveler had brought news of a murder in the hall of the Wolf Folk at Rendlesham, but the murderer's family had just given the victim's a milch cow, and that was the end of it. Now he could see why Penda was known as the Mad Dog. He was savage, crazed. But then a small voice spoke in Essa's head, saying, *But are you any different from Penda? You have killed, too. You are a killer.* And once again, he was in the beech coppice, thrusting his knife backward into the belly of the man choking him.

Heart racing, Essa bowed his head and said, "Father, do I have your leave?"

Cai shrugged. "Of course." Then he left, following Penda back to the tent.

Wulf had already taken the heads, with swift cuts that

made the blade of his sword sing through the air. "You don't have to help. I know it's a mucky job."

Essa shrugged in as Cai-like a fashion as he could manage, trying not to look at the slumped, headless bodies lying on the cold mud, their limbs tangled together. The boy's fingers had uncurled: a wooden crucifix rested in the palm of his hand. "I don't mind," he said. "They deserved it. Traitors."

Wulf did not seem to have heard. "I always try to give them poppy wine when he makes me do this," he said, dragging a blanket from the nearest tent. "I go over when no one's looking and slip them a draft. It dulls their senses, you see. But the girl wouldn't take any."

Essa nodded. He did not know what to say.

But he did know that nothing would prevent him from putting a stop to Wulf's father. One way or another.

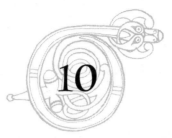

10

From Mercia back into Wixna-land

CSSA sat up. The tent was cloaked in darkness and quiet: everyone had gone to sleep, and all he could hear was the sound of people breathing heavily. He was meant to be leaving, with Wulf, at dawn. Would there be enough time?

He stepped outside and ran through the maze of tents toward the stables. Wulf had taken him there the day before to choose his mount, but it was not the dappled gray mare he went to now.

"Melyor!" He whispered her name into the dusty, straw-smelling darkness. She was standing in her stall, nosing at the latch on the half door as if she had been waiting for him. He caught her long, intelligent face between his hands and rested his head against hers.

Knowing that Cai slept nearby, he led her out of the stall, wincing at every creak of a hinge, every soft thud as her hooves struck a stone embedded in the earthen floor.

He had only one chance to get this right.

The men guarding the gate were sleeping. It had not been hard to guess where Wulf hid his poppy-wine draft; Essa had found it in the leather bag that hung from Wulf's belt, and had taken the little silver bottle while he slept. The dogs were another matter.

He pressed himself against the fence, feeling the rough wood against his shoulder blades. He could hear the dogs breathing, feel the rhythm of their heartbeats, swifter than those of the sleeping guards. Melyor waited silently beside him. He'd have to be quick: it was one thing to find a boy skulking around the gate, but there would be no excuse for a boy and a horse. There would be another head on a pole by the gate. The British boy's and his sister's were there now, still trailing long black hair. He found he had to look at them, absorb the horror of it, to stoke his courage. Penda had to be stopped.

He closed his eyes; one of the dog heartbeats grew louder till he could feel it himself, the blood pounding in his ears as if it were his. Then, the familiar tug in the pit of his stomach as dog senses grew more acute and his own senses were left behind in the shell of his body. He could smell fresh blood. He felt the dog's thoughts.

Old chief two-legs has mauled some of his pack; left bits of them just out of reach. Two-legs who leaves meat is asleep, him and his two brothers, all snoring like cubs. No good. And there's another, too, a cub one, and flying-tail. Should not be there. No. Flying-tail flicks back her ears. She hears.

Lie down and sleep, Essa thought. *Never mind the cub one; let him go.* He felt the dog's confusion and unease, almost as if it were aware of his cuckoo-like presence in its body.

I must call, it thought. *Call for more two-legs.*

The smell of blood grew fainter. *Just let the cub one go.* Then, in a heartbeat, Essa was back inside his own body, cursing himself, wishing there were someone who could teach him how to do this properly. It was one thing for his spirit to slip into the body of a dog, quite another to steer the dog's free will to his own course. It was like being in a boat but having no control over the sails; he was just pushed by the wind, by the force of the beast's own being.

He slumped forward, grinding his fingers into the dirt, thwarted. He had to get back to the village, and he was not going to be stopped by a couple of mangy hounds. He got up, leaning back against the wall. Fenrir. Where was she? If she called, maybe they would go to her. He let his spirit drift again — he could feel her presence, somewhere out there in the marsh.

Come on, girl. Call to them, call to your brothers and sisters by the gate, make them run with you, hunt with them.

Then, faintly, he heard her answering cry.

Yes!

One by one, the three dogs slipped through the open

gate, leaving the sleeping guardsmen alone at their posts. He mouthed silent thanks to Fenrir.

It felt good to ride Melyor. Better even than sneaking past the sleeping guards. They would pay with their lives if Penda found out, Essa was sure, and he felt a flash of guilt. Then again, his life would be forfeit too, if Penda ever discovered what he was about to do. Despite all this, riding Melyor was better than knowing he had gotten clear of the fortress and that there was nothing but the marsh between him and the village. He was free.

They trotted silently through the sparse woodland surrounding Penda's fortress, drawing closer to the marsh. Essa listened carefully; he could hear the high keening howl of hunting dogs in full chase, and he was glad Fenrir had some pack brothers to run with. He just hoped the dogs would not suffer for it later, and that he would not have to call Fenrir back when he returned. There was hardly enough time as it was, and he wanted to make sure she was outside the gates at dawn, ready to join him and Wulf on their journey west.

He dug in his heels and Melyor surged forward. He clutched at her mane as marsh water flew up at his face. He breathed fond words into her ears, then sat back, gripping with his legs. There had been no time to saddle her, but he knew he would be safe. One of his first memories was of Cai propping him up on Melyor's bare back, walking alongside the horse as she carried him safely. It felt as if he were joined to her, even after all these years.

"Go on, girl," he whispered. "Go faster for me, just this once. I'll never ask again."

They tore across the marshy flatland, stars blurring in the sky above, cold wind whipping at his face, and it felt as if the huge dome of night above was absorbing his anger. These men might think they could play with him, moving him about like a goose piece on a gaming board, but he was not beaten yet. He would not be part of their game. *Whatever that might be.* Who did Cai think he was, leaving him like that? What was he doing? *He could've come to get me anytime. He just didn't want to.* For years he had thought that his father was dead and that nothing could be worse than that. But he was wrong. This was far worse.

He had to get back to the village.

He slowed Melyor to a canter, watching her sides heave as the willows started to thin out on the Anglian side of the marsh. He let her drink from the reedy water as they approached dry land, and he dug in his heels again when he caught sight of the village walls through the trees. His stomach surged when he saw Egric's standard, the running wolf, hanging limply from the flag mast. No need to ask what was the penalty for treason, for disobeying a ring giver, for running off to do the bidding of an enemy king. It would be far worse than being exiled, sent into the wild-wood as Egric had threatened. In his mind's eye, he saw the British boy slumping forward into a pool of his own blood, heard his sister's dying curse torn off, rising to a ragged scream. He just hoped it would be quick when it came —

97

a thrust of cold metal between his ribs, his heart bursting. *If it comes,* he told himself angrily. *It might not happen. Don't think on what might not happen.*

There was no choice. He had to do it. He had to go with Wulf, or Cai would face questions he would not be able to answer without losing his life. Egric would just have to understand that there had been no choice. Was that a grey sliver of dawn he could see on the eastern horizon?

"I'm sorry, girl," he whispered. "But I've got to be quick."

Melyor obeyed his touch, but he slowed her again as they neared the alder coppice. Under the cover of the trees, he put his fingers to his mouth and whistled, hoping Cole or Red would be awake. Melyor shifted beneath him, as if she were eager to move again.

"Wait, girl," he whispered. "Easy, easy."

Moments dragged by. No sound came from within the great earthen walls. He whistled again, his heart thudding. If he didn't get back to the camp by dawn, if they discovered Melyor was missing, what would Penda do? Penda wasn't stupid: he *knew* Essa hadn't arrived in the camp with Cai. He had guessed. He was playing some kind of game, just as Cai himself was.

Maybe Penda would kill Cai. Did he already know he was a traitor?

Feeling desperate, Essa lifted his fingers to his lips to whistle a third time, when he heard something: footsteps, someone running lightly across the yard to the gate. Hild? No. She didn't know the whistle signal. Essa dismounted and, leaving Melyor in the alder coppice, scrambled up the mound to the gate. It creaked open, leaving a tiny crack.

It was Lark.

He stood there, the breath torn from his body by the sight of her. Her face had changed, the coldness gone. Lark had come to life again before him, as if she had just been released from some elvish binding.

"Essa!" She slid through the small gap and wrapped her arms tightly around him, squeezing the breath from his chest. "Where have you been?" she cried.

For a moment, she was all. Just Lark and the heat of her body, the scent of her skin making him feel drunk. There was nothing else in the world. He fought the urge to lean down and whisper in her ear, "Come away with me," and ride out into the wide world with her in the saddle before him. But he knew he could not.

Then he wanted to laugh with relief that after all these years of not speaking, of not even looking at each other, she was here in his arms. But everything now depended on silence. "Shh." He stepped back, clutching at her hands. "Listen. I can't stay. I got caught."

"What? Who by?"

"You won't believe it: Cai. He was there, with Penda."

Lark's face was pale and frightened in the silvery darkness. "Cai—your father? What was he doing in *Penda's* camp? I thought he was Seobert's man. Essa, I thought he must've been dead by now, he never—"

"Shh. He's a spy—for both sides. I don't know who he's

really loyal to, but he's there. Now, look, Penda's sending me away with his son—to Powys. Cai just let him do it. We leave at dawn." He gripped Lark's fingers even tighter, to silence her. "If I don't go, Penda will doubt me. I need to leave here straightaway, only you've got to help me. I need—"

"But Egric, Hild—they've been waiting up all night, and all last night, too."

Essa shook his head impatiently. "When I've gone, tell them Penda's got a camp full of fighting men, and he's mustering his troops. He's marrying one of his sons to the king of Powys's daughter—so he doesn't get attacked from the west while all his men are riding out to the east, to here."

Lark's eyes grew bright. "Here? Oh, no—"

"I'm going to try to stop it. I don't know what I'll do, but something. Tell Egric if they don't rouse Seobert to fight or pick another king, then we're finished. And tell him I'm sorry for going, but I've no choice. I'll be loyal to him, I swear."

"You're not being, though," whispered Lark. "You're being loyal to Cai. But why should Egric have chosen you, anyway? That's what I can make no sense of. I had such a misgiving when he gave you that ring—"

"It's to do with that day in the beech coppice," Essa said quickly. "When I killed that man. I'm sure of it, but I don't know how. Egric knows something about me. He knows—" He wanted to tell her about Egric speaking to him in British, calling him Aesc, son of Cai, but he felt sure the sky had lightened already. "I must go, Lark. It's not a question of being loyal to Egric or Cai — I want to find out what I am." He stepped away, letting go of her hands.

"What you are? Essa, don't talk nonsense. You're just yourself."

"I know that," he said, wanting to tell her about his spirit journey, but there was no time — he would be lucky to get back before he was missed. "It's only that Egric's using me for some reason — I'm sure of it — and I want to know what kind of game he's playing. Now I must go."

"Essa, be careful."

"I will, and you too. And tell Cole to look after you."

"I'll look after him!" She smiled unhappily, her face wet with tears.

Essa held her tight. He saw that the gray line on the eastern horizon had widened just slightly. Not long till daylight. He knew that when he let her go, it would hurt as much as it had done the day she walked away from him in the stable, the day he had taken a man's life. But there was no choice; he had to go. Would he get back in time? "Listen," he said. "I need you to get something for me — my sword, the one with the black-and-silver scabbard. Can you get it? Run!"

Lark looked at him gravely, then pulled away and ran back into the village. Essa sprinted down the slope into the coppice, where Melyor was waiting, swung himself up onto her back, then trotted back to the gate. He heard the sound of hinges creaking as Lark let herself into the smithy, where the weapons were stored, then creaking again as she let herself out. He imagined her standing on tiptoe in the darkness, silently lifting the sword off the two nails banged into the wall. Then, after what seemed like ages, she was back, handing it to him with silent misery etched across her face. She offered up the sword, and the silver dragons chasing each other around the scabbard glinted in the moonlight. He leaned down to take it from her, his fingers closing around the familiar shape of the handle as he buckled the Silver Serpent to his belt.

They clasped hands briefly.

Lark looked at him, a strange, hard light in her eyes. "Go," she said. "Go on. And swear you'll come back."

He nodded, unable to answer her, and went.

Cai was waiting for him outside the stable when he got back. He squinted up at the pink stripe of light in the eastern sky. "Cutting it fine, are you not?" he said.

"Oh, hold your talk." Exhausted, Essa dismounted, the muscles in his thighs screaming after the blistering ride across the marsh and back. "I could hardly not go, could I?" He led Melyor into the stable, not bothering to see if Cai would follow.

"It's dawn." Cai stood in the doorway of Melyor's stall, watching as she dipped her great roan head to the water trough. "You'd better go and break your fast. It's a long journey. I'll look after her."

"What's your little game, anyway?" Essa spun around to face him, whispering harshly. "I thought you were meant to be loyal to the Wolf Folk! What are you doing here, getting all friendly with Egric's worst enemy? You're hardly singing songs." He snorted. "Some scop you are. Who are you really working for—Seobert or Penda? You're just a traitor."

Cai smiled. "How can I be a traitor, dear child, when I have no king?"

"What?" Essa stared at him, then laughed. "Because you're British?"

Cai raised his eyes heavenward, a faint, mocking smile playing at the corner of his mouth. "I have one Lord, and He rules them all. When the day comes, I will be judged by Him alone."

Essa shook his head in disbelief. "Well, if I'm dead before the year's out, I hope your *Lord* knows who to blame."

Cai looked at him with an expression of faint surprise, as if he thought he had been alone in the stable and had only just realized Essa was standing there. "Well, go on, then," he said. "Go and get something to eat—you won't last the day if you don't. It's a long way to Powys."

West through the wildwood of Mercia

ESSA leaned back in the saddle, feeling the reins rasping through his palm. He held them loosely and closed his eyes.

They were in the middle of the greenwood, the great forest that stretched from the Anglian marshlands to the foothills of the western mountains, and he was looking for a bird. A finger of breeze teased his hair, brushing across his forehead. Far above his head, branches danced in the wind, filled with rich sap aching to break free of winter's frozen clutch. In the distance, he heard the coughing bark of a roe deer, and he knew Fenrir would soon start thirsting for a hunt and a kill. *But not yet, my girl. Not yet.*

In his mind's eye, he saw a song thrush perching high in the branches of an old beech: she was oyster-shell pale, splattered with dark speckles. The song thrush raised her head, the inside of her beak a splash of flame-bright orange. Her call rang out across the forest, and Essa's heart wanted to burst from his chest with the joy of it, because winter was losing its battle with the sun. The earth was slowly warming as the Aesir breathed life into it again.

He felt the swift tug in his belly as his spirit left his body, and then, looking down, Essa saw folk on the forest floor — two boys. He felt the stretch as the song thrush spread her wings, darting from branch to branch, and he willed her to fly free of the trees so he could see where they were. *Go, go.* But the song thrush just shot down to the ground, knocked a snail off a log, and started tapping it against the moldy bark.

Opening his eyes and tweaking the reins, Essa cursed. They'd been lost for at least a day. He had been sure it would work, that he would be able to slip inside a bird and fly up above the trees and get some sense of which way they were heading. But it was not like with Myfanwy, whom he had trained for years to come to him for food; the thrush was wild.

They were lost. They should have been on the right track: they had ridden for twelve days with the sun at their backs in the morning, then straight toward it as it set. But they were still deep in the middle of the forest, Essa was sure. The trees were woven together as thickly as ever. And what was the use of being able to slip the shackles of his body and fly with the birds if all they wanted to do was eat snails?

"It's that hound slowing us down," said Wulf, laughing. "I can see why your father told you to get rid of it."

Fenrir had appeared just after they'd ridden out of the

fort, and Wulf had swallowed Essa's lying explanation without question. Nothing seemed to ruffle him — he was content to ride about the forest, getting nowhere, but it was starting to drive Essa mad. The longer he was away, the worse it would be with Egric when he got back.

"Don't talk foolish," he said. "Fenrir won't slow us down — she's a deerhound. She's fast enough. And if we went any quicker, we'd tire the horses."

Wulf snorted derisively. Essa ignored him. Had the sun really been at their backs each morning? In truth, the canopy of trees was so thick that Essa could not swear to it. They might have ridden too far to the north or south. There was no way of knowing. If only he had Myfanwy here, or could get inside the right bird, one that would fly high enough to break out of the trees and allow him to see where they were. But that could take days. Days and days, and Wulf would start to wonder what was wrong with him.

What was the point in being different from everyone else, of having this strange gift, if he could not use it? He wished now he had told Cai the truth back in Penda's camp. Onela had been right about Cai; he had some kind of elf gift too, Essa was sure. The way he had of drawing out your most secret thoughts was no ordinary skill, and there was a strange light in his black eyes. Maybe Cai would have known how Essa could learn to command the will of wild creatures. Perhaps the skill had come from his mother's family, but it was no good wishing she were here to teach him the way of it.

So we're stuck. We'll just have to keep going.

Penda's men and Cai had told them the great forest would start to thin by late morning on the tenth day. Then they would be out of Mercia, with the wide plains of the Magonsæte, the border people, between them and the western kingdoms of the British. They should have been able to see purple mountains on the horizon when they came to the wood shore: the gates to Powys. Essa had tried all the tricks he knew; cutting markers into tree trunks with his knife to make sure they were not going around in circles (they were not), keeping the north star on their right-hand side (useless: the night sky was full of cloud and always hidden by the trees). Nothing worked.

"Oh, well," muttered Wulf. "The longer the delay, the better. She's probably going to be some pox-faced toad with a face like a dog chewing a wasp. Let's slow down even more, and Eiludd Powys can keep his wretched daughter a few days longer. I hope she's not a complaining, sickly wench with too much religion. I don't understand you Christians. What a miserable death for the son of a king, getting nailed to a cross. Why did your Lord let such a thing happen to his own child?"

Essa felt the color flood to his face. "It was for our wrongdoing," he said. "Jesus died for our sins, so that we might have the chance to get into heaven when we die."

"What's heaven?"

Essa struggled to remember. What Cai had once taught him he had forgotten. "It — it is not hell, which is torment and punishment and misery."

Wulf shrugged. "I'll place my trust in the Aesir," he said. "There's enough misery in life without having to concern yourself with it after you're dead."

But Essa was no longer paying him any heed. "It's not right," he said. "We should be near the western edge of the wood by now." The moon had been just a silver hook in the sky when they left Penda's fortress, and now it was almost full: round and cold when he glimpsed it between the branches.

"Maybe we are," Wulf said. "It's that dark, we might be anywhere. We should stop soon, fill our bellies, and get some sleep."

"We're not at the wood shore," Essa replied. The air was still thick with the musty reek of rotting leaf mold: if they were near the wood shore, that smell would have faded, stirred up with the sharp, heathery scent of grassy moorland and the distant, cold smell of the mountains. It had been a long time since Essa had been in high country, but he remembered the clean, clear edge to the air. No, they were still in the heart of the forest, but there was something different. What was it? He was tired, and his thoughts trickled slowly through his mind like stiff honey on a cold day.

"There's no really big trees," he whispered, more to himself than to Wulf. "This is new woodland. Someone was here; they cleared the land, and then when they left, the trees grew back." A prickly feeling settled across Essa's shoulders, as if someone were watching him and he could not see who it was. He remembered that day in the beech coppice with Lark and the man who had come to kill him.

"Wulf, we must get out of this place now." He struggled to keep his voice steady. Fear had him by the throat, and he could barely breathe.

"Ah, do you stop jumping and fretting like a girl," said Wulf as he guided Balder, his white gelding, through the lattice of birch, elder, rowan, and ash. "You're like an unbroken horse, you are, frighting at shadows."

Maybe he was right. Maybe Essa was just being foolish, flapping and squawking like a chicken. Fenrir let out a small, purring growl. He glanced down at her: her ears were flattened against her head, her gait stiff-legged, as if she had just caught the scent of another roe deer, far away in the trees, and was about to run for it.

Essa listened, ears alert for a cracking twig, a footfall, a sharp drawing-in of breath — anything that might betray an unseen watcher. Nothing. Although it was not even very cold, he shivered. Ahead of him, Balder looked like a ghost horse, Wulf just a smudge of darkness on her back, partially concealed by a crisscross pattern of thin, whippy branches.

There was something wrong; he knew it.

And then Wulf turned around to face him, his teeth shining in the darkness. "Look," he said. "Stones. Walls of stone, over there in the clearing. Oh, the air must be thick with spirits around here."

The ruined buildings loomed up out of the trees like trading boats Essa had once watched sail out of the mist onto a beach in Rheged. Beside him, he heard Wulf whistle in admiration.

"Stow your gab, will you?" Essa's shoulders were still prickling.

"There's no need to be afraid of stones and ghosts," said Wulf cheerfully. "They can't hurt. Come on, let's have a look."

"No!"

But Wulf had already dug his heels into Balder's sides, and the tired horse moved on. Essa whispered an apology to his own horse and followed, whistling for Fenrir.

It had once been a great hall. Now it was a ruin. Trees grew where the roof used to be, and shutterless windows gaped out of crumbling walls. Wooden buildings rotted within the courtyard, as if people had tried to carry on living there, rebuilding and pretending everything was normal, but without the knowledge or the desire to repair the sprawling stone house. Essa felt his stomach tighten, and warm spit flooded his mouth.

Wulf dismounted, leaving Balder standing. Cursing under his breath, Essa followed him. He whistled softly; Fenrir turned and padded toward him, her head hanging low. She was tired, too. As he ran his hand along her knobbly spine, he felt her sides heaving. Her ears were still flattened against her skull, and she let out another low, rumbling growl.

Wulf clutched at Essa's sleeve as they approached the silent house. "Look," he whispered. "It's all blackened and burned. There must have been a great fire." He put his hand to the wall, and it came away dark with age-old soot.

Essa nodded. It must have been a huge blaze, turning the woodland surrounding the house to ash on the wind. The trees here now were young: no more than a few generations of growth. What of those who had survived the fire and stayed, building shelter from the ruins? Had they just died off, one by one? Had they taken to the sea, or chosen the route across the mountains to Powys, as he was doing now?

"Wulf, we should leave this place." He turned to glance over his shoulder at Balder and Grani, who were nosing in the undergrowth for something to eat. "It's bad here. Fenrir's unsettled, too."

"We'll move on at dawn, get our bearings straight," said Wulf, stepping lightly through a gap in the wall. "We can't be that lost."

Essa felt the cold shiver settle about his shoulders like a frozen mantle of deerskin.

Someone watched, yet no one was there.

A quick, hot thrill of excitement flared in his belly as he followed Wulf into the ruins, but he was still uneasy, unable to shake off the feeling they were not alone. For a moment, Fenrir sat back on her haunches, barking twice, but followed when she saw he was not coming back, catching up in a couple of long strides. He glanced over his shoulder as they clambered over a fallen stretch of wall, but he saw only the horses.

"Look at this!" hissed Wulf, standing in the center of a

courtyard flanked on three sides by the walls of the rambling villa and on the fourth by a roofless outbuilding. The stones shone pale under the moonlight, like ghosts. Essa could not picture living in a house of stone, so cold and unforgiving.

Give me a wooden hall any day, he thought, *with the tales of the Aesir carved into the beams and dragons with golden eyes watching from the roof, and the wide doors open to the sun.*

Rickety shacks rose drunkenly from within the walls of the villa, poking up through the gap left by the collapsed roof. Wind and rain had torn away the plaster, leaving a crisscross of lathing open like the exposed ribs of a dead sheep Essa had once seen rotting at the bottom of Long Acre.

"How long do you think people stayed, I mean, afterward?" Wulf said. "Look at the floor! This place must've been a fair sight."

Essa looked down: they were standing on a school of playing dolphins, laid out in hundreds of tiles barely bigger than his thumbnail. How long would that take to do, he wondered? He couldn't imagine anyone back in the village having the time to spare. In the center of the courtyard, a young woman, hewn from solid rock, held a basin above her head. The large bowl at her feet was still stained with lichen, the water long since dried up and gone. Every detail of her face was perfect, her eyes downcast as if she were about to look up at any moment.

Then Fenrir barked, again and again till it sounded like a howl.

Essa grabbed Wulf's arm, glancing around for her. A moment ago, she'd been right beside him — now she was nowhere to be seen. The still night air was filled with her voice. "Look, we've got to get ourselves gone. Fenrir's seen something."

"Come on, don't be foolish," said Wulf. "She's just howling at the moon. Our dogs do it all the time."

"She's not!" Essa tugged him back toward the horses, calling, "Fenrir, Fenrir, come, girl, come!"

But Wulf was still staring at the fountain, at the beautiful stone girl with her empty stone bowl. "It's like elf magic." He drew in a deep breath. "I've not seen anything like it. Could we lift her off the base, do you think? She'd make a fine gift for—"

Essa felt the blow before it connected with the back of his skull: the quick rush of air displaced by a heavy weapon, then the burst of pain. Before he fell, he saw Wulf crumple to the floor beside him, and dark figures rose on all sides, drifting from the shadows of the ruined buildings.

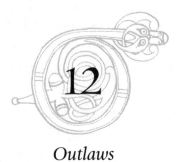

Outlaws

CSSA lay on his back, unable to sleep. The blankets were full of stones, and they moved beneath him.

"Stop moving," he muttered. He tried to fling out an arm and realized his hands were bound. His shoulders blazed with pain as he was dragged along the ground, and he felt a warm, thin line of blood trickle down his right arm, where the skin had been torn from his wrist by a rope. The air was thick with the baying of a hound, a wild, bloodthirsty sound. His heel caught on a tussock, and above his head someone swore.

"That cursed dog. Why don't we just kill it?"

"You try! She looks like she could have you for breakfast, my friend."

Fenrir. Where was she?

He forced his eyes open. The back of his head throbbed and pulsed, and greenish spots blurred his sight. Someone was hauling him along like a dead sheep being taken out to hang. He drew a deep breath, praying his captors had not noticed he was awake. The long sword still hung at his belt, dragging through the leaf mold, bouncing over knotted tree roots protruding from the soil.

Fool, fool. You knew *there was something wrong. . . .*

Who were these people?

He squinted across to his right and saw a heavyset man with long, matted trails of hair hauling Wulf unceremoniously across the forest floor. Wulf's body was limp, and his head dangled at an odd angle. Essa's heart bunched up like a bloody fist — *Wulf can't be dead.* The man dragging him glanced across and grinned at Essa's own unseen captor. A long scar ran down one side of his face, and there was something wrong with one of his ears. Essa squinted, fighting the pain in his shoulders and head, forcing himself not to cry out. The ear looked as if it had melted and unraveled down the man's neck — the lobe snaked down in almost a straight line. To his left, a third man, short and wiry, led Grani and Balder.

They'd hooked a rich haul, all right, with all the gifts for King Eiludd's daughter stuffed into the saddlebags: garnet brooches, a silver bowl from Constantinople to hang from the high rafters of her father's hall, bales of fine white linen, and a long sword.

Then he saw Fenrir, and relief coursed through him. She was prowling stiff-legged around the group, ears pricked up. She'd stopped barking but was growling now, a low, menacing sound that seemed to shake the ground.

115

Wulf's captor, the one-eared northerner, turned again and spoke. "We should take care, *kaveth*. These ones look rich. I don't want to bring anyone big and powerful down on top of us." His accent was northern, and he had used a British word, *kaveth*, mixing tongues just as the northerners did. *It's in tha face.* Essa felt a fresh jolt of fear. For a moment, he was back in the beech coppice with Lark and the dying man who had tried to kill him.

Then Essa's own captor spoke, "It's more than dangerous, but they've fallen into our hands." He had the same accent as Wulf; he was Mercian, but Essa could have sworn the man leading the horses was a pure-blooded Briton: shorter than the others, fine-boned, wiry, and dark.

Outlaws. They'd been taken by outlaws: men banished from the halls of their fathers, rings torn from their fingers. Men forced to dwell in the forests and mountains, in the high, wild places where no one else went. They were traitors, murderers, thieves, or sometimes they had just fought on the losing side of a battle, their lords dead, their gold rings worthless. They were kingless men, beyond the reach of the law and the warmth of the hall.

He almost wanted to laugh. He was going to be just like them, if Egric did not kill him first, for his treachery.

If *they* did not kill him.

Rage flashed through his body like the shock from a burn. He would not die like this, like a beast going out to slaughter. He let his mind go blank for a moment, took a deep breath, and kicked out with his legs, twisting his body like a salmon. His hands were tightly bound; he could feel the rope biting into his wrists, but the shock of sudden movement tugged them from his captor's grasp. He heard Fenrir baying again, one of the men yelling in fear, and he prayed she would not try to bring one of them down like a deer. Then they would certainly kill her.

A shout of fury echoed through the darkness as he rolled across the ground, staggering to his feet. His bound hands became a weapon; he forced them up into the face of the man who came running at him, smashing both fists into his nose. Essa could hardly see; he let out a bark of laughter as the man staggered backward, his face splattered with thick, dark blood.

He wheeled around to face the two other men. "Do you want some, too?"

The northerner let Wulf drop to the floor, and Essa heard him groaning. At least he wasn't dead.

"Grab him, you fools!" yelled the Mercian, wiping the blood from his mouth. He stalked over to Essa, reaching for his knife. "Give me one good reason why I shouldn't cut your throat, *maw*."

The Briton and the northerner came closer, drawing short, clawlike fighting knives from their belts. They circled him; he was surrounded. Then Fenrir came tearing from the shadows and cut them off, leaping up, pawing their chests, howling with rage. Cursing and screaming, they fell back, flinging up their arms to shield their faces.

"Down, Fenrir, down!" Essa yelled. She dropped back

and stood there, rigid, teeth bared. *Good girl, there's my girl.*

The rope around his wrists was looser now; he flexed his fingers and yanked his hands apart. Closing his fingers around the handle of the Silver Serpent, he drew her from the scabbard. The gleaming metal sang a hissing note as she sliced through the air. He laughed, breathless. "Who wants a taste?" His voice was harsh, unrecognizable. Had he spoken in his own language or not?

It was as if he were floating above his own body, watching a stranger leap at the Mercian, sword raised.

"He's crazy!" the Mercian yelled, jumping back out of the way, his face still smeared with blood.

Essa swung his sword, the blade sang through the air. On the ground, Wulf groaned again and sat up unsteadily. His eyes went wide, and he scrambled to his feet, tall and wolfish, moving with the contained passion of a hound about to spring.

"Essa, watch your back!" he yelled, trying to shake his bound hands free of the rope.

Essa whirled around, and the northerner leaped out of the way, knife still raised in his fist. Dodging Fenrir, the Briton ran at Wulf, but Wulf sidestepped him, using his bound hands as a weapon just as Essa had done, and piled both fists into the man's face. Then Fenrir spun around, leaping, and brought the northerner down.

"Get her off me, for God's sake!"

Essa caught a glimpse of her standing on his chest, and

he knew she was thirsting for blood, longing to rip out his throat. It had been a long time since she had brought down a deer, and her need to kill was strong. *No, girl, he'll put a knife in your ribs, my honey—*

Where was the Mercian? Essa could not see him; one moment he had been backing away through the trees, the next he was gone. The Briton fell, clutching at his face and cursing Wulf, and Essa felt a hot line of pain down his side. The Mercian was behind him, laughing, tossing the knife from one hand to the other.

"There's a little taste for you," he said, and Essa glanced down at his tunic. Where his cloak had fallen away, he saw a dark stain spreading across the pale linen, and the line of pain intensified. It felt as if someone had drawn a line on his bare skin with a burning branch, but the two things did not seem connected.

"Essa!" yelled Wulf. "He's going to get you again! Get out of the way!"

His mind went blank; suddenly everything seemed very clear, sharply defined. The Mercian had a small birthmark on his forehead, the shape of an acorn. He was smiling, and Essa could see one of his teeth was chipped at the front. Bright points of light in the night sky peeped down at the earth between the tapestry of branches: Lady Frigya's discarded jewels. A high, singing noise pierced the silence, and something flashed before his eyes. His hand jerked down the sword handle—the blade had connected with something—he nearly dropped it. A bloody, animal scream ripped across the night, and the Mercian fell to the ground.

Essa stepped back, breathing heavily. He glanced over his shoulder: Fenrir was still standing over the northerner, who had twisted over onto his side and was watching in horror. Essa whistled through his teeth, and she came running to him and stood panting by his side. He reached for her and stood there for a few moments, running one of her long gray ears through his fingers, unable to look.

"Is he dead?" He expected the northerner and the Briton to rush at him now that he had called off Fenrir, but they did not. Everyone stood very still. Wulf was staring at Essa as if he had never seen him before, a grim little smile teasing the corner of his mouth.

On the ground, the Mercian rolled to one side, letting out a deep groan. He had left behind one of his hands on the forest floor, fingers clawing up at the night.

Essa had cut off his hand, just above the wrist.

"I'm sorry," he said, uselessly.

The Briton and the northerner shoved past him, the Briton tearing a strip from his tunic, kneeling by his friend to try to stop the bleeding. The Mercian was moaning, a low, deep noise that made Essa's guts freeze. Blood pumped from the wrist stub in thick, dark globs.

The northerner looked him up and down. "Where'd tha get that sword, *maw*?" he said. "Where'd tha steal it from?"

"I didn't," said Essa. Suddenly he remembered finding it lying in the trough in the stables, and realizing that Cai had left him. The silver dragons on the scabbard had glinted at him in the gloom. "My father gave her to me. King Edwin gave it him."

The northerner stared at him, his eyes pools of sorrow. "Ah, Edwin was my lord, my ring giver," he whispered. "But now he's dead, and Ad Gefrin, my hall, burned to the ground by Penda's barbarians. And I must wander like this forever." He looked down at the sword. "But that was never given to your father by Edwin. That's the Lady's sword. Tha hast the Lady's sword, *maw*. May God forgive you."

"What?" said Essa, but Wulf was beside him, holding the horses by their leading reins. "Come you *on*, let's go. There might be more of them, a whole nest of outlaws living in the forest; we won't stand a chance if the rest get here."

The northerner was still staring at Essa, scrutinizing his face as if he were looking for someone he knew.

"Essa!"

He felt Wulf's hand on his arm and swung himself into the saddle. Pain knifed his side, and he slumped forward, letting Grani carry him into the night.

They found their way out of the woods more by chance than by skill. Wulf made some pretense of squinting up at the stars and nodding in a knowing fashion, but Essa knew that he was just trying to reassure him. His tunic was soaked with blood, and he felt as if his brains had leaked out of his ears, leaving an empty space in his head. The right-hand side of his body was alight with pain, and every step Grani took made him want to scream. Wulf had torn a strip from the white linen intended as a wedding gift for King Eiludd's daughter and had insisted on binding it around Essa's middle to stanch the blood flow, muttering that, luckily, it didn't look too deep a cut, or Essa would have been good for nothing by morning. He pressed his lips together and rode in silence as the sky lightened toward dawn. Fenrir trotted behind them, her muzzle nearly scraping the ground. She was exhausted, and Essa was racked with guilt at bringing her. *I should've sent you back to the village, my honey. I'm sorry.* But he knew that if Fenrir hadn't brought down the northerner, they would probably all three be dead.

"Look," said Wulf. "The trees are getting thinner again. I think we're all right."

Essa nodded dumbly. In his mind, he could still see the severed hand lying pale among the dead leaves on the forest floor, fingers clutching at nothing. But Wulf was right. The air smelled different. He could smell grass, and he heard the cry of the linnet rising up from the dawn song of the woodland birds, so he knew they must be quite near open grassland.

For days, Essa had been longing for the sight of a clear horizon, clear of the trees, but when it came, he felt so dizzy and sick that he could hardly even return Wulf's grin.

"We've done it," Wulf said. They stopped the horses at the wood shore, staring out across the rolling, bare green hills tumbling toward them from the feet of the great white-capped mountains in the distance, the gates of Powys. At their backs, behind the great forest, the sun was rising.

"The marches of the Magonsæte," said Wulf, helping Essa to dismount. "Father said he'd grant me the western marches if I do well against the Wolf Folk." Essa stood leaning on his arm, breathing heavily. For a moment they stood together, looking out toward the west.

Beneath his tunic, Egric's ring hung cold against Essa's chest, chilling his skin.

"Essa," said Wulf. "Look, I know you and Cai aren't bound to any king, but if you fight with me against the Wolf Folk, I'll grant you lands out here. You saved my life earlier on, and I owe you. Will you fight with my father and me, when we get back?"

Essa drew in a deep, wheezy breath, fighting the urge to laugh.

He shook his head. "Wulf," he said. "I can't."

Wulf looked hurt, lowering his eyes to the ground. Then he smiled. "You've more sense than I thought, then," he said. "It'll be a bloody fight. My father's given orders that we kill every man, woman, and child until we cross the River Deben and torch the hall of the Wolf Folk at Rendlesham."

Essa dropped to his knees, fighting the urge to groan out loud. He stared at the dewy grass soaking his clothes. A gossamer-thin blanket of spiders' webs glittered at the tips of the grass, spreading out before him as if it had been left by the elvish.

"It's odd," said Wulf thoughtfully. "It's not like you haven't the courage. The way you fought in there, you were like a berserker. I can't make you out, Essa."

Essa closed his eyes. He saw the hand again, lying dead on the floor, the wrist stump dark with blood. He would have to clean his sword today. The rush of nausea grew stronger. Then he could hold it back no longer and spewed on the grass, then lay back, letting the dew soak through his clothes until everything went dark.

Across the plains of the Magonsæte

They rode on in the early afternoon, bleary-eyed, having slept through the rest of the morning at the wood shore. Wulf was troubled now about the time they had lost, saying that he just wanted to get it done, and if his new wife was fat and looked like the back end of a horse, so be it.

Essa felt bad. A burning line of pain stitched through his flesh down the right-hand side of his body. The linen bandage was blood-soaked and clammy against his skin. His head ached as he urged Grani to a fast trot; sharp jolts of pain slid from the back of his skull, down his neck, right to the base of his spine. Fenrir ran alongside them, her stride long and loose, and Essa could tell she was sated, for the moment. She must have killed something while they were sleeping.

The sky above was gray, hiding the sun, and the distant mountains seemed to creep farther away rather than closer as the afternoon passed. Holding the reins with one hand, Essa clutched his cloak tight about his shoulders, but it was no good; the wind found its way in, sliding icy fingers through the ragged cut in his tunic where the Mercian's knife had torn it, pinching at his flesh until he thought he would never feel warm again.

The wind grew stronger as they left the last straggling reaches of the forest and rode out onto the tumbling plains of the Magonsæte, where the grass was churned up by the wind, and the sky rose above them, huge and high like a giant bowl of pale light, upturned over the earth. Essa's hair was whipped away from his scalp; the dusting of copper-colored freckles on the backs of his hands as they clutched the reins stood out like a spattering of dye against his white, frozen skin. He stared at his hands as the landscape flashed by: a blur of green hills cowering beneath a sky growing heavier, grayer as the day passed.

He had cut off someone's hand. How would the Mercian live now, if he even survived the wound? What would it be like to ride with one hand, to climb a tree, skin a rabbit, hold a girl?

It began to rain, and the snow-capped tips and great, dark shoulders of the forest-cloaked mountain were lost in a fog that settled across the plains, thicker near low ground, hanging like skeins of raw sheep's wool just above the grass everywhere else. Fenrir was lost in the mist; he could hear her ragged breathing. They would have to stop soon, or she'd begin to fall behind. Essa could hardly see Wulf ahead of him; Balder had faded altogether into the fog, her rider a dark shape riding on nothing, like a spirit. Wulf was singing, massacring the story of Beowulf descending deep into the swamp to kill Grendel's mother. Essa mouthed the words to himself, thinking of his father playing the cherry-wood lyre, reeling off the old stories, Anglish and British alike, line by burning line.

They stopped before it truly got dark, and Essa squatted down in the rain and took his strike-a-light from the pouch at his belt. The iron was cold in his hand, but he managed to coax a few sparks from it with the flint and spill them into the pile of dry twigs Wulf had taken from one of the saddlebags. They sat shivering around the leaping yellow flames with Fenrir lying spent at their feet, and skinned a hare Wulf had shot from his saddle in the last of the light. When it was done and Essa had forced the naked, purple body onto a sharp stick and hung it above the fire, Wulf insisted on looking at the knife wound again.

"You were lucky." He tore off another strip of linen, batting Essa's hands away from the blood-soaked bandage and stripping it off in one swipe so that Essa gasped, breathless with pain. "That's the best way to do it, nice and quick. They probably would've killed us both if you hadn't gone crazy with your sword. I can't believe you did that."

Essa shrugged. "It just happened," he said. "Shouldn't you be saving that linen for your wife? Don't worry about me; I'll be all right."

Wulf groaned. "She'll have what she gets — wasp-faced

slut that she is, or I'll bet, anyway. Shut up and let me bandage it. It's not really bleeding anymore, but it looks angry, like it might rot if you're not careful. And then we'll have to get the maggots in there, won't we?"

Essa shuddered. Cole had once cut his hand falling off one of the grain mounds in the village. When the cut started to rot, his mother had bound maggots into the open wound until they ate away the poison, leaving only living, clean flesh behind. Cole had not minded too much, although he'd said he could feel them wriggling.

"She might not be wasp-faced," Essa said. "Maybe she'll be fair and charming, like your father reckons."

Wulf snorted. "Some chance. You should see the heifer he married my older brother to. She's got arms like tree trunks; I swear my brother's in terror of her, and he killed the king of Kent's son the summer before last, *and* one of his bishops. Where'd you learn to fight like that, anyway? Cai doesn't seem a fighting man. He's too clever."

"I suppose I just taught myself." Essa shrugged, suddenly back in the courtyard outside the hall, sparring endlessly with Cole and Red, clouting and parrying and thrusting with wooden swords until they were all covered in bruises. The Wixna were serious about fighting, but he could not admit that to Wulf. He stared into the leaping yellow flames, watching the hare's flesh char.

"You really scared that northerner, didn't you?" Wulf leaned over and turned the spit. "It was odd, like he was more scared after speaking to you than he looked after you chopped off his friend's hand." His tone was light, but Essa wished he had been sent away with someone a little less questioning. "What was it he said again?"

"That I've got some woman's sword," Essa said. "I think he was mazy in the head."

"Where did it come from, that sword?" said Wulf. "It's finer than anything I've ever had, and I'm the son of a king."

"My father gave it me. Are you calling me a thief?"

Wulf grinned, shoving him lightly on the shoulder. "Did I say that, hothead? Look, I just think it's strange. He said you had 'the Lady's sword,' didn't he? And Cai gave it to you. Maybe he knew your mother."

Essa shrugged, trying to ignore the little knot of pain in his belly. He had almost forgotten it as he'd grown older and tried not to mind he had never known her, that he could not even remember her face. Hild was the only mother he would ever have.

But it isn't the same, is it?

"She's dead. I really don't care."

"What was her name?"

"Elfgift!" Essa snapped. "But I know nothing about her. That was the only time my father's ever beaten me, when I was about seven, one day when I just kept asking about her. He went crazy."

"Don't you think that's strange? That he wouldn't talk about your mother?"

Essa shrugged, wincing as the movement pulled apart the lips of the long cut down his side. "I've always thought he just could never bear it, knowing she's dead."

All he knew was that she had red hair like his and that she was called elf-shining: fairer than any earthly woman.

Wulf pulled the hare off the spit, blowing on his fingers. He tore off a leg and tossed it across the fire to Essa. "We'll be at Eiludd's fort tomorrow. This is my last night of freedom: let's celebrate with burnt hare."

Essa took a bit of hot, stringy meat and chewed, staring into the flames. What would he do once they had the girl?

If Penda would not attack the Anglish till he had the west secured, with Powys's daughter safe in his camp, then somehow Essa had to make sure that Penda never laid eyes on the girl.

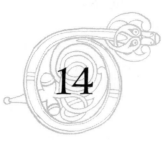

14

*From the marches of the Magonsæte
into Powys*

They came to the feet of the mountains in the early afternoon. The sun was high above them, lancing down through clots of gray cloud. Pale gold lines of light seared through the fog, burning it away. They drew to a halt at the brow of a hill, looking down into a valley dipping deep into the earth, the mountainside a wall before them. If he craned his neck and looked right up, Essa caught glimpses of the snow-covered peak as the clouds moved across the sky. Below them, the valley was thick with fog: it looked like a boiling white lake.

He felt them coming, the riders. The ground shuddered beneath their horses' hooves, like the old oak boards in the hall whenever someone walked across the floor. For a moment, Essa even thought he could hear their voices, whispering on the wind.

"Look!" Wulf pointed down at the valley floor. Essa followed his gaze, and the breath froze in his chest as, one by one, cloaked riders emerged from the mist, traversing the gully faster than ghosts, thumb-size men at this distance, bareheaded, with long hair streaming out behind them. Fenrir sat up, ears cocked, and let out one of her low growls.

The leading rider suddenly reined in, coming to a halt facing in their direction, pointing up at the hillside.

"They've seen us," said Essa, heart pounding. "Who are they?"

Beside him, Wulf sat back in his saddle, grinning. "It's the Magonsæte, the Westerlings. They're always riding out on the border marches. My father told me they spend their lives in the saddle, probably even sleep on horseback. They *breathe* horses. We should go down and meet them before they start shooting arrows at us."

He raised a hand in greeting and Essa followed him down the hillside toward the Magonsæte. There must have been at least twoscore of them. They moved silently through the trailing mist; by the time Essa, Wulf, and Fenrir had reached the valley floor, grim-faced men on horseback surrounded them, spears lowered, hands on sword hilts.

"Who goes there?" said the leading rider, smiling sarcastically.

Wulf shrugged, waiting until they noticed the heavy gold-wrought boar brooch holding his cloak together at the neck.

"Oh, you're one of Penda's brats. Which?"

"Wulfhere," said Wulf.

"Mereleor, lord of the Westerlings. What brings you so far west, Wulfhere of the Mercians, with only one little friend and a pet dog? Don't tell me your father's sent you to exact more tribute from us. It's getting so tiresome, and our coffers are empty." He turned and looked around at his men, eyebrows raised.

They all laughed.

"I don't see what's so funny," Wulf said.

Essa pretended not to have heard, whispering, "Do you shut up!" from the corner of his mouth. Fenrir sat up on her hindquarters, showing her teeth, but the hall dogs had been trained not to frighten horses, so she didn't move.

Mereleor's smile vanished, and Essa felt the skin on the back of his neck crawl in horror as the Magonsæte closed their circle, their spearheads only a thrust away.

"You could easily go missing out here, little atheling; it's wild country. Anything could happen."

"Not this time," said Wulf lightly. "I'm promised to Eiludd Powys's daughter, and she won't like to be kept waiting. You can tell us the way to Caer Elfan, though."

Mereleor laughed. "All right, then," he said. "No one could say you've not got spirit. We'll show you the way. You're a lucky boy — half of Powys is in love with her, but I'm warning you: although she's passing fair, they say she's a mad-crazy girl her father can't wait to be rid of."

"Just my luck," said Wulf. "Ah, well, as long as she's not ugly, I don't care what she's like."

"Take the northwestern passage between those two hills; you'll find Caer Elfan at the foot of the high peak." Mereleor pointed with his spear at a pair of boulder-bestrewn hills with silvery-white streams crisscrossing their sides. "It'll be sundown when you get there, so watch that your horses don't stumble, or you'll be in trouble. These hills are full of outlaws."

Essa and Wulf exchanged a quick look. "All right," said Wulf. "Let's go, then." He saluted Mereleor and rode a few paces ahead, staring up at the fog-shrouded peaks.

Essa hung back, mouth dry. He had to do this sooner or later. It was what he had been planning all along. So why not start now, with the Magonsæte? Heart hammering in his chest, he turned his back on Wulf, bringing Grani alongside Mereleor's horse. Mereleor was leaning forward in his saddle, adjusting his horse's bit. "My lord," Essa said, stumbling over his words. "There's something I must tell you." He lowered his voice. "You—you don't have to live like this, in thrall to Penda and his children."

Mereleor sat up and looked at him. "You're playing a dangerous game, boy. What is it? What do you know?"

Essa glanced over his shoulder. Wulf was joking with one of the Magonsæte, laughing and cupping his hands by his chest, saying, "Well, I hope she has a good shape!"

Mereleor sighed. "Good luck to him," he said. "If half what I hear of Eiludd's daughter is true, he'll need fate on his side with friends like you and a wife like that. Not that I'm complaining—come, spit it out."

Essa felt his face grow hot with shame. "Eiludd's daughter, she's going to be more of a hostage than a wife. Do you know what I mean?"

"What of it? Happens all the time."

"As soon as Wulf takes her back to Mercia, Penda's army moves east, to take the throne of the Wolf Folk. Most of his men are already garrisoned along the East Anglian border, in the marshes."

"I'd heard Egric the Atheling's been trying to coax that cousin of his out of Bedricsworth monastery. So Penda thinks he's secured the west by taking the girl?" Mereleor laughed quietly. "Maybe now's the time for the Magonsæte to stir up a touch of bother out here, while he isn't looking. Well, I thank you, boy—whoever you are. Now go, and may God save your skin, because if Penda finds you out, no blood price on earth will buy your life."

Mereleor reached out, and they clasped hands. "If you'll hear my counsel," he said in a low voice, "stay away from the affairs of kings. It's a bloody game, and you're just a lad. Whoever put you up to this must be a fool. Who's your lord, then, if not Penda's brat? You don't wear a ring like an honest man."

"I'm not an honest man," said Essa. "And the rest I can't tell you."

Mereleor shook his head, grasping Essa's hand tightly. "You're either brave or brainless, boy. May luck stay by your side."

Essa nodded and forced himself to smile, as if pretending not to care meant he actually didn't. He rode on after Wulf, guiding Grani up the tussocky hillside, whistling for Fenrir, who came loping out of the mist like a wolf. He turned once and looked back after their Magonsæte escort, dark figures on horseback, melting back into the fog. A moment later, it was as if they had never been.

"Doubtless they've sent us off the wrong way," said Wulf when Essa caught up with him. "The Magonsæte hate my father more than anything."

"If it wasn't you, they'd be paying tribute to someone else," said Essa, sure that Wulf must be able to sense his betrayal, to smell it oozing from his skin like sour sweat. He and Wulf were bound now, whether he liked it or not: they had fought back-to-back and defeated an enemy together. Betraying Wulf was betraying a friend.

But he had to stop Penda.

He pictured Cole running to the top of the village wall, his broad fingers stroking his sword hilt, fiddling with his belt. He would be exchanging jokes with the men next to him, laughing a bit, but they were waiting for the Mercians, for death to come striding across the marshes. He thought of Hild, her hand resting on Meadowsweet's old, gray-muzzled head as she listened for the sound of hoofbeats coming from the west.

And Lark: Lark running light and quick to the top of the wall with the women and girls, ready to string her bow and send arrows streaming down. But a bow would be no use once the Mercians breached the village wall — which they would, eventually. They would come streaming over the top, cutting down every man, woman, and child in their path. He could not bear thinking of Lark, sure that if he did, he would turn his horse around and ride back east till he reached her.

Essa sucked in a deep breath, closing his eyes as the dull, throbbing of pain in his knife wound grew deeper.

If Penda were not to ride east until Eiludd's daughter was safe in his hands, Essa would just have to make sure that Wulf did not return. Filled with misery, he looked across and watched Wulf leaning back in the saddle, yawning and twisting the reins around his long, clever fingers as he squinted into the twilight.

It would not be easy to kill him.

Then, just as the last of the light was fading, the wind picked up, playing with Grani's gray mane and lifting Essa's own hair from his shoulders, stirring it like waking flames around his head.

The cloud boiled away to one side, and they saw Caer Elfan at last: a bright-windowed hall high in the hills, sitting in the lap of a white-crested mountain. The westering sun threw a rich crimson wash of light onto the white peak, and Essa's heart swelled at the sight of it and the high-gabled hall below. He was filled with a sense that anything was possible: he was in command. He would think of something.

They reined in the horses, drinking in the sight after long days in the wildwood and on the lonely plains of the Magonsæte, away from the warm brightness of human company. "She's in there," said Wulf. "My wife."

"Well, do you come on, then. Let's go and fetch her."

15

Caer Elfan, Powys

JUST before the gates, Essa and Wulf stopped to untie the leather peace bands they'd worn looped around their wrists since leaving Penda's fortress and wound them tight around the hilts, pommels, and scabbards of their swords.

"I hate this custom," Wulf muttered. "It gives me the chills going into a place knowing I can't draw my sword."

"Hide a knife, then," Essa said, tying his last knot firmly. "I'll wager every one of Eiludd's men does it, peace bands or not."

Wulf grinned. "Oh, I already have," he said. "Two."

"Such craven dishonor," said Essa, and unbuckling the bone-handled knife and its wooden sheath from his belt, he slid them down the inside of his boot.

"Such a strong desire not to get my throat cut," Wulf said.

And, laughing, they rode on.

After the plains of the Magonsæte and the sharp, clear

mountain air, Caer Elfan was overwhelming. The silvery rush of Essa's own tongue, spoken all around him by a crowd of curious, questioning people was like the crashing swell of the sea, pounding over him in great waves. The accent was thick and hard to understand: it was like trying to listen to someone speaking underwater. Women and girls walked around with spindles leaning against their shoulders, and his head whirled with the thrum of spinning wool. Men's voices rose in song and laughter. Children shrieked and ran around the long table.

They were borne through the crowd, and he knelt before Eiludd himself, Eiludd Powys: a tall, snake-thin man with long, strong fingers and swirling blue clan tattoos on his cheeks. "Why do you speak our language, boy?" he said, raising Essa to his feet. "Who're your people?"

"Cai of the Iceni is my father, my lord. He's a scop."

Eiludd laughed. "He's that and more. I'm knowing him. There isn't a king in the land who does not. He's a clever man, your father, but I hope he does take care."

And Essa felt a little burst of fear for his father then, and he wished he had seen Cai ride away from Penda's fortress on Melyor, bound for the safety of the Wolf Marches.

Then there was Eiludd's sister, a spare-boned woman with a glazed look in her eyes that Essa had seen before, when he was in Kent with his father, selling green glass bottles to the bishop of Augustine's church. A crowd had been throwing stones at an old woman laying gifts at the foot of an ash tree. Eiludd's sister had the same masklike expression as those folk, as if God had stolen their faces, their thoughts. Her hand when he held it in his felt like a claw, bony and cold.

Then Eiludd's men came forward, some of them his sons. They were outwardly cheerful, their faces traced over with blue clan tattoos, clasping hands with hard, gripping fingers.

And Essa thought, *We cannot trust them.* He had not thought of it before, but he saw now that Eiludd most likely had the same plans for Wulf that Penda had for Eiludd's daughter. *What if Eiludd means to take Wulf hostage? Or even kill him?*

Eiludd's sons made much of Fenrir, calling her a fine beast, slapping her flanks and dropping shreds of meat to the floor for her. She whined, looking up at Essa, and he felt a flash of guilt. She was tired and hungry; she had covered a vast distance without complaint, but now, it seemed, she'd had enough. He ran his hand down her back, grubbing his fingers into the thick fur around her neck, whispering, *Go on, my honey. Go by the fire and sleep.*

Then, when he looked up, there was Eiludd's daughter, standing between her father and aunt.

She wore a red gown, the crisp pale sleeves of her underdress grazing the backs of her hands. Her skin was milk white, black hair hung past her waist in long, loose curls. Her eyes darted toward Essa, and she lowered them quickly to the floor.

Beside him, Wulf seemed to slacken suddenly, as if the air had been sucked from his body.

"Sweet Lady Frigya," he muttered. "Oh, may you preserve me."

The girl looked up and stared at Wulf, her face expressionless for a moment. Then she smiled, and Essa saw that she was not looking at Wulf, but at him.

Oh, no, he thought. *Not me.* He felt a great heat wash through his body and wanted more than anything to be holding Lark in his arms, to feel her head against his shoulder and her arms around his waist, pulling him closer. He had to fight a strong urge to turn around, take Grani from the care of Eiludd's horse boy, and ride till he was in Wixna-land again. But then he recalled the heads of Dai and his sister rotting on spikes by the gate to Penda's camp, and he thought of how angry their spirits must be, lonely and wandering the Land of Mist till their shameful deaths were avenged. And he thought of Penda and his cold arrogance, and of all the Wixna at home in their marsh fortress, nothing more than ticks to be squashed beneath Penda's foot on his way east to the heartland of the Wolf Folk.

He is a murderer, and a robber king, Essa thought, *and I will stop him.*

He looked back at Eiludd's daughter and, though the light in her eyes made him yearn again for Lark, he just smiled and bowed his head.

Eiludd said, "Wulfhere of the Mercians, I give to you my daughter Anwen."

Wulf did not answer; Anwen had silenced him. He knelt

141

before her, speechless. And until the moment Wulf moved, her dark eyes were fixed on Essa.

He had to get away. He smiled his way through the crowd until it felt as if his cheeks would crack. He finally reached a side door that let him out into a courtyard. The great white mountain shone in the moonlight, watching over the hall like a fond grandmother, and people were milling about, laughing and calling greetings to one another. Nobody took any notice of him. In the dark, with the color drained from his red hair, he could have been anyone. It was not like the village here: people would always be passing through Caer Elfan to pay homage to Eiludd, to beg his favor, and to sell him secrets. People just like Cai.

Just like me, he thought.

There was no ash tree in the courtyard — Powys had been Christian for generations. He could see a light burning in the smithy shed opposite and heard the sound of grating metal. Someone was still at work, then. The wooden wall at his back vibrated as a loud cheer went up in the hall, and he imagined Anwen raising Wulf to his feet, Wulf drinking in the sight of her, kissing her hand. Essa felt so alone; even Fenrir was asleep by the fire without him.

He leaned against the thick wall, breathing deeply. The cut down his side throbbed: a dull, nagging pain. His head ached; it felt as if a hot iron band was tightening around his skull, and the sticky, cloying taste of mead clung to the back of his throat.

He let out a long breath. He had to stop Wulf from

returning to Penda with Anwen. He would have to kill them both, Wulf first. He tried to imagine the shock of impact thrumming up his sword arm as he plunged the blade into flesh.

That's if Eiludd doesn't do the job for me. And my life means less to him than one of his dogs'. He'll have my throat cut without thinking twice.

Essa would grieve the rest of his life for it, he knew, and Wulf's green eyes and wild laugh would haunt his dreams till the day he died. Only what choice was there? He closed his eyes and fixed his mind on the rattling of loom weights echoing from the torchlit weaving shed, clay weights clinking together at the end of the warp threads. What would Hild be doing now? Hild, Lark, and the other girls in the village, chattering as they worked at the great standing looms leaning against the walls of the weaving hall at home.

Lark. He wished he could kiss her in the orchard among the pear trees, beneath the grapevines. How could they have lived side by side for so many years without doing so, without even speaking? It was what Hild, and Lark's mother, had wanted to prevent by breaking apart their friendship, he saw now. He did not understand why, though. Red had put a child into fair, smiling Freo. Cole spent his evenings by the fire with Helith. *So why did they want to keep me away from Lark?* Surely not because he was half British, not truly Anglish — a cuckoo in Wixna-land?

He wished Wulf might meet Lark and that they could all sit around the fire together. But that would never happen, because Wulf was Penda's son. Then Essa pictured his home again; the weaving hall empty, the looms smashed, their frames broken and bitten by axes, half-finished fabric torn on the floor, flames coming closer, licking, burning.

Stop it — stop letting it take over your mind, he told himself. He knew that such thoughts would allow fear to enter his body and freeze his limbs at the moment he needed to act. If he tried to kill Wulf and failed, how could Wulf spare him? One or the other of them would have to die.

He opened his eyes. The courtyard was empty now. In the hall, someone had started singing of Bran, Lord of the Ravens, and his seven ships. Everyone had gone in to listen. He wondered if Wulf found it tiresome, unable to understand. He smiled in the darkness: Wulf probably had not stopped staring at Anwen.

The light in the smithy had gone out, the forge fires banked down with turf. But another light had been lit, farther away, on the far side of the courtyard.

The interior of the god house was cool; iron sconces cupping flames threw out flickering circles of light, casting the shadows surrounding them into deeper darkness. The air was thick and sweet with burning incense, brought all the way from Constantinople in a trading ship. He expected the priest to be inside, but he was alone.

A stone font guarded the door, lidded with thick, oiled oak. Essa ran his fingers over the rough stone: it looked as if it had been hewn from the mountain outside, its sides carved with images of a martyr on her knees.

"Saint Eluned," said Essa quietly, tracing the long, twisting shape of the saint's body with his forefinger. The stone felt rough and cold against his skin. Cai had told him this story long ago: how fair Eluned had been killed for loving God more than an earthly prince. Looking down at his hand made him think of the Mercian in the wildwood. Was he dead?

Then Essa did something he had not done in years. Leaving the font, he walked up to the altar. Dropping to his knees, he kneeled on the floorboards, pressing his forehead against the dusty wood.

Oh, Lord, oh, Jesu, forgive me what I'm about to do. I must take two lives, but I'll be saving many.

He thought of Lark, gripping his hand, looking up at him with hard bright eyes. He had to do it.

He woke, his left-hand side stiff and cold from lying on the bare floorboards of the god house. He had fallen asleep. He rolled onto his back, wincing. The knife wound was not healing well: the skin not knitting together properly. *It shouldn't hurt like this.* He sat up, groaning, and peered down the front of his tunic. The bandage was blood-soaked, but luckily it had not seeped through and ruined Wulf's spare clothes.

"Essa! What are you doing?" Wulf came running in,

long-legged and stoop-shouldered, loping like a hunting dog, like Fenrir. "The god man found you here this morning — he nearly had a fit. He thought you were dead. Why did you creep off so early last night?"

Essa struggled to his feet, cursing under his breath. "I'm tired, that's all — I had to sleep." He tried to say something about Anwen, and how lucky Wulf was, but the words stuck in his throat. Had he just imagined the longing way she had looked at him? "What's the fuss about, anyhow? You're not getting married until the afternoon. It's barely dawn."

Wulf gazed up at the ceiling. Essa barked out a laugh. "They're going to christen you, aren't they?"

"May Lady Frigya forgive me — yes, they are. And if only that were the worst of it." Wulf handed Essa a piece of bread wrapped around cold beef left over from the feast he'd missed the previous night, and he crammed it into his mouth.

"Anyhow," said Wulf. "There was I, thinking my father's actually done me a favor for once in his miserable life, marrying me off to Anwen." He lingered over her name, as if it left honey on his lips.

Essa said, "Well, it's as well she doesn't look like a horse's arse."

"Don't call her a horse's arse! She's going to be my wife!"

Essa sighed. "But that's what *you* said —"

"She's the fairest girl I've ever seen in my life, and you'll talk about her with respect."

Essa fought the urge to roll his eyes. "Oh, do you stop.

You sound like a fussy old man. What've you to moan of? It's all working your way, isn't it? The wyrd's in your favor." The words felt like stones in his mouth. The wyrd was not moving Wulf's way at all, because Essa was going to kill him.

He looked up, half expecting Wulf to have overheard his thoughts, but he was smiling, as usual. "The aunt," said Wulf. "Remember her? Looks like she's been chewing hornets — sort of dried out and corpse-ish?"

Essa nodded, swallowing the last of his bread and meat. It filled him with strength: his head was suddenly clear and his belly full. Wulf handed him the wooden cup, and the cool, watery cider slipped down his throat.

Maybe I can talk to him, he thought, *persuade him not to go back. Wulf's not like Penda.*

Maybe everything would be all right.

"Well, do you hear this: she's coming along with us!" Wulf said, his eyes wide with horror. "Back to Mercia! To make sure Anwen doesn't sink into our heathen ways."

Essa let out a snort of laughter, but his guts were churning. He really did not want to deal with the aunt too. He remembered her cold, masklike eyes and shuddered. "Maybe she wants to convert your father," he said, trying to sound lighthearted.

Wulf shook his head, moaning quietly. "Good luck to her. The last person who tried that ended up with his head on a spike. See, this is the thing, Essa. They're christening me this morning, and, well, you're Christian, aren't you?"

"Well —"

"You're in a god house, aren't you? Communing with the Holy Ghost or whatever it is you folk do. Although how you keep your god trapped in all these different houses I'll never know." Wulf grabbed Essa's hands, gripping them tight, gazing at him with wild green eyes, the brown freckles on his nose standing out stark against his pale skin. "Look, you've got to be my godfather. Promise to teach me the ways of the Lord. Not that I care for them, but I'd rather it was you than that old hag. She's threatening to pray for my soul! Well, she's free to, so long as I don't have to listen to her talk on about it. She wants to be my godmother, but I said I'd already promised you the honor of teaching me."

"Oh, Holy Christ," said Essa. Wulf gripped his hands even tighter. "Oh, well, enough then. I'll do it."

It was not, he thought, as if he had much choice.

Wulf grinned and slung his arm around Essa's shoulder. "I knew I could count on you, Essa. And don't you fret — we'll think of a way to get rid of the old sow somehow. If she comes back with us, I'll end up with a blood price on my head."

Essa went to bed after Wulf's wedding feast swollen with wine, beer, and mead, bloated with roasted meat, sausage, ham, and preserved fruits boiled in cream and bread rolled in salt and dried herbs. When Essa had left, Wulf was still dancing with his lady in the hall, her black hair flying, his green cloak swirling about their legs. Essa felt trapped in the hall by the closeness of unfamiliar bodies squashed against his. The stink of fresh sweat and beery clouds of breath drove him outside. He took a thick blanket and the sheepskin from beneath Grani's saddle, whistled to Fenrir, and went outside. She followed him with a last beseeching look at the warm hearth, but followed all the same.

They lay in a cocoon of warmth behind the smithy shed, Fenrir sleeping, Essa staring up at the glittering lights smeared across the night sky, leaning into the warm bulk of her body. He could not seem to shake off the cold: it was coming from within, from deep in his body, and the whole of his right side was numb with pain. When he moved, he could feel the bandage tugging against the broken skin, and the pain made him close his eyes and grit his teeth.

He listened to the roaring laughter and cheering from inside the hall, guessing Wulf was taking Anwen off to bed behind the curtain of deerskin. He closed his eyes.

His mind slid back to the village, to the hot pressure of Lark's hand against his on that desperate morning. He remembered how she always rinsed her hair in lavender water, how the smell followed her about, growing richer on warm days or when she shook out her braid. He remembered standing in the hall, alone among strangers when Cai had left him, and Lark saying, *I don't care, I like lice.* She had smiled at him.

He did not fall asleep for a long time.

Escape from Caer Elfan

ESSA woke the following morning with a sore head, turning his face into the sheepskin to shield his eyes from the light. His eyelids felt as if they had been boiled in oil. His side ached still. He could not face peeling back the bandage to look. When was he ever going to get a night's sleep?

But it was as if the pain had heated up his mind like a forge; as the discomfort of waking ebbed, a plan emerged like a new-honed knife, still glowing red from the fire.

We must get out of this place, he thought. *It's like sleeping in a den of vipers.* He did not trust Eiludd. What if Wulf became the hostage, and not Anwen after all? Or, at any moment, one of those hard-eyed sons of Eiludd's might slide a knife between Wulf's ribs. *Or mine.* And word would be sent to Penda, asking if he still meant to send his son for Eiludd's daughter, for the boy had never come.

It would have saved Essa the job of killing him, but

waking on this new morning, he saw no reason why Wulf should lose his life for the sake of his father. Wulf was his friend, and none of this mess had been of their making. Essa would not kill him, and he would not allow anyone else to do so. Once they had gotten clear of Caer Elfan, he would find another way of stopping Wulf from going back east with Anwen.

Then Essa thought of Egric, how angry he must be that Essa had disobeyed his order to come straight back to the village, and he smiled to himself in the gray dawn. He would suffer for it when he did return, but it felt good to have shown that arrogant princeling that his word was not the law.

And Cai, too.

He staggered to his feet, and his legs felt drained of blood, like shreds of dried meat. Whistling to Fenrir, who shook off sleep like droplets of water after a swim in the mere, he crossed the yard to the hall and let himself in by a side door.

He brushed his hand over the back of Fenrir's head, running one of her rough, woolly ears through his fingers. *Do you wait here, my love. I'll not be long.* And he closed the door carefully behind him, not wanting the gray dawn light to wake anyone within.

The air was thick with stale breath and the stench of spilled honey wine. Stepping quickly over humped bodies sleeping in the gloom, Essa made his way to the curtained-off part of the hall where Eiludd's family had their quarters. Where were Wulf and Anwen? He did not want to surprise Eiludd or one of his sons.

Essa stopped when he drew near the deerskin curtain. The air hummed with the sounds of people breathing. But he had spent many nights sleeping by Wulf's side, and he knew what to listen for. Wulf slept on his back, arms sprawled above his head, as if he were not at all afraid that someone might come in the night and stick a knife in his belly. Sometimes the breath caught in Wulf's throat when he was most deeply asleep. There he was, off to Essa's right-hand side. He made his way toward the back of the hall, walking along the length of the curtain. He just hoped that Eiludd and his sons would have drunk enough last night to keep them wound in sleep till the sun was high.

Closer, closer.

Then, there was Wulf, right behind the curtain. Essa could hear Anwen breathing softly too. He pulled the flap of deerskin to one side, letting it fall behind him, and found Wulf and Anwen, twined in blankets and sheepskin. She lay curled up on one side, her back to Wulf, one white arm drawing the blanket close under her chin. Wulf lay on his back, dark hair spread loose. Essa felt a rush of pity for them both, seeing the gap between their bodies as they lay. If it were him lying there with Lark, he knew they would wind around each other as they had done when they were children by the fire in the Wixna hall. Kneeling, he gripped Wulf's arm, and his eyes snapped open. Wulf's other hand shot under the sheepskin beneath his head, and he sat up, holding his knife.

"Hush," Essa said softly. "It's me."

Wulf laughed quietly. "I'm restless in this place," he whispered. "I wonder why."

"I don't trust Eiludd either," Essa said. "I think we should leave while we still can."

Wulf looked at Anwen, still asleep beside him. "I know. Now?"

Essa nodded. "Do you think we can trust *her*?"

Wulf shrugged. "We don't have much choice. She's my wife, and I won't live long if I have to tell my father I left her here. And, well—" he broke off, and at that moment Anwen rolled over and sat up, clutching the blanket to her chest, black hair tangling over her shoulders, still twined with ivy leaves from her wedding feast.

"What is this?" she said.

"Wulf, do you tell her," Essa whispered. "I'll meet you at the stable." Wulf nodded and, without looking back, Essa slipped through the curtain and made his way outside, heart thumping. All now depended on Anwen. If she were her father's daughter, she would rouse the whole hall, and he and Wulf would not live to see the sun set.

Expecting at any moment to hear shouting coming from inside, Essa kneeled by Fenrir, running his hand over her bony head, digging his fingers into the silky fur behind her ears. She let out a tiny moaning sound, licking his hand with her broad, rough tongue. *Now, my honey, we must go softly, softly.* And he ran to the stable with Fenrir at his side, but all remained quiet. By the time he had Grani and Balder saddled and bridled, he could hear footsteps outside in the yard. *It might be two of Eiludd's men,* he thought. *Wulf might be already dead. At a word from her, they could have held him down and slit his throat.*

Essa dropped to one knee and slipped the bone-handled knife from its hiding place in his boot. He could see every little dust mote caught in the early morning light, and the footsteps seemed to grow louder and louder till it felt as though his body shook with each one. He turned around to find Wulf and Anwen dressed and wrapped in traveling cloaks. She wore a linen shift with long white sleeves and a heavy wool gown fastened at the shoulders with a pair of iron brooches.

Relief washed over Essa, and he smiled.

"You'll come, then," he said to Anwen.

She looked up at him, and her eyes were dark and shining like blackberries.

"Why would I stay?" she said. "They'd feel worse about losing a horse. And it means we can leave behind my aunt Beton. I hate her."

Essa nodded warily. Anwen, he saw, was not simply going to be part of the baggage.

"I trust you've worked out," she said, "how we are going to get past the guard?"

Essa and Wulf looked at each other. Essa shrugged. "Well, I—"

Anwen sighed. "I thought not. We'll have to lie. Wulf, go to the bird mews and fetch a goshawk. The man there will be asleep. If you are not too clumsy, you should be able to manage it. We're going hunting."

Smiling fondly at her, Wulf flitted out of the stable.

"There's no cause to speak to him as if he were some kind of half-wit," Essa said, in British. "It's not Wulf's fault you've married him. He was forced into it just as you were. You may as well make the most of it."

"Who are you to tell me what to do?" Anwen turned on him, her face blazing with high red color.

Her hand flew out to hit him, and he caught her by the wrist, pushing her away and hissing, "And it is not my fault, either, so do not blame me because you've been sold to Mercia."

Afterward, he could never recall quite how it had happened, but before he had drawn another breath, she was in his arms, whispering, "You are my kind—you speak my language! You must help me!"

"Hush," he said. "All I can do is get you out. And Wulf's my friend. He's *good*; he won't do anything to harm you."

But all she did was hold him tighter. He looked down at the top of her head and breathed in the scent of her hair— rosemary. Lots of girls rinsed their hair in rosemary water— but it was wrong. He thought of Lark, drying her hair by the fire in the hall after a swim in the mere. He suddenly had a very clear picture of her in his mind, sitting on the hearth-stone in her shift, the scent of lavender and the fresh, salty smell of her body rising up as she moved to stretch out her legs, wiggling her brown toes. The way she had looked away when she saw him, and he had done too, thinking, *Cold-hearted sow*, because it had been easier than admitting what he really felt.

He stepped back, gently pushing Anwen away.

"Jealous of your master's treasure, are you?" Her voice was shaky, hurt.

Oh no, oh no. "Wulf's not my master!"

Then Fenrir barked, but Essa could hear it was a greeting rather than a warning, and he looked up to see Wulf coming toward him, crossing the courtyard from Eiludd's bird hall, a goshawk on his gloved wrist.

"At last!" Anwen looked up, smiling, as if she and Essa had been talking about nothing more than the weather. "You won't have thought about food, either, I'm sure. Wait here."

She fled out of the stables and into the courtyard.

They rode to the gate, saddlebags bulging with twice-baked bread, sausage, blood puddings, and dried fruit, all stolen from Eiludd's stores. The goshawk was hungry for the kill, and so was Fenrir. Essa could feel their hunger for the chase and for hot blood. He was still feeling faint with the pain of mounting up. It had hurt so much he'd felt tears start to his eyes. He had been cut before, only never this deep, never so long and ragged a wound. But he should not feel this sick.

There was nothing he could do about it now.

Two men were at the gate, muffled in cloaks against the dawn chill, watching them come closer.

"Are you sure that hound isn't going to slow us down?" Anwen said quietly. "Would she not be best off here? She's a fine dog—it'd be a shame to lame her."

"No," hissed Essa. "We're meant to be hunting. It would look strange not to take a hound. And even so, I'd bring her. She'll not go lame."

Wulf nodded his agreement. "She's fast—and she saved our lives in the greenwood, didn't you, Fenrir?"

The guards got awkwardly to their feet, stiff, Essa guessed, with sitting outside all night in bone-aching cold.

"A fine morning!" Anwen called out. "I'm showing my lord how well is the hunting out beyond the Black Wood."

One of the guards caught her bridle. Essa sucked in a breath.

The guard laughed, patting the white mare's flank. "Glad to see you have plenty of food, my lady," he said, nodding toward a bulging saddlebag.

Anwen smiled, and Essa saw the guard's eyes dim slightly, as if her beauty had knocked the senses from him. "Well, I would not want my lord to go back to Mercia thinking we do not know how to give pleasure to our guests."

"No, indeed, my lady," said the guard, and Essa saw that they were safe for now. Looking mazed, the guard let go of Anwen's bridle and the three of them rode out of the gate.

Leaning forward, Essa whispered, *Go well, my dear*, into Grani's ear. *Soon we will have a fine gallop.*

They picked their way down the mountain path, and he silently prayed that the horses would be surefooted on it, that none of them would slip one of the new shoes King Eiludd's farrier had fitted outside the smithy the previous morning.

They rode away from Caer Elfan into the dawn-lit mountains, facing back toward the plains of the Magonsæte and the east. Wulf and Essa rode on either side of Anwen, Grani and Balder flanking her white mare, Fenrir striding along beside Grani, taking long, easy steps. They had just reached a wider, grassier path when Essa felt a sudden chill. He gasped, and his spirit flew free. He felt the stretch as the goshawk perching on Wulf's wrist spread her wings, and the thrill as she rose into the air. Up she went, higher and higher. And when Essa looked down, he saw, through the goshawk's arrow-sharp red eyes, a beetle moving laboriously through the grass, a gray flash of warm fur as a hare cowered in the heather.

They flew higher, and then he saw the riders bearing down the path from Caer Elfan.

He made the goshawk turn her gaze back to his body, slumped in the saddle on Grani's back: the rusty flash of his red hair, the pale sweep of his arm. And then Essa was back inside himself. "Stop!" he said. The others reined in their horses.

"What?" said Anwen.

"Down the path—" He could hear them now, too. He could feel the earth shuddering beneath their feet, shaken by horses at gallop — how many? Eight? Ten? Judging by the stricken expression on Anwen's face so could she.

"My brothers!" she said. "He's sent my brothers."

Essa caught Wulf's eye, remembering those hard-faced young men in the hall, their gripping handshakes.

"Let's not head for the woods," Essa said quickly. "That's what they'll be thinking we'll try. Let's go north instead. We can double back later."

They urged their horses to a gallop. Looking down, Essa could just see Fenrir, a blurred gray shape, running as though she were a spirit hound, a dog of the Aesir. He could hear hounds howling behind them, but she did not reply, she just ran, and he wondered how she must feel to be prey.

But we're not prey, he thought. *We're going to get away.*

It was a bruising ride: fast and violent, thundering over loose tussocks of earth, scattering mud and dried heather as they went north through the grassy foothills of the mountains. And at last, a long, spirit-draining age after Essa had last heard their pursuers, they slowed down and shared a flask of water without dismounting. The horses were exhausted, their flanks dripping with sweat, their eyes rolling, ears flattened back against their heads.

Anwen laughed. "They can't get me now."

"You weren't supposed to enjoy it," said Wulf, passing Essa the water bottle. "How's that cut?"

Anwen looked chastened for a moment. "You should let me have a look at it when we stop," she said. "Wulf told me. Why didn't you say anything when we were at my father's? I packed the right herbs — I can make a salve."

Essa shrugged. She seemed to have gotten over her anger with him, at least — unless this was all just a show for Wulf's benefit. He felt faint with pain, but it was clear they could not stop for long yet. There were still many more acres to put between them and Anwen's brothers before he might feel safe.

They rode on, a slow trot this time. But still farther and farther away from Caer Elfan.

Essa could not keep up. He had fallen a little way behind, so he was watching them, riding along together. Anwen held the reins loosely and had the easy seat of a practiced rider. The mare's sleek sides were the color of new milk, her legs strong and elegant, her black eyes like smudges of charcoal on her face. Anwen's fingers trailed in the long white mane, and many times she leaned forward in the saddle and whispered into the mare's ears.

When Essa was very young, no higher than Cai's waist, his father had taken him to a green hillside in Wessex. In the gathering dusk, they had climbed the grassy slope until they came to a ridge and saw a great white horse cut into the chalk hillside. Standing there with his father, Essa's heart had sung, soaring high at the sight of the great running mare, pale chalk glowing in the near-darkness.

"Kneel, little cub," Cai had said, and Essa followed his father's movements: they dropped to their knees and fell to the ground, breathing in the scent of warm grass, and Cai had prayed to the horse goddess. The British would never forget her, despite their god houses and their adopted Lord.

When Cai had finished his prayer, he looked down at Essa and gave him a rare bright, flashing smile, laying a hand on his head. "There, now she'll keep us safe. It's a good thing Elfgift doesn't know we've been here. I don't think she'd have liked it!"

Essa always remembered that long-ago dusk, because it was one of the few times Cai had mentioned Elfgift without being asked.

Essa, Anwen, and Wulf rode in silence the rest of the afternoon, squinting into the sun.

Anwen and Wulf were silent. Last night, they had lain together behind the deerskin curtain in Eiludd's hall, and Wulf had put his seed in her while the whole hall cheered and clapped and sang of the fine sons she would bear him. They had known each other for less than the time it took for a new moon to be born in the sky and die there, and already she might be carrying his child. It was no wonder, Essa thought, that they had little to say.

But he could not bear the quiet: it gave him too much space to think, and it had not taken long for his thoughts to turn from his father and settle on what he was going to do with Wulf and Anwen. How could he stop them from reaching Penda? He would not kill them, so how else?

His thoughts moved slower as the afternoon rolled

toward eventide, thick like porridge without enough milk. His heart ached with the desire to be back on that Wessex hillside with his father and the great white mare, safe and free beneath the billowing sky.

Time slipped by, and he fell into a kind of trance, only dimly aware of their journey beyond the mountains and the reaches of Caer Elfan. The pain in his right side spread through his body in slow, relentless waves, rippling across his skin, eating into every bone. He caught snatches of talk between Anwen and Wulf—they seemed to grow less awkward as the day rolled toward evening. She complained of the ache in her thighs, as she had not ridden so far or for so long in ages; but later they were arguing cheerfully about something—Essa could not make out what; his ears felt full of water. Hitting something, a man with a black eye, running on frozen ice—they were talking about the rules of bandy.

And then, in his mind, Essa was back at home, racing with Red across the frozen marshland, crashing into Cole and Ariulf as Cole smashed the ball with his bandy stick. He remembered throwing himself belly down on the ice to catch the ball before it hit the crabbed hawthorn they had chosen for a goal, being filled with burning joy when he caught it. He and Red had won.

He wished he were there with them all now.

"What do you know, anyway?" Anwen's voice was high and clear, but Essa could not see her. He had fallen back even more, and the other two were riding on, a length ahead of him. His sight grew clouded and the landscape fell away, a tumbling mass of green and gray. He could see only the two pale horses in front of him, tails swishing, their riders dark, indistinct shapes. Their voices sounded as if they were coming from above, bouncing off the hills, swept away with the wind. He was so cold. Why would not the wind stop? A dark mist clouded his eyes, and an iron ball of fear settled in his stomach. He did not want to die like this, away from everyone he loved. He did not want Wulf to bury him out here on these wild, lonely marches with nothing to keep him company but the whispering of the grass in the wind, and the lonely keening of the curlews circling above.

And if he died out here, the Wixna would die too — every one of them, without warning, without help. Penda's orders echoed inside his head, *every man, woman, and child until we cross the River Deben.*

He closed his eyes and felt his fingers let go of the reins. Then he fell. The last he heard was Fenrir baying as if she had just sighted a deer, then Grani's panicky scream, and the sound of her hooves striking the ground about his head, like the beating of a funeral drum.

Someone was carrying him through the darkness. His body was alight with pain, and colored lights danced inside his eyelids. Faces came at him out of nowhere: the Mercian, eyes dark with horror, the severed hand on the forest floor; Wulf smiling, flashing his sharp, white teeth; Hild putting her shawl around his shoulders, saying, "See, Meadowsweet has had her cubs"; Cole, long ago, looking up as he showed Essa how to thread a blue jay's feather onto a fishhook, every line and shadow of his serious face so dear and familiar; and Lark as she handed him the sword outside the village gate.

He could smell lavender now, and he called her name. She must be here.

Oh God, let her be here. He would have done anything to see her again. He imagined her running up the side of the village wall with her bow, scaling the great earth rampart like a cat. He saw arrows flying from her bow, and he flew with them, piercing the breasts and arms and legs of the Mercian warriors.

But they would reach her in the end.

He cried out, and a voice said, "He's with the spirits. He's walking with the spirits."

"Quiet, you're scaring me. He's just ill."

He could hear someone breathing in awkward little starts, feel the muscles contracting in the arms that carried him.

Wulf was carrying him. *It's a good thing he doesn't know I wanted to kill him not long ago,* Essa thought.

"What ails him, for God's sake?"

"It's my fault. I knew it wasn't healing properly. We ought not to have let him talk us into this. I ought to have made him wait a couple of days."

"Who's this Lark he keeps calling for, anyway?"

"I don't know."

Then it went dark again, and he heard nothing.

17

Northern marches

ESSA was lying on a sheepskin with a blanket pulled over his legs, up to his waist. Fenrir lay sprawled at his feet, her head resting on her front paws. Anwen knelt beside him, the blood-sodden linen bandage in a heap beside her. A bolt of clean linen lay folded next to it. He felt a jolt of anxiety, remembering the look in her eyes as he had stepped away from her in the courtyard at her father's fortress. What was she going to do to him?

Her black braids hung over her shoulders, their tips tickling the skin on his bare chest as she leaned forward. His skin felt cold; she was dabbing a wet wad of cloth against his knife cut. It did not pain him so much now. Maybe she was not going to hurt him after all: perhaps she was trying to help. Early evening sunlight slanted in through a doorway cut so low a grown man would have to stoop through it. He had slept in bothies like this with his father many times. Little green huts like the mounds left by moles, cut into the hillside for shepherds to shelter in when the night or a storm beat them home. He felt safe and at peace. He could do nothing.

She did not know he was awake. She twisted the lid off a clay jar, breaking the wax that sealed it. Then she tore a strip off the bundle of damp cloth and dipped it into the jar. It came away trailing a golden stream of honey, and the sweet scent mingled with the smell of lavender. Anwen was treating the wound with honey and lavender water: honey to keep out the rot, and lavender to make it heal faster. Lark was not there. He had known she wouldn't be, not really.

But it did not stop him from wanting her.

The honey dribbled onto the raw wound, warm and thick. Soon the whole area was coated. Then, with gentle fingers, Anwen covered it with a long strip of clean linen.

She looked up, and he closed his eyes. He wasn't ready to speak.

"Yes," she said in British. "It's best for you to sleep, *cariad*."

Time slipped by, darkness fell and went away again, sunlight came and faded. He dreamed of his father, the great white mare running across the hillside, the firelit god house at Caer Elfan. He dreamed of the ash tree in the courtyard of Hild's village, Yggdrasil, the World Tree. He dreamed the serpent in Yggdrasil's roots was coming for him, its great shining coils seething across the ground. He could not run. He could only wait.

Then, after a spell of darkness, he dreamed of his spirit journey again, soaring high above the earth, looking down on the hall below. *I'm not a wolf*, he told himself frantically. *I'm not a real member of the Wolf Folk.*

So what am I?

Morning came once more. Anwen sat beside him with a bowl of porridge and a cup of water. Fenrir was lying by his side now; she was sleeping, but one of her ears lay flat against her head, and her eyelids were twitching.

Anwen smiled when she saw he was awake. "We lit a fire outside — lucky we packed lots of food. We've been here days. Come, see if you can't sit up and eat some. It's got honey in it."

Essa's first thought was to wonder how many days. Long enough for Egric to send word to the monastery? Had there been time to bring the king to the border? He wished there was some way of finding out, of talking to Lark or Hild, even Egric himself, though Essa dreaded facing him. But they might as well have been in another world. He wanted to laugh. He had spent all that time worrying about how he was going to stop Wulf and Anwen from reaching Penda, and it was as easy as falling off a horse.

"So did you not put all of the honey on me?" The words came out stiff and awkward, his throat dry. He reached out and rested his hand on Fenrir's head, stroking her ears.

Anwen smiled, but she looked worried. "You were awake,

then. I kept some. It's good to put on wounds, though; did your mother not tell you that?"

"No, she didn't." He sat up and took the cup of water, draining it in one go. Sitting up was hard; the bandaged wound throbbed, but it was much better. The hard part was moving his legs and arms: they felt weak and useless. He managed in the end and leaned back against the bare earth wall. He was wearing a loose white tunic now, and suddenly he felt ashamed of being so helpless, and that Anwen had done so much for him — even after what had happened in the courtyard at Caer Elfan.

Silently, she handed him the porridge, and he spooned it up, his hand shaking. The oats were thick and creamy; they must have used the last of the milk or stolen some from a ewe on the hillside. The honey was warm and sweet in his mouth. It was bringing him back to life.

"I'm sorry," he said. He was half thinking of that moment in the courtyard when he'd pushed her away. "I mean, thank you. What you've done—"

She smiled. "I'm in no rush to reach Mercia. I've heard what they say about Penda. They call him the Mad Dog."

"You'll manage him. Where's Wulf?"

She stared at the floor. "He's outside."

Essa saw his sheepskin boots lying in a pile next to his pack and grabbed them, binding them firmly around his legs with the leather straps.

"Essa—"

He got to his feet, sucking in his breath as the movement

disturbed his wound. He could feel that the skin had knitted together at last, though. "I must speak to him. I owe him my life as well as you."

She sighed. "Best you see him sooner rather than later." He did not ask what she meant, just stepped outside, blinking as daylight flooded his eyes. They were staying at the bottom of a shallow, grassy gully, partially sheltered by a line of wind-whipped hawthorn trees. The sky was laced with tendrils of white cloud, the ground splashed with pale snowdrops; a breeze stirred up the grass. Spring was moving in at last.

He could hear a stream running along the far end of the gully. Wulf was crouching next to it, tending a smoky fire with his back to Essa. His shoulders were hunched. He turned away from the fire, wrenching a tuft of grass, about to start cleaning the porridge pot. But he saw Essa first. He sprang to his feet, face set and angry. There was something else there, too — sadness. He looked hurt. He must have argued with Anwen, Essa thought.

"I'm sorry," he said, walking over to him. "I know you needed to get back."

Wulf strode over until they were very close. The blood had drained from his face, and his cheekbones stood out like knives. "Just who are you, anyway?" he shouted, his voice ragged with anger. "*Who are you working for?*"

Essa's breath turned to ice. Wulf was holding something. Something on a string of blue glass beads that glittered in the morning light.

Wulf was holding his ring.

"Whose is it?" His voice was thick with rage. "Who's your lord, Essa?"

"Egric the Atheling."

Wulf reached out and struck him in the face with the flat of his hand. Recoiling from the blow, Essa lunged forward and snatched the string of blue beads, clutching the ring tight. The leather thong snapped, and beads bounced in the grass. He stepped back, feeling his breath escape in a long, raging hiss. The inside of his cheek had torn where Wulf had hit him, and his mouth filled with blood. He spat. His hand flew to his knife, the bone-handled knife. But before Wulf could reach his own, Essa threw it to the floor, chest heaving. He turned and walked off down the gully, expecting to feel a cold iron blade at his back. Wulf might easily grab him now and cut his throat. Essa was weak and could not fight back.

But Wulf did not.

"How could you do this?" he yelled. "I thought we were friends!"

Essa shook his head and carried on walking. His head was spinning, and he sat on the bank, holding the ring and three of the glass beads. He pushed the ring down the middle finger of his right hand and sat there staring at it: the band of gold that had brought him so much trouble. What was he meant to get in return for this? Egric's love, generosity, and protection; the warmth of his hall; the bounty of his harvests; and all the ale and mead he could drink. Essa had not seen much of that.

"I'd rather be free," he said out loud. He wanted to laugh. All he had done so far was betray his friends, betray Egric himself, even — and none of it by choice. He felt hot with rage. He hated Egric for binding him so, but most of all he hated his father. He was tired of being used, moved around at their whim like a goose piece on a gaming board. A warm, thick feeling burst in his nose, and blood dripped on the grass. He wiped his face, and his hand came away smeared crimson.

Then Wulf was standing in front of him, holding a wad of grass. He sat down.

Essa took the grass and dabbed at his nose. They did not meet each other's eyes. He heard footsteps and looked up to see Anwen running toward them down the gully, black hair flying around her shoulders.

She turned on Wulf. "How could you *hit* him! He nearly died."

"It's no matter," said Essa. "I deserved it. It's my fault. All of this is my fault."

And he told them everything, starting from the day Cai had left him in the village, right up until his betrayal of Wulf — telling Mereleor that Penda had dispatched most of his fighting men to the far-off eastern borders of Mercia, where he waited to pounce on the Wolf Folk.

"I would've told your father, too," he said to Anwen, "but we left so fast there was no time."

Wulf stared off into the distance, fiddling with a leather bracelet on his wrist.

"To think I asked you to fight with me, to wear a ring for me," he said. "I suppose you meant to kill us, to stop us from getting back."

"I don't think I could have done it. I'm sorry. If there'd been a choice, I would have worn your ring."

Wulf turned to face him, laughing. "You're my god-father!"

"I know — it's all madness. I'm really sorry; I never meant for any of this to happen. I only wish there was some way of *stopping* it all."

"Have you told him?" Anwen demanded, leaning across Essa to pinch Wulf's arm.

"Oh, all right," said Wulf. "If it makes you feel any better, I was supposed to kill *you*, out here. But I decided not to after what happened in the forest, when you saved my life. My father told me you were a spy; he guessed Cai was still loyal to the Wolf Folk. But I was going to defy him and bring you back as my ring bearer instead." He sighed. "It was a crazed plan anyhow — he would've killed me."

Essa's stomach lurched. "What about Cai?"

Wulf shook his head. "I'm sorry, Essa, but he's probably dead by now. They were going to kill him after we left."

Horror gripped him. He thought of the British boy, Dai, and his brave sister, who had died screaming curses at Penda. Had they killed his father the same way: a quick slash across the throat — or worse? And Wulf had not even been there to offer a poppy-wine draft to ease Cai's passing — *not that he would have taken it.*

Essa wanted to get up, walk away, but he could not move. Hot tears splashed to the grass, pink with the blood from his nose. He leaned forward and clutched his knees, resting his head on his arms. All those years in the village, he had gotten used to the idea that he would probably never see Cai again, that he was certain to be dead. But he had never expected it to feel like this: as though he had been stabbed in the belly. He felt hands resting on his heaving shoulders, Wulf and Anwen trying to comfort him. But he knew there'd be no comfort. When he woke up tomorrow it would still be the same: Cai was dead.

They sat there, staring down at the grass, Wulf and Anwen with their arms around his shoulders. Essa glanced up, saw Fenrir weaving her way toward them through the hawthorn trees. She stood before him, nosing at his hands, his head. He felt her tongue rasp at his forehead, her wet nose against the tip of his ear. He reached out and stroked her lean, brindled flank.

One day, even she would leave him and cross into that other land from which no one returned. For a moment, the thought made him despair: what was the point in anything, if it would all end in that strange, distant country? In the village, they called it the Land of Mist. For the Christians, it was heaven or hell. But then a strange calm washed over him: in time, everyone would be called to its gates, far below in the roots of Yggdrasil. If they were lucky, they would find the Hall of Warriors, and feast till the end of the world. If not, it would be a long, lonely wandering through a cold land. But that was not for Penda to determine, or any other king.

Suddenly, Anwen sprang to her feet, pacing frantically up and down. Essa jumped — for a moment, he had almost forgotten they were there. "I can't bear it!" she said. "Why do we let them treat us like this, forcing us to carry on with their fighting and killing? There's nothing in it for us."

"What else can we do?" said Wulf, reaching over to play with Fenrir's ears.

And then Essa knew. He got to his feet, his head clear. It was so plain to see.

"We'll go north to Ad Gefrin," he said. "To the High King. We'll tell him everything, get *him* to rein in Penda. Mercia's beholden to Northumbria, just the same as everyone else. Your father pays his tributes to King Godsrule, doesn't he?"

Wulf laughed humorlessly. "Well, yes, but that didn't stop him from burning Ad Gefrin to the ground, did it? Essa, my father *killed* the last High King. The only reason he didn't take Edwin's place is because Kent, East Anglia, Wessex — all the powerful kingdoms — are gone to the way of the Lord or whatever it is you call it, and they won't pay homage to my father. Why else do you think he hates you Christians so much?"

"But now you're one!" said Anwen, sounding as though she were about to cry. "And so am I!"

And then the three of them were laughing, lying back on the grassy bank and howling with laughter until Essa's belly ached and his jaw hurt. He felt weak, as though he were made of water. This was madness, lurching from misery to resolve to wild laughter all in the space of a moment, and somehow consumed by all three at once.

They lay watching wisps of cloud chase one another across the big sweep of blue sky. "Up till now," Essa said. "Everything's been laid out by others — Egric, our fathers, everyone but us. It's time we chose ourselves what's to be."

"So what'll we do?" Wulf said. Anwen nodded, and although Essa knew they had saved his life, he felt responsible for theirs, for getting them through this mess safely. They were together now, the three of them, bound to one another.

He looked down and saw that Anwen and Wulf were holding hands, and he was glad Anwen no longer looked at him in that hungry way she had done at Caer Elfan. It made him think of Lark, though, waiting with the rest of the village for the Mercian attack. If only she were here with him, and he knew she was safe. He sat up, raking his hands through his hair.

"We must try stopping this war," he said. "If we can bring a messenger from Northumbria, that might work. King Godsrule won't want this — he surely knows that if Penda takes all Anglia, he'll look to the north next. The Christian kings might refuse to wear Penda's ring, but sooner or later he'll take their lands if he's not stopped. And it was an East Anglian king that put Godsrule's family on the throne, so there's a debt of allegiance too. Penda must be as fond of his gold as the next man — if Godsrule threatens to double his taxes, he'll stop. Won't he?"

Wulf sighed. "I don't know. Sometimes he does, sometimes not. A few years ago he decided he'd had enough of paying tribute and sacked the place. His moods change. He'll not be an easy man to stop. And we don't even know where Godsrule is — my father moves around from hall to hall all the time. Godsrule won't stay in Ad Gefrin all year. He could be up on the border with Dál Riada for all we know."

Essa shrugged. "But if we go to Ad Gefrin and Godsrule's not there, they can tell us where he's gone to, or get a message to him."

"Oh, wonderful," said Wulf. "So we trek around Northumbria looking for the High King, like children chasing a frog? In the meantime, my father gives me up for dead and takes Anglia anyway. And he's my *father*. How can I just turn on him?"

"But Essa's right," said Anwen. "We've *got* to try to mend this mess, Wulf. They're all using us; we don't mean anything to them. If your father would have killed you for bringing Essa back as your ring bearer, what does that say about him? He doesn't care for you — he's just like the rest of them. All they care about is themselves, how much power they've got, and squabbling over their borders, as if anyone cares. And I bet that Egric's just the same, Essa."

Essa did not answer; he knew she was right.

Wulf stared at her, stunned, his hair hanging over his face. She leaned across and brushed it out of the way, but he hardly seemed to notice. Essa looked down at the ring on his finger and took it off, holding it out to him.

"I—I can't." Wulf said. "I can't take it."

"I don't want you just to take it," Essa said, heart pounding. He suddenly recalled the moment he'd knelt before Egric in the hall, so low his forehead touched the floor. "Do you give me yours."

Wulf stared down at the grass again and sat like that for what seemed like half a day. No one spoke; even Fenrir sat silently watching and at last flopped down in the shade, head resting on her front paws, one ear twitching. Close by, Essa could hear a lark singing.

Finally, Wulf looked up, and when he did, he had taken his ring off, and it was lying flat in the palm of his hand. Mercian gold, Penda's gold; it should have been poison. Essa half expected it to burn his skin when he picked it up. But it did not. It was just gold: a cold metal ring that slid down his middle finger, slightly looser than his own ring.

It meant that all had changed. They turned to each other, Anwen watching, solemn-faced for once, and clasped hands, gripping each other's fingers hard, as if that would make it a stronger pact.

Essa tried to think of something to say. Cai would have known, and a stream of brave and noble words would have slipped forth from his tongue, each one of them probably a lie, knowing him. But at least he would have known what to say. In the end, Essa just said, "All right. All right."

And it was Wulf who said, "Ad Gefrin, beware, and beware, High King."

And then he laughed.

18

From the far west of Mercia
to the northeast

"DOES anyone really know the way?" Anwen said. "Essa — surely you've been to Ad Gefrin with your father?"

It was the following morning. Essa had been out with Fenrir the evening before and walked till he felt the life coming back into his legs. He had watched the sun dying on the western horizon till the cloud, seething up from behind the mountains they had left behind, was suffused with golden and crimson light. He had shielded his eyes, watching Fenrir streak through the long grass after a hare, and for a heartbeat he knew her joy at the chase and her hunger for blood. That night he had slept a deep, dreamless sleep.

Essa shook his head. "No, never." He had often wondered what it was like — everyone had heard tales of the High King's palace nestling in the green fells: the great wooden hall, patterned with beaten gold. He had heard of the sparrow flying from one end of the hall to the other, and of the bishop Paulinus telling Edwin, the old High King, that the sparrow was like human life, flying from the unknown to the unknown. That Jesus Christ had the answers. Cai had been the one who persuaded old King Redwald of East Anglia to stand by Edwin when he took refuge at the court of the Wolf Folk, an exiled prince in fear of his life, and put him on the Northumbrian throne. Essa banished the thought from his head. Cai had plotted his last intrigue, and now he was dead.

"My father told me Ad Gefrin was the brightest light in Britain until Penda put it out," said Anwen.

"They rebuilt some of it, didn't they?" said Essa.

Anwen nodded. "I heard it will never be the same again, though. So what'll we do? We'll have to find the Magonsæte and ask them — they'll know."

Wulf smiled awkwardly. "No need for that," he said. "I was there when we burned it. I'm Penda's son, remember? I'd say it's northeast of here. Sun at our left shoulders, days and days to ride. It's a long way."

The air smelled different on the way north: it was cold and sharp, edged with the smell of heather and gorse. They galloped across untamed moorland under vast skies skeined with cloud. They skirted green forests and rode along fellsides that plunged dizzyingly down to dark, deep lakes. On the shore of one of the lakes, they stopped at a little village hugging the water's edge and traded one of Anwen's new linen dresses, sewn for her wedding, for twice-baked bread, dried fish, and some of last summer's dried apples and berries. The people were dark-eyed and wary of Wulf, even of Essa, despite the fact he spoke to them in British. The dried fruit tasted dusty, but Essa knew they would welcome the sweetness later.

It was the wrong month for traveling, so they came across no others, but the song of spring was everywhere: frogs shuffling in the bracken, calling as they moved from bog to puddle, larks wheeling above the heather, their urgent, bubbling song lasting from dawn till dusk. Late in the afternoon of the seventh day, the clouds gathered in gray fists and threw down rain. The rain did not stop; Wulf and Anwen complained bitterly, but it suited Essa's mood.

He was wracked with misery, aching with grief at the loss of his father. His dreams were plagued with visions of Cai choking out his last breath, drowning in his own blood. His dreams showed him the village, too, the way he had first seen it — just a hump on the horizon as he sat before his father in the saddle. But the hump was growing larger: now there was smoke, and he could make out the flag mast by the gates. The air was filled with blood-freezing screaming and the stinking sweat of men hungry to kill.

He was riding with the Mercian army.

Penda had released his hordes, and Essa was riding with them.

When he woke each morning, bathed in sweat, Essa had to remind himself that it had not happened yet, that it was just a dream, that he would never betray Hild and the village, even though he had double-dealt with almost everyone else. *We're going to stop it from even happening,* he told himself. *Penda's men won't ride out this time.* But the fear that it already *had* happened never left him. What if Penda had not waited for Wulf to return with Anwen? Essa had to push the idea to the back of his mind and think only in terms of their present: finding shelter, summoning enough strength to ride.

A few more days passed, and their supplies started to run low. There was no sign of a hall, village, or even a shepherd in his bothy to trade with. They were somewhere in Elmet now, one of the northern kingdoms of the British loyal to the High King, but harried constantly for tribute by Penda. Essa remembered Dai and his sister, the British spies. They had been from Elmet. Did their family know what had happened to them? he wondered.

"We've not seen a single village since the lake," Anwen said miserably. "I wish we could sit by a fire just to dry out our clothes."

"These people move like smoke," Wulf told her. "They're always on the run from my father's men, and their villages are hidden. We'll see no one if they see us first."

A lot of the food they'd packed at Caer Elfan had been used up during Essa's illness; they ate just once a day now: a piece of sausage or dried fish, a handful of oats boiled in water if they could find enough dry twigs to get a fire going. It was not enough.

"I wish I was a horse!" Anwen said, watching Grani, Balder, and her white mare cropping the grass. They all laughed, but they were hungry and getting weaker.

"I knew we should have bought more at that village," Wulf said one night as they laid out their damp bedrolls. Once again, they had been forced to give up the struggle to light a fire in the rain. There was no way of drying out, no fierce heat to draw the ache of the day's ride from their bones.

Essa shrugged. "What with? The clothes off our backs?" But he was cursing himself and the Mercian who had cut his flesh in the first place.

"God's wounds!" Anwen stared bitterly at the wild, empty moorland sweeping away from them on all sides, now rendered eerie by the oncoming night. "Why does Godsrule have to live so *far away* from everywhere?"

Suddenly, Fenrir whined and stood up, shaking out her wet fur. Her body went rigid.

Instantly, the three of them huddled closer together. Essa was fixed by a nameless, bone-chilling fear.

"What is it?" whispered Anwen, screwing a corner of her blanket into a tight coil. "What's she heard?"

Essa had already guessed, but when he heard it next, he was still unprepared for the jolt of fear that shot through him—an unearthly howling in the distance that made his bowels freeze and his scalp prickle. The sound grew louder, tearing across the night sky: *wolves*. He reached out for

Fenrir and caught her flicker of desire. They were her kin, and she wanted to run with them, but she was afraid for her companions. And she was afraid of her kin, too, because they had never known the warmth of a hall, and they were always hungry.

That was the other thing about fire: it kept wolves away. And they had no fire.

Essa sat silently, huddled in his damp cloak, running his hand along Fenrir's flank, teasing out her rain-sodden, tangled fur with his fingertips.

"They won't bother us," said Wulf. "Sounds like they're a way off."

Anwen nodded, but Essa was not comforted and knew Wulf was not either.

"I wish we had spears," Anwen said, sounding much younger than usual.

Wulf put his arm around her shoulder. "Don't be afraid. It isn't wolves. It's just the Great Lord, riding around the night sky and howling away with his ghostly warriors. The Wild Hunt, they call it, when Woden takes to the skies with the battle madness upon him. He'll ride the length of the hawk's path by morning, wielding his hammer till his battle rage is sated, and then he'll go back to his learning and his poetry as though it'd never happened. He's tricky, but he's the greatest of the Aesir, is Woden, and he won't hurt you, Anwen, see. Have you heard the story of how he found the first song?"

Anwen shook her head, and Wulf began quietly telling her the tale of Woden hanging upside down in the branches of Yggdrasil for nine days and nine nights till the knowledge of the runes came to him: fiery butterflies alighting in his mind's eye.

Essa had heard the tale before, hundreds of times. But even if it had been a new story, and the most gripping ever told, he knew he would have been unable to listen. The lonely howling of the wolf pack was growing quieter.

He looked away awkwardly as Wulf crouched next to Anwen, squeezing her shoulder, stroking her wet, tangled hair. He stirred the damp pile of kindling with a hawthorn twig, trying to wake the flames, knowing it was useless. Wulf and Anwen had lain together behind the deerskin curtain: they wanted to be alone, and here they were, stranded on a moor with him and his dog.

For a moment, he wished he could leave them, go to Ad Gefrin by himself, but then what would stop Wulf from riding back to his father? They had made an agreement — swapped rings. They would go together to the High King. And yet, a cold little thought trickled into Essa's mind: *Can I really trust him?* All Wulf's life, he had been trained to obey Penda's every word. Yes, they had swapped rings, chosen to take their own path and stop this foolish war before it even started. Yet Wulf was sixteen summers old. Was a few days really enough to undo the fear and loyalty Penda had wrought in Wulf's heart since the day he was born?

But no one else knew the way. They were in Wulf's hands.

And that night, Essa dreamed again, only this time, the Mercian army was over the village walls, the great hall was burning, and neither Hild, nor Red, nor Cole, nor Lark were anywhere to be seen.

19

Northumbria

ORE than twenty days after leaving the bothy, they were riding across rain-soaked green fells, and Essa sensed they were close.

"It ought not to be long now." Wulf's face was set and serious, and Essa knew that in his mind he was watching Ad Gefrin burn again. He could see children running, screaming, women and men fighting, hacking at the Mercian army with sword, ax, staff, anything they could lay their hands on. "Ah, Frigya," said Wulf, after a while. "They say it's always the same with the first fight. It haunts your dreams, even after you've fought more battles than you have fingers and thumbs on each hand and killed more men than you can count."

Essa nodded but did not answer. It would be the same with his first battle, and unless King Godsrule put a stop to Penda, Essa would be fighting Wulf. Then he felt hoofbeats shaking the ground and looked up sharply, scanning the horizon. Anwen turned, watching too.

"Is it just our skill?" Essa said in their own language. He kept his eyes on the rich green hillside rising up before them.

Anwen shrugged, answering in a rush of silvery, songlike British. "An old skill it is. British or nay, I'm not knowing." He was growing used to her strange accent now, and the words closed around his heart like comforting hands.

"There's someone coming," he said to Wulf. "Listen."

"How do you hear so sharp?" said Wulf. "It gives me the cold chills. Well, you know what they say—you British mate with the elves, don't you? No wonder you're strange. It's elvish blood."

Anwen laughed. "Two sets of hoofbeats."

Then they heard a horse whinnying and the sound of human voices laughing.

"Outriders," said Wulf. "Well, I don't blame them for being cautious after the beating they took from my father's men."

"What if they know you?" Anwen twisted the reins in her hands. She leaned forward, peering at the two approaching riders. They were fair-haired, easy in the saddle.

"They won't. I was barely more than a child." Wulf rubbed his fingers in the short growth of bracken-rust beard on his face. "I must be twice the size, too." He laughed. "If there's anyone left alive who knows me for Penda's son, I'll be dead before I can blink, so it shan't bother me."

Anwen smiled, but her white fingers twisted the reins around and around.

"Too late now," Essa whispered. "They've seen us." They rode on, the horses picking their way up the steep fellside until they were within hailing distance of the outriders.

"Who comes?" shouted one of the horsemen. He was bigger than his companion, but both were broad-shouldered, with long pale-red hair whipped about in the wind.

"Travelers with news, no more!" Essa yelled. He sounded strong, sure of himself, but his guts were sloppy with fear.

"Ride in, ride in!" called the outriders, and they stayed their horses until Essa, Wulf, and Anwen had reached them.

They were young men, hardly older than Wulf—both had freckled faces flushed with color, and pale eyebrows. They gripped their reins with strong, broad-fingered hands. One looked several years younger than the other, built on slighter lines, and his hair was a deeper red, more like Essa's. He fidgeted in the saddle, as if he hated to be still. When they noticed Anwen, they both slumped slightly, the breath sucked from their lungs by the sight of her.

Anwen smiled. "Are you brothers?"

Both outriders smiled at her. They each had the same wide, square-toothed grin.

"Aye, lady," said the elder. "Godsway and Godsgift, house of Ad Gefrin."

"What's left of it," said his brother, and his bright face darkened.

"That's Godsgift, though they call him the Fox—he's that cunning."

A smile flashed across Godsgift's face, but Essa was watching him closely, and he could see it had not reached his eyes. *He's a deep one, all right,* he thought.

"Then we are honored to be met by the High King's athelings," said Anwen. "Is he your father?"

Godsway shook his head. "Nay, he's our half brother. We lost so many at Penda's fight, but he'll pay for it in the next life, the heathen bastard." He glanced at Essa and Wulf. "Are your blades peace-bound or not? Now's the time to make them safe—tha'll be safe in our hands if tha's not armed."

He rode closer, and Essa and Wulf showed the peace bands on their swords, and Essa felt glad of the bone-handled dagger hidden safe in his boot.

"Well enough," said Godsway. "Are you honest Christians, or keeping the old ways still?"

"Oh, we're honest Christians, praise the Lord," said Wulf. Essa fought a strong urge to laugh.

"Good, for there's powerful hatred against the old ways in our hall, and the old ways may blame Penda for that," said Godsway. "I must ask your names and what you want here now that you're on our land. If you would come closer, it'll be with us or not at all. Nor far, the least. The way is guarded now with hidden archers."

They gave their real names, but said Essa and Wulf were cousins from East Anglia, Anwen Wulf's wife, and that they'd news for the king.

"What's tha news, then?" said the Fox. He glanced down at Fenrir. "It's a long way to travel with tha hound, all the way from Wolf Folk marches." His eyes narrowed slightly. "And the king's enough to think on as it is."

He knows we're not telling them the whole story.

Essa put the idea out of his mind. They would have to deal with that later, if at all. Now they just had to get in that hall. It was making his toes curl with frustration, knowing the High King was only paces away after so many days of riding. He glanced across at Wulf, and they exchanged a look; they had not thought of this. What if they were not actually allowed to see Godsrule? There must be hordes of people seeking an audience with him: there was every chance they would be turned away.

Anwen smiled serenely. "It is news for King Godsrule's ears only."

"News?" said Godsway. "What's the price?"

"We give it free," said Essa.

Godsway and the Fox stared at him. "There's something about your face," said the Fox. "Where'd tha say you come from?"

Essa felt a bubble of fear rise up his throat, and he heard that long-ago voice once more: *It's in tha face —*

"You're mistaken," he said. "I've not been this far north before."

"Aye, well," said Godsway. "Ride on with us, then."

But the Fox stared at Essa a moment longer: long enough to turn the blood to ice in his veins. *He can't know you,* he told himself angrily. *And besides, it's Wulf they'll kill if they find out who we really are. Nobody cares any which way about you in here.*

Ad Gefrin lay settled in a green valley amid high, soaring fells. The land surrounding it was bright with new grass, and the great earthen palace walls rose high above a deep, dark ditch, dotted with snowdrops. It was spring: the fells were covered with flowers, and new life was everywhere. Essa heard the crying of lambs born on the hillside and smiled at their keening, the song of spring. There would be no fighting now, no bloody death. He was going to put a stop to it all.

"We dug deep and built the walls high after that heathen bastard came," said Godsway as they neared the gate. "You should have seen Ad Gefrin before these days. They say the earth ran with molten gold as the hall burned, and Edwin's golden dragons melted right off the walls."

"Were you not at the fight, then?" said Essa lightly. Wulf was grinning and sitting back in his saddle, swinging his legs so that the iron buckles on his stirrups sprayed raindrops. Essa wondered how he did it; it was as if he had never laid eyes on Ad Gefrin before, far less helped his father burn it to the ground.

The Fox shook his head. "Na, more's the pity. We were fostered down in Kent and never knew of it till a month had passed."

Essa felt a thin trickle of fear slide down the back of his

neck. It was unlikely anyone would recognize Wulf, so why did he suddenly feel as if he were walking into a trap? Godsway and the Fox rode on either side of Anwen as she told them about the "little East Anglian hall" she had grown up in. "It's so wonderful to live by the sea," she said. "Apart from the Frisian pirates." He could tell they weren't listening to a word she was saying; they were spelled into silence by her face, watching her red lips move. For a moment, Essa wanted to laugh and had to stare at Godsway's solid, square back to distract himself. There was a sooty black stain on his cloak—he must have brushed against a cooking pot.

We ought to be safe here. This should work. They'll listen to us.

But when the Fox excused himself from Anwen and rode on a few paces to bang on the huge, oak-hewn gate, Essa had to fight a strong urge to turn Grani south, whistle to Fenrir, and ride away. Maybe it was the ghosts of the fallen making him feel uneasy, he told himself. Maybe Penda's victims had never left Ad Gefrin, tied here by the sorrow of their passing, and the passing of their great, golden-banded hall.

The gates swung open. Godsway exchanged a few words with the guard, and they rode in. Ad Gefrin lay before them: a great hall still, new wood, built over what had been burned. It was a huge place with soaring thatched roofs, smaller halls surrounding the largest as if it had spawned cubs. Some of the trees nearby were blackened, others just young saplings.

Despite the spitting rain, the courtyard thronged with people: gangs of men and women with long, curved bill-hooks, back from laying hedges out in the fields; a pair of sulky-looking boys heaving baskets full of manure from the stables to the dung heap; a group of older girls sweeping across the yard with hooded hawks on their wrists. A group of shouting children ran in circles around the great flag mast, playing a game beneath the fluttering dragon standard of the High King. Two little girls jumped in puddles, shrieking and laughing, skinny bare legs streaked with muddy water. They stopped and stared when Godsway gave the signal to dismount, gazing at him devotedly. When everyone was out of the saddle, Godsway jerked his head at the girls. "Here, Thryft and Unna, isn't it? Take these horses to the stables, take the hound to the dog shed, and honor our guests."

The girls dropped to their knees and scrambled up again. One of them was dark eyed, and Essa saw that there must be a lot of British blood in Northumbria. He remembered the northern outlaw in the forest, the way his speech was veined with the old language, old words. One of the little girls reached out a hand to Fenrir, but she backed off, growling softly.

Don't fret, my dear one, go on. Go with her. Fenrir stared at him, as if to say, *Are you sure?* And Essa felt another pang of unease. He glanced quickly around the courtyard. In the corner, a small boy was leaning over the fence into the pig-pen, scratching a black hog with a stick. *It's fine,* he told himself. *And, anyhow, you have no choice but to go in if you want talk with the High King.*

The girls darted curious looks at the three strangers over their shoulders as they splashed off, leading the horses, Fenrir following close behind.

Essa felt powerless without Fenrir and Grani, and let his hand rest on the sword handle at his belt. He felt a fresh shock of grief as his fingers rested in the hollows and shapes left in the bound leather by his father's hand. But there was no time for that now. Anwen and Wulf were already following Godsway and the Fox toward a dark doorway. They went in. A pair of women sitting spinning in the shelter of the dripping eaves stared at them without much interest. Wool thrummed as their clay spindle whorls fell, twisting the wool into thread. Again, Essa had to fight the need to run like a sprung deer as far away from here as he could get. Taking a long breath, he went inside.

The hall was huge and dark, most of the wide doors closed against the rain. Weak, gray daylight followed Essa in; he could see dust floating in the air and smell burning pitch from the torches guttering in iron sconces on the walls. A group of men sat on the floor on a pile of skins, leaning against the wall as they played knucklestones. He heard a sharp intake of breath as he passed them and murmuring voices whispering about him. The men let their knuckle-stones fall as he went by. All the better to stare, thought Essa. Did they not see strangers here, in the hall of the High King? This was not some marsh village. What was wrong with these folk? He quickened his step to catch up with the others, but he could still feel the men watching him.

A fire burned in the center of the hall, surrounded by flat, gray riverbed stones. A couple of heavy iron pots rested on the stones; savory-smelling steam drifted from beneath their lids. A great silver bowl hung above the fire, suspended from one of the high ceiling beams on a thin chain, just like the one from Constantinople that Wulf had given Anwen at their wedding, only bigger, richer. A woman passed him, carrying a copper pan of cream. A thick braid of gray hair was coiled around her head; her face looked kind. *Let's see if they're all gapeseeds*, he thought, and looked up, smiling broadly at her.

She dropped the pan. Time seemed to melt, slow down. A low note sang out as the copper pan struck the floorboards, and a wave of white cream splashed her feet, but the woman just stood there, staring at him.

"I'm sorry." Essa reached down to pick up the bowl. When he handed it back to her, he saw that the old woman's veined hands were shaking. She opened her mouth to speak, but at that moment Godsway said, "Brother, this is the lad with news. Says it's no price, too. Essa — that's your name, isn't it? — speak up, then! The king's got enough to think on without waiting for your news, whatever it may be."

Essa walked toward him. The air in the hall felt heavy, pressing down on his head. Anwen and Wulf were on their knees, bowing their heads before a man sprawling in a chair near the fire. He stood up, unfolding himself slowly. He was tall, as tall as Essa, with gray-streaked red hair hanging loose around his shoulders, and a gray beard. His eyes were gray too: hard and sharp like flints. A gold-wrought crucifix swung against his chest on a fine chain.

So this was Godsrule, High King of all Britain. Essa knew he should be kneeling but could not move. Godsrule stepped close to him, taking Essa's chin in his hand. Essa could smell the stale wine in his breath, the sweat of his body. The king's gray eyes were flecked with amber, as if the red in his hair ran through his body like a vein of bright metal, and they traveled across Essa's face so slowly that he wanted to tear himself away. Somehow, Essa knew that to speak would be the end of him, that this man would kill him at once if he said a word. It was too late to run now.

"Show me tha blade." Godsrule's voice was dry and hard, the rustling of winter leaves. The words of the northern outlaw echoed in Essa's head, *Tha hast the Lady's sword*, maw.

Essa unbuckled his sword belt and, kneeling at last, he laid the sword in her silver-dragon-patterned scabbard before the High King's feet, waiting to see what would come.

The king stared down at it, and the lines around his mouth seemed to grow deeper. "I trust tha isn't such a fool as to come into my hall bringing a sword not made safe with peace bands, boy. Unwrap them now, and show me the blade. I've a fancy to see it."

Essa felt strangely calm as he dug his fingers into the

knotted leather that bound the Silver Serpent in her scabbard. Within moments, the bands were undone.

Well, my lord, he thought. *You asked to see it.* Heart hammering, Essa closed his fingers around the sword hilt and pulled her from the scabbard. The blade shone as she sang through the air, and Essa laid her at the High King's feet, naked in her beauty.

The king stared down at her, a small, tight smile on his lips. "Get up, that I might look at thee again," he said. "What is tha father's name, boy, and where do you come from?"

Essa stood up. "I'm Essa. Aesc, son of Cai. He's a scop and a trader."

The king's cold gray eyes narrowed. "That's not all he is."

A sudden, thick silence settled on the hall like a fall of heavy snow. Someone dropped a wooden spoon. It struck the floorboards with a noise like a drumbeat.

Essa felt his skin crawl, as if someone were tracing a line down the back of his neck with a feather. *What's happening?* he thought. *Why is he looking at me like that?* "With respect, my lord, but he is dead now. Killed by King Penda—we have come here to—"

Suddenly, the king turned away and laughed. "Well done," he said to Godsway and the Fox. "Tha hast brought me the bitch's whelp. After all these years, he walks into my hall. This is the working of God, I swear it."

"My lord," Essa said. "I do not know what you mean. We have come with news of Penda—he waits to march on the

Wolf Folk. His host of fighting men is gathered at the border, and Seobert will not come out of his monastery—"

Godsrule laughed again, an airless hiss, and gestured with one long-fingered hand so that Essa turned. Behind him, a silent crowd had gathered, staring at him as if he were a spirit. "Oh, how they adored her," said the king. "How they loved their Lady. And I did too, for she was my sister. I am your mother's brother, *kaveth:* your uncle."

Essa turned away from them, a nameless feeling creeping through his body: part thwartedness, part burning excitement. He could not take his eyes off the king's face now: the long, slightly hooked nose, high cheekbones, arched red eyebrows, skin spattered with freckles. He had seen it before, down by the mere with Cole, threading blue jays' feathers onto a hook, looking at his own image in the still water.

"Yes," said the king. "You see it now, don't you?"

Essa stood silent, breathless, thinking of the dragon standard fluttering at Godsrule's flag mast outside. In his mind, he flew high above the village again, watching the Mercian forest stretch out to the west, the flatlands reaching east across the marches of the Wolf Folk for the coast.

Essa's spirit journey had lifted him to the skies because he was a Silver Serpent—born of the house of Ad Gefrin.

This was what he was.

Somewhere, a voice in Essa's head said, *Remember what you came here for.*

He could feel the crowd watching him; their eyes were like needles in his back. What did they *want*? He heard lambs calling outside on the fellsides. A side door creaked open, and he caught the hot, yeasty smell of a bread oven. High above his head, a starling flew from one beam to another.

"My mother," he said. "She is dead."

"Dead to me, to my family," King Godsrule said. "Edwin should have had her strangled, and you drowned in the water butt—he was always too softhearted. But Elfgift's still alive, last I heard. The bitch ran off to a nunnery after she'd been gotten with you—she sits there now at Bedricsworth with that useless fool, Seobert."

The Silver Serpent

ESSA gasped when he heard his mother's name spoken.

"My lord," he stammered, "you are mistaken. My mother is dead."

By now Wulf and Anwen were standing; Wulf's face was slack with shock. Anwen had folded her arms across her chest, shaking her head.

"With respect, it is plain to see you are kin, to look at you all," she said, gazing from Godsrule to Essa, then to Godsway and his brother.

Wulf opened and closed his mouth a few times, then said, "But does this mean that Essa—"

"He is one of us," said Godsrule sharply. "Traveler's leavings or no. Lucky for you, boy, that Penda killed so many of my house, else I'd cut tha throat." By now, the watching crowd were staring and pointing openly at Essa, muttering to each other, some holding up their children for a better view.

"It's the Lady's child," a woman said.

"It's a miracle, the working of the Lord!"

Godsrule wheeled around to face them all. "Get thee gone!" he hissed, and even though he had not even raised his voice, everyone backed off, slipping away to listen from dark corners of the hall where they would not be seen. He turned to Essa. "Now that you're here, boy, you'll stay. I need all the men I can get, though your friends may do as they please. For he's no more your cousin than I'm a goat, and I'll only have people by me that are useful."

Essa only half heard him. She was alive. His mother was alive. Everything Cai had told him was a lie. He wanted to laugh—Cai had lied to everyone, so why not to his own child? Elfgift was alive, at Bedricsworth monastery. And Bedricsworth was in Wolf Folk land, near the coast. It was no more than a few days' ride from the village. All these years she had been so close to him. Anger burst in his chest, and he fought to swallow it back.

"I don't believe it!" He stooped to pick up the sword, the Silver Serpent who had been sleeping all these years, just hanging on the wall of the smithy. Metal hissed against leather as he resheathed her. "Anyone could have a sword like this. And many people look alike who are not kin. With respect, my lord, it proves nothing."

"But you said yourself Cai's tha father!" said Godsway. Essa stared at him. If Godsway and the Fox were the High King's half brothers, they were his kin too, his uncles. "And that's what the man who dishonored my sister was called."

The Fox nodded. "Everyone knows the tale." He did not look pleased, and Essa realized with a jolt that it was because he now stood just as close to the throne of Ad Gefrin as the brothers. *His uncles.* The Fox could not be old enough to remember Elfgift, but Godsway must have been able to.

Essa ignored the Fox, turning to the king. "I have come here to ask your help, and if you cannot give it, I must return to my lord, Egric the Atheling. Penda will not wait forever, and I will have to fight."

The king raised a thin red eyebrow. "So Egric's your lord? He was fostered up here with my uncle when we were boys." He laughed. "He's always been a cunning one — trust him to get thee for himself, an atheling from the house of Ad Gefrin."

Essa remembered Cai smiling, saying, *A sly move, Egric.*

It was true, then. Elfgift was King Godsrule's sister. Suddenly, he saw in his mind Hild meeting them at the gate of the village all those years ago, looking at him so curiously, saying, *Is it—?*

She had known, too. Everyone had known who his mother was, and that she was alive. Everyone but him. So why should he care what happened to the village? He could trust no one but himself.

Not even Lark. The thought made him breathless with anger and sorrow.

"My lord. Any day now, Penda will march on the Wolf Folk. He has scores and scores of men at the border. He waits only for his son to arrive with Eiludd Powys's daughter as a hostage, to stop the British coming from the west while he looks to the east." Essa paused, half sure someone would guess who Wulf was, that they would be denounced. But no one did. No one was paying any attention to Wulf and Anwen — all were staring at him, even the king. "My lord, if Penda attacks the Wolf Folk, there will be war the rest of the year till none are left alive. Will you send a messenger to the border, ordering Penda off?"

Godsrule laughed, and Essa felt a chill of horror. They had come all this way so that the High King could laugh at them. He glanced at the others. Anwen's face was set in anger; Wulf looked close to tears. Their eyes locked. Essa knew now that the rings on their fingers and their pact meant nothing. *If there's no way of stopping Penda, then we've no choice but to fight each other.* Wulf was first to look away, and Essa thought perhaps he was relieved that he could go back to obeying his father's every word, loyal to Mercia till the end.

"My lord," Essa said. "Is there nothing you will do? Will you send a messenger to Penda? You could threaten to double his taxes!"

"Who are you to tell the High King his business?" said Godsway.

But Godsrule just laughed again. "Nay, lad. Let them fight. I'll not bring Penda up here again, not till I've a host to crush him. He killed so many last time it'll be years before I meet him on the battlefield again. Why should I move, when I have the biggest prize of all, here in my hall?"

The Fox looked angrily at his brother; Godsway shook his head.

"Well, then," said Essa. "If it pleases your lordship, we will stay one night to rest our horses, and ride south. We must fight." He glanced at Wulf again, who looked away. *We must fight, and on opposite sides.*

Godsrule's smile faded. His face was hard and lean, as if it had been carved from one of the gray fellside rocks. "It does not please me that you should go, Aesc, son of Cai. Tha's Edwin's kin, my nephew, and you'll stay here, beside me. Tha's bound to Egric the Atheling no more, for you're an atheling, same as him."

"I will not hear this!" Essa knew he was risking his life to raise his voice, but he could not stop himself. "My lord, you must help! If Penda takes Anglia, what is to keep him from —"

"Ah, shut tha mouth. Tha's just like that bitch your mother." The king reached out and cuffed the side of his head: a sharp, ringing blow that made his ear sting. Essa hissed through his teeth, stepping backward. Squinting, he found that he could not see; his sight was clouded by red shadows, and his breath felt hot in his lungs. He moved quickly, full of elf magic, curled his left hand into a fist, and let it fly. There was a shout of rage, and he felt another blow, hitting his nose this time. Hot blood filled his mouth. People were shouting, screaming in horror. He was fighting the High King of Britain. He was going to die, but he did not care; his fists flew; he kicked out in a frenzy. Someone grabbed his arm, and he snatched it away, wrenching around and digging his knee into someone's crotch. A stunning blow to the back of the neck sent Essa to his knees, and both his arms were wrenched behind his back.

He heard someone say, "Jesu, he's mad." Now they were dragging him along; he writhed and twisted like a landed fish, but the hands that gripped his arms were strong, and he was weak after the long journey and limp with shock. The hall rang with voices; people were shouting, but he could not make out the words. They dragged him past the long table, the mead benches: the Silver Serpent left behind on the floor. They were probably going to take him out into the yard and cut his throat. Bright rugs hung on the walls; torches flickered, sending long coils of smoke up to the high beams crisscrossing above his head. He could see the carcass of one of last winter's pigs hanging up there, cured and blackened by the smoke from the fire. That was all he would be in a moment — just a carcass, a piece of meat.

They dragged him outside, and all the while he expected to feel a blade at his throat, but the cold touch never came. He caught glimpses of shocked faces, watching as he was dragged across the yard; a door opened. Shoved forward, he fell to his knees just as the door slammed behind him. He heard the bolt being drawn home, and then, all around him, a ragged howling noise rose up: hounds baying and barking.

They had shut him in the dog hall, and the hounds were hungry.

The air was thick with their scent. Their feelings flashed through him — they were tired; they had been chasing deer through the greenwood only that afternoon; and they were hungry, so hungry. He felt their anger at being invaded by a stranger, their curiosity too, but mostly anger stoked by the intense need for meat.

Was he to be torn to pieces? As he kneeled there watching them, his eyes grew accustomed to the gloom in the dog hall. Thin streams of evening light poured in through small, high windows. The hounds were all around him — a score or more, long, lean shapes writhing about each other. Where was Fenrir? He could not see her. He would have to find her later.

Staying on his knees, he looked up. A host of liquid-dark eyes stared back. He picked out their leader, the dog closest to him — a black-haired deerhound a good hand-span taller than Fenrir. The hound sat back on his haunches, and his lips peeled back from his teeth as he let out a low growl that made the ground hum. He was enormous — nearly the size of a yearling colt. Essa drew in a breath — if they knew he was afraid, he would be finished. He could feel their hunger. Some hunting men did this: kept their hounds without enough meat so they were always ready for the chase. But these dogs had killed recently; he could feel it in the air, the savage thrill of the hunt, the trace of blood like the taste of wet iron. They had killed, but no one had fed them yet. *What a mad thing to do, throwing a prisoner into a shed full of starving hounds.*

He felt naked without the weight of the sword belt at his waist and shoulder. This was the first time he had been without the Silver Serpent since the day Cai left him in the village, five years ago. She had hung on the wall in the smithy, too heavy for him to lift at first, but always there, always within his reach. And now she was gone.

At that moment, the huge black hound stepped closer. Essa did not move. The bone-handled knife was hidden in his boot, but he did not want to use it. He reached out his hand instead.

Come, my friend, I mean you no harm. Essa closed his eyes, let his thoughts spill from his mind like dried barley from a sack; he had to do this now, had to fly free of his body and get inside one of the dogs, see if he could steer its thoughts. Nothing happened, and he felt sick with the fear that he would not be able to do it. But then came the twisting feeling in his guts.

For a moment, he was a pack of hounds, all gathered around the kneeling figure of a boy. They had been running in the greenwood all that morning and afternoon, and they wanted to eat: they wanted fresh meat.

So that's how it works, he thought. *When they're all together, their spirits mix. That's how they hunt in packs. Maybe it's how men hunted, too, long ago.* For a moment, he felt a flicker of regret. It was cruel, really, this trick of his: these were such noble creatures, and he was like a cuckoo edging into another bird's nest. *But you must do it.* Then he was inside the body of the black deerhound — he could feel its fiery spirit flickering all around him, only Essa's was stronger, and then he felt its thoughts.

Two-legs over there smells of rage. What's he doing in here with us? He'd best do no harm to my brothers and sisters.

Then the new female came forward, the stranger. *That's my brother,* Fenrir said. *Harm him, and I shall not take pity on any of you.*

The pack's voice rose in disgust, in shock. *She shan't speak so to us.*

I shall.

The pack leader had a strong spirit; in the forest on the way to Powys, Essa had been unable to make even a thrush fly above the trees. How could he hope to quell the spirit of a huge dog, even with Fenrir's help? He felt the hound's fiery essence crackle around him and sent out a thought: *The newcomer's brother means no harm. He means no harm. He means no—*

But the pack leader's anger was strong; Essa was consumed by it. Why had he and his brothers and sisters not been fed? Where was their reward for running so fast and for so long through the greenwood, for bringing down six spotted roe deer between them? And now this stranger thrust into their midst, sending off waves of rage and fear. *Take him instead. We shall feed on him if they give us nothing else.*

But he means no harm; he means no harm.

At last, he felt the black deerhound's anger abate.

Maybe they will come soon with our reward. He's scrawny anyway: not much to enjoy there.

Essa gasped for air, back in his own body, slumping foward. Then the pack leader stepped toward him, and Essa reached out and laid his hand on the hound's head. *Thank you, my brother.*

The hounds were all around him now, pushing forward, nudging his legs with their noses, tails thumping against his thigh, his outstretched hands. And suddenly, he no longer had the strength to sit up. Lying on his back in the corner, he drew in a deep, shuddering breath, full of relief that he was still alive. His body quivered like a plucked string on his father's cherrywood lyre. Where was the lyre now? Probably broken in the mud, somewhere outside Penda's fortress — wherever they had thrown Cai's body. Essa wrapped his arms around his knees, still sucking in deep breaths, knotted with rage against the arrogant, red-headed man who had struck him across the face. His uncle, the High King of all Britain. The gods were playing one of their tricky games with him, just as men set cocks in a ring to fight. But he was angrier still with Cai: for his lies and for being dead.

Elfgift was alive, though. His mother lived, and she was with Seobert at Bedricsworth.

21

Elfgift and Cai

He **heard** women calling the children in for their food and drew the rich scent of it in through his nostrils: deer stewed with vetch and coriander, and fresh-baked bread. He heard the men go off up the hills to bring in the sheep with their dogs, muttering about wolves, telling a lewd tale about a woman one of them had been with. Night was falling, the light from the tiny slit windows had long faded, and with every moment he waited for the dog hall door to open. They would come for him and kill him. No one could insult the king in front of his people and expect to live.

How unfair it all was, he thought, that just as he learned his mother was alive, he was about to die. How would they kill him? He hoped it would be quick. Other than the British spies in Penda's camp, he had never seen anyone put to death. What was the point in taking a life as payment for a crime when a blood price was to be had instead? Sheep, or barrels of wine, or cattle were of more use than the corpse of a villain. But there was no blood price high enough to pay his debt. He had raised his hand in violence against the High King. *His mother's brother.* He whispered the words "my uncle," trying to make it seem more real, but it did not.

Then, at last, he heard the bolt lift on the other side of the door.

His gorge rose and he stood, Fenrir on her feet beside him in a heartbeat, a deep, low growl coming from the back of her throat. Surely they would take him outside. No one was ever killed in a dog hall. They would take him outside. It was all so foolish: Anwen and Wulf had tried so hard to keep him alive after the knife wound, and here he was, about to have his throat cut. Or perhaps they were going to throttle him, or bury him alive, weighed down by stones. He had heard of men doing that. Dying with the breath stolen from his body would be worse than anything he could think of. It made him think of that sun-dappled, terrifying afternoon in the beech coppice, of hard fingers closing around his throat.

It's in tha face. Anyone can see—

And then Essa knew that the man who'd tried to kill him that day had *known who he was.* He had not been an outlaw driven out of his senses by loneliness. He had been looking for Essa.

Oh, Tasik, he thought. *Oh, my father—when I follow you into the next world, I shall not rest till I find you. I will be seeking answers.*

Feverishly, he wondered what had happened to Wulf and Anwen. Were they already dead? If so, he'd as good as killed them.

He expected Godsway and the Fox to burst in with a gang of young men of Ad Gefrin, ready to avenge the insult to their lord. But instead an old woman came in alone, the one who had dropped the pan of cream when she first saw him. The hounds must have known her well; none barked or howled — most of them were dozing, nearly asleep, dazed with their chase through the greenwood and their hunger.

In one hand the old woman held a bowl covered by a cloth, with a piece of flat bread resting on top. In the other, she held the knotted neck of a large sack. It must have contained the hounds' food, because she was soon surrounded by lithe, wiry bodies, questing for the sack with their long noses.

Essa, not knowing what else to do, took a couple of quick steps back, hand resting on Fenrir's neck. She was tense, ready to spring.

"Tha's alive, then," said the old woman. "You must have a way with hounds — talk was they'd tear thee to pieces."

Essa felt another flicker of scorn for Godsrule. What kind of man sent an old woman to find a corpse torn to bits by dogs?

"Peace, child," the old woman said. "Take tha food that I may feed the dogs. And sit down a while. I want to look at thee."

Light-headed with relief, Essa took the bowl from her

and sat on the floor, watching her shake out the contents of the sack. A large pile of scraps mixed with raw meat slid out onto the floor. The hounds gathered around, their great hunger sated at last.

The old woman came and sat down beside him on the sacks, passing him a spoon drawn from her belt. "Tha looks just like her, though you're a man. But tha face is same as hers. You walked in here like a ghost, like her spirit."

"What's your name?" Essa said, cupping his fingers around the warm bowl, swallowing his pleasure at being called a man instead of a boy or a child.

"I'm Roe; I was tha mammy's nurse, for I'm bound in service to this hall. But I missed my freedom less for the love of my little Elfgift. I was there when tha came into the world, here in this hall."

"I was born here?" Essa could hardly believe he had been to Ad Gefrin before, let alone that it was the first place on earth he had ever seen.

Roe nodded. "Tha shan't remember. Tha was such a tiny scrap when you were taken away, out of Godsrule's sight. Elfgift was to marry, you see; he and Edwin had arranged it all, and then she was got with you."

Essa spooned in a few mouthfuls of stew. "Is Godsrule going to have me killed?" Oddly, the fear of death did nothing to lessen his appetite. This was his first real meal in nearly a month, and the rich, dark deer meat was hot and good.

Roe shrugged. "He may wish to, but he won't. I'll get tha out of here the way I got tha and Elfgift out, fourteen year ago and more."

"How?" Essa tore off a piece of bread and scrubbed it around the inside of the bowl, sopping up every last smear of juice. "And you'll be in danger if anyone finds out."

"I'll do it for tha mammy." Roe took the empty bowl and held it in her lap. Her hands were thin, blue-veined, spotted with age, her eyes dark with sadness.

"Well, I must go to my lord. I think he's at Bedricsworth monastery."

"Then you'll see her there, too. She'll be so glad of it."

Essa felt a quick, hot flame of excitement, and for a moment, the pressing need to return to Egric paled against the thought of seeing his mother. But it all must happen quickly, quickly. Surely Godsrule's men would come for him soon? "Can you help me get out, then? I'll need my horse."

"We'll let thee out when night's full and all are sleeping."

Essa stared at her, shocked. "But —"

Roe shrugged. "Godsrule's our king, but there were many here loved our Lady, and they've not forgiven him yet for driving her away. Even old Edwin wept when she went. She were the light of Ad Gefrin, tha mammy, and there's plenty here loyal to her still."

"Why did Edwin not stop him?" Essa's throat felt tight, his escape forgotten. "He was still alive then, and Godsrule

215

must have been just an atheling—Edwin was the High King. He should have stopped him."

"He were angry with her too, for he loved tha mammy above all else, and she'd defied him too, by going with Cai. But he wept when she'd gone, all the same. Godsrule didn't, though." Roe shook her head. "He's no true Christian, is Godsrule. He'll not forgive anyone even the smallest slight."

Essa nodded. "And my sword? I can't go without it. I must get it back—I'll have to do it while everyone's asleep. Where did Godsrule put it?"

"Na, na," said Roe. "Tha must not. The risk's too great, but don't tha worry; it'll be brought you before tha leaves, and it shall go with thee down the coast."

Essa jigged his right leg, trying not to let his impatience show in his face. Surely the men would come soon? And what would happen to Wulf and Anwen? They'd be spending the night in the hall with everyone else—those who were still loyal to the Lady, to his mother, and those who were not. How would they get out without anyone seeing? But Roe had been waiting nearly fifteen years to tell her story, and Essa knew he must hear it.

"Tha daddy begged her gan with him when he fled this place, though she wouldn't. But when tha was born, Godsrule wanted to have thee drowned like a pup. A girl might have been useful, he said, to marry off to some other king. But he knew a boy were just a danger to *him* being king when Edwin died. And Edwin agreed, though he were the better

Christian, and his wish was just that you'd both go to Francia and live in a monastery there.

"So she went in the end. Cai came back and stole thee both away one night, and you gan on a trader boat down the coast with tha mammy and daddy. She went to the god house, to be safe, and tha daddy took you, that Godsrule might never seek thee out. They say my Lady wept for thee a year and more."

Essa stared at the ground. All these years, he had longed to hear this story, his story. Now he wished he did not know it. Roe put her hand on his and squeezed.

"And that's how we'll get thee away from here this time. You'll gan to the sea, my dear."

He looked up sharply, hardly believing his luck. "To the coast?"

"It's quickest if tha wants to go south from here. Over a whole moon it takes to ride direct."

Essa's heart clenched — he was going to be racing against Wulf, racing south. Every moment would count. He had scant memories of sailing with his father and a crew of dark-skinned southern traders from the northwest coast of Rheged down to Wessex. He remembered Cai kneeling to tie a rope around his waist, lashing the other end to the mast, saying, "There, little cub, if you fall in, we'll pull you out. We'll run down the whale road and be in Wessex in half the time it takes to ride." The cowhide rope had dug uncomfortably into his belly, and he had been seasick.

One of the traders, a man with black hair wrapped in hundreds of tiny braids that looked like snakes, had given him a piece of dried ginger to suck.

Sailing would shorten the journey by more than half. There was still a chance he could get back before Wulf and Anwen.

He slept fitfully, sprawling among King Godsrule's hounds, waiting for the darkest part of the night, for someone who remembered his mother to come and quietly draw the bolt. Drifting in and out of sleep, he thought of Wulf and Anwen. What would happen to them? Had they already left? He remembered meeting Wulf's eyes in the hall earlier, each of them knowing their alliance had broken with Godsrule's refusal to rein in Penda. But still they wore each other's rings. Nothing would change that. *Even when we're both old men — if we live that long — we'll have the rings, and we'll always know we tried.*

He tried to picture what would happen if the three of them were to just go away, but the blood-stained dream of the Mercian army bearing down on the village rose again in his mind, and he knew he must return to Egric, to his lord. Egric would be back at Seobert's side now, in Bedricsworth. What would Egric say when he saw him? Essa had been gone almost two months. Or perhaps Seobert had listened at last to Egric's pleading, and there was already a host gathered at the western border of East Anglia, with Cole and Red and Ariulf, and all the men from the village among their number.

But Elfgift was at Bedricsworth. He would go there first.

Essa was coiled in sleep when he felt Fenrir butting his arm with her nose. He rolled over, wincing as his weight rested on the long scab down his right side. The dog hall was wrapped in darkness shot through with silvery lines of moonlight streaking across the ground, picking out the humped, sleeping bodies of the hounds. Then he froze: someone was outside the door. Fenrir nudged him again, and he was on his feet in a moment. *Come on, my honey, it is time.*

They stepped silently across the straw-strewn floor, weaving around the sleeping hounds. A soft scraping sound came from outside — they had bolted the door to keep him in, and someone was gently, gently lifting the bar. There was a dull thud as it was placed on the hard ground outside. Essa felt more than heard it, a soft trembling of the ground below. His hand rested on the back of Fenrir's neck, more for his own comfort than as a warning. He reached the door and stepped back slightly, a sword's length away from it. This might easily be a trap. Roe had seemed true, but maybe she was not. Perhaps this was his death waiting on the other side of the door. His death, come to meet him.

The bolt eased. Essa's hand felt for the knife hidden in his boot, strapped to his calf, his fingers closing around the bone handle. He muttered a silent prayer, a garbled plea to the Aesir, and Jesus Christ too, for good luck.

A hooded man came in, cloak wrapped around his body against the chill night air. "Come," he said softly. His voice was cracked with age. He closed the door behind him, and from beneath his cloak the old man drew the Silver Serpent. "Be quick," he whispered.

Essa hooked the sword belt over his shoulder and fastened the buckle at his waist, his heart singing with relief as he felt the familiar weight of his sword. He let his fingers rest on her hilt, and he could almost feel her twitching at his touch like a hound, thirsting for blood. The Silver Serpent had come home: this was where she had been woken out of dead iron and steel, great ropes of metal beaten and twisted and hammered till the blade shone like the side of a fish. The Lady's sword — his mother's sword.

"Come," the old man said again, touching Essa's arm lightly. "Tha hast no time, lad." For an instant, Essa did not want to follow him. He was so tired. He had ridden across the length and breadth of Britain. He wanted to rest.

"Where is my horse?"

"I'm taking you up the fellside; she'll be there. Now come, for the love of God. If tha's caught, it'll go bad. Now walk along of me. If someone comes out of the hall for a piss and sees two people running, they'll remember tha, and we won't know if they're loyal to tha mammy before it's too late. So don't tha run."

Essa swallowed, and thought of dying with the air

snatched from his body. Looking back to check that Fenrir was behind him, he slipped out of the dog hall, helped the old man replace the bar, and followed his unknown rescuer across the silent courtyard. For an old man, he moved quite fast, his gait uneven—some old leg wound, Essa guessed. The man said nothing, but Essa knew why—when he glanced back at the dog hall, with Godsrule's huge hall towering behind it, he saw a light glowing through one of the high windows at the far end. He walked faster, his breath coming in short gasps as though he had been running.

Every shadow threatened to melt into an armed man, and the courtyard stretched before them. The old man seemed to be heading for one of the boundary walls, near the great cattle enclosure. Essa could smell the warm reek of cows, taste their sleepy breath rising on the air. At any moment, they would be caught, and this poor old man who had loved Essa's mother would die with him. The wall seemed to get farther away, not closer, and Essa longed to break into a run and drag the old man with him.

At last, they reached the bottom slope of the great earthen wall. Essa looked up and saw the palisade fence stretching along the top.

"Must I climb?" he whispered.

The old man shook his head. "Follow me." He led Essa and Fenrir along the foot of the wall—they were behind the stables now; the sweet scent of horses mingled with the cow smell, and he thought of Grani. The way was overgrown with brambles; the old man pushed through them, but Essa's forearms were quickly crosshatched with scratches. Behind him, Fenrir whined softly: she hated brambles. Once, he had to turn around and ease one out of a tangle of long fur on her flank. The old man did not stop, and Essa had to push even faster through the undergrowth to catch up.

Then, finally, they came to a halt.

Essa had expected to find a gate with guards loyal to his mother ready to let him through, but there was nothing, just the great earthen wall rising up above them on one side, and beyond a huge thatch of brambles, the back of the stables. The old man had picked up a stick and was poking away at the brambles. "What do you mean me to do now?" Essa whispered, instantly regretting it. This man had risked his life to get him out. "I don't mean to be ungrateful," he said quietly. "But where do I go? I don't understand where I—"

"Gan, lad." The old man pointed with his stick at a dark space behind the tangle of thorns. "Godsrule had us dig it through the wall after Penda burned this place—so now we've a way of getting the children out if the heathen bastard comes up here again. I lost four of my sons in that fight, and they cut my woman's throat."

"I'm sorry." Essa did not know what else to say.

"It comes out halfway up fellside—Godsgift's waiting for you there with tha horse."

"*Godsgift?* The Fox?"

In the darkness, Essa thought he could just see the old man smile. "Aye, he's been waiting years for a chance to get the better of his brother. There's no love lost between those two. Now gan, lad, and God speed tha way."

He gave Essa a little push, and when he turned around, the old man had melted into the black night like a ghost. Essa looked down at Fenrir and rubbed his hand along her knobbly spine. *Well, my honey. It's just you and me once more.* He pushed through the bracken and ducked into the tunnel.

From Ad Gefrin to the east coast

he slipped down into the cool, dark tunnel, breathing in a rich, earthy smell like old mushrooms going soft. Fenrir came afterward, her claws scraping on the flint in the soil. Essa stood in the darkness for a moment, feeling the cold earth walls with his hands, listening. Had it all been a trick? What if this was not a tunnel but a cave? A trap. Any moment, the old man would return with armed men and . . .

Fenrir whined, pushing forward, nudging at the back of his thigh. *Go on, go on.*

Then he felt it: the cool touch of breeze on his face. It wasn't a cave. He started to run.

The tunnel seemed so long, he began to think Roe and the old man had tricked him after all; that they were in league with Godsrule. They had surely led him into a trap. But after his run in the dark had slowed to a walk, and the tunnel had turned so many corners he felt sure it had gone around in a circle and he was back behind the stables again, he saw a thin, silvery shaft of moonlight. He wished it were still dark. Pale sacs hung from the tunnel's roof in white drifts. Essa looked up, unable to stop himself. The roof was alive with spiders bigger than his fist.

Shuddering, Essa scrambled up a rocky slope, Fenrir close behind as he whispered fervent prayers of thanks for the brightness of the moon, for showing him the way out. But it meant he had been away nearly two whole moons. It must be getting close to Eostre month now — in the village they would be spreading dung on the fields and ploughing. They would be making spiced buns and rising at dawn to hang the ones they did not eat from the branches of the ash in the courtyard, tempting the great goddess Eostre out of her winter sleep.

They probably thought he was dead by now.

A dull ache lay heavy in his chest when he thought of Lark. He tried to recall the way her hands had felt when they had said good-bye outside the village gate: her long, lean fingers entwined with his, her palms hot and dry. His forehead and temples turned hot with longing. Did she think of him in this way? Or was she mourning him as she would a brother, like Cole?

The Fox was waiting, lying on the fellside, whistling and drinking from a leather bottle. Grani and another horse were tied to a hawthorn tree, hunched against the wind. Grani whickered when she saw him, and the Fox sat up. He was not alone. Anwen and Wulf were standing with him, by their horses. They turned to look at Essa, speechless.

"Took tha time," the Fox said, swigging from the bottle. He stood, offering it to Essa. He ignored it. Anwen ran over and threw her arms around him.

"Essa! Oh, I'm so sorry! We tried so hard, didn't we?"

He nodded, stepping back, letting her go. He turned to Wulf, wanting to clasp his hand.

"You must believe me," Essa said, "I knew nothing about any of this. I'm glad you haven't gotten back to your father with Anwen, but I swear I didn't know Godsrule's my uncle. And I really thought he might help the Wolf Folk somehow."

Wulf smiled wryly. "I know. The way you ploughed your fist into his face gave that away."

Essa tried to smile back.

"I can't believe it," Anwen said. "When I saw you standing there in the hall with all of them I just *knew*. You all look so alike."

"It's the wyrd." Wulf shrugged. "The wyrd takes us where she will."

The Fox took another swig from his leather bottle. "If tha doesn't get moving, the wyrd's gan take you all the way to a broken neck, my friend."

Wulf looked down at Anwen. "We must go, dear heart."

She nodded, hugging Essa again, so tight he thought she was going to squeeze the breath from his body; she kneeled and hugged Fenrir, crying as the dog licked her face. Then it was just Essa and Wulf, looking at each other.

"Keep my ring," Wulf said.

Essa nodded, fighting a sudden wish to cry. Next time they saw each other, it would be on the battlefield. He wanted to say, *Go well*, but how could he? He did not want them to go well. He did not want them to go at all. He watched, dumb with misery, as Wulf and Anwen mounted up and rode off, picking their way down the fellside.

The race had begun.

He turned to the Fox. "Let's go."

"About time too," said the Fox. "Hurry on, mount up. We'll be riding the rest of the night, else tha'll miss tide, and be waiting till evening. He'll have men after thee by morning."

"I don't understand why you're doing this."

The Fox laughed. "Because tha did what I've been longing to do since I've worn the bastard's ring, that's why. I've lost count of the times I've longed to punch him in the face. And I don't want thee around, getting in the way of me and Godsway. Now come on, if we miss tide it won't be my fault. Can tha hound keep up? If not, you'll have to leave her."

Essa whispered yet another silent apology to Fenrir. *Do it for me, my honey. Run as if you were running with the Great Hunt, all the way across the sky.*

Essa swung himself up into the saddle. Looking back

down the fellside at the great hall, at the firelit windows under the eaves, he wondered if he'd ever see Ad Gefrin again. After the welcome at his first visit, he hoped not.

It was a quiet, fast ride, and the air around them seemed to crackle with urgency. The Fox was silent, and Essa missed Wulf's talk, but he knew he'd never cross the fells without a guide. *My kinsman*, he thought, staring at the Fox's hair flying out behind him, drained of color in the moonlight. For years, he had longed to hear of his mother's people, but Cai would never speak of them, and there had been no use in asking anyone in the village. But Hild had known who he was. He felt a flash of anger: *She kept me for herself, away from my real mother.* But no one could keep him from finding Elfgift now.

Not long after they were out of sight of Ad Gefrin and high up into the fells, a great bank of cloud drifted across the moon. They rode at a heart-stopping pace across wild, bosky moorland, at every moment in danger of a horse breaking a leg. Fenrir was only paces behind them, her powerful body streaming in long, bounding movements. The sky was turning gray in the east when the air started to smell different, and Essa caught a tang of salt that sent a thrill snaking through his body.

He did not want to race against Wulf, but if he must, he might as well win.

When they reached the brow of the next hill, a glittering expanse of sea stretched out before them, silvered by the moon. The hill swept down to a wide beach, pale in the moonlight, where shadowy figures moved busily around a pair of wooden skiffs, loading them with nets. At the foot of the hill glowed the dim lights of a village.

The Fox slowed his pace at last, sitting back in the saddle. "You'll make it," he said. "They're going out on the dawn tide for cod, and the trading boat's due by any moment."

"How do we know for sure it's coming?" whispered Essa.

The Fox laughed. "Tha's cautious, *maw*. There's no one here to hear tha. The trader's due today, but to pass, not stop by — that's why tha must go out with the fisher boats. And if they don't like it, this'll talk them into it." He held out his hand, showing a clutch of gold sceattas. "Give half to the fishermen and save the rest for the traders — if they think they're full enough already, they'll soon change their minds. Tha'll need it. I don't think they're used to sailing with hounds."

"You really are making sure I go, aren't you?" Essa said, taking the sceattas, and marveling at their weight. "It's not even as if I want to be king. I'm lucky you've not finished me off out here."

"Finish you off?" said the Fox. "Not after the sport you gave me earlier today. I don't know when I've enjoyed myself the more. Now gan, the tide's coming on and the fishermen won't wait. You'd best give the horse to me, and count it payment. Tha hast no use for her now."

Essa dismounted and, handing the reins to the Fox, he walked around and buried his face in Grani's mane, whispering words of thanks into her ear in British, in the old language, because horses always seemed to understand it best. He felt worse than when leaving Anwen and Wulf— this was another betrayal: another heavy price to pay.

He turned and ran down the hillside, Fenrir bounding ahead of him; he called out to the fishermen to wait. They had dragged the skiffs to the shoreline now and were stowing the nets, shipping oars, coiling ropes, all moving with brisk skill. His ache at leaving Grani faded when Essa saw that they had no reason to listen to him, a wild-looking stranger with a handful of gold coin. He should have asked the Fox to come with him. They would know him for Godsrule's man and listen. Since Essa was alone, they'd more likely hand him over to their lord in the hall, in case he was a wanted man. *Which I am*, he thought, and fought the need to laugh. *Penda wants me dead, and now Godsrule too.*

The fishermen all stopped what they were doing when he called out. Five hard, wiry-looking men stood watching his approach, hands on the dagger hilts at their belts.

"What's tha game, lad?" called one of them.

"Funny¬°° time of day to be out with tha hunting dog," said another, laughing. "What's tha hunting? The moon?"

Essa put out his hands palm first, to show he had no weapon. "Is the trader ship coming?" he asked.

"Sighted up the coast this afternoon, she was. What's it to you?"

"I need passage out to her." Essa held up one of the gold

sceattas, and the men whistled, lifting their eyebrows with mocking admiration.

"What's a stripling like you doing with coin like that?"

"Run away, hast tha?"

"Stolen goods, I'm guessing, or worse. And he wants us to send him safe on his way! Shameless."

"Got some girl in trouble, I reckon."

"We should take you into the hall and hand you over to our man."

"Do you listen to me," Essa said, as forcefully as he could. "I'm not running away. I'm trying to get back. My lord's Egric the Atheling, and I must reach him—he's at Bedricsworth, down the coast."

Four of the men laughed, disbelieving, and turned back to their nets and ropes. But one, a white-haired ancient, stood looking at him, shaking his head. "Nay, I believe the lad. I've heard of Egric; he was fostered at the big hall ten winters back or more. I recall he were brought out here by old King Edwin, God bless him, so he could have a look at the boats. I say we take the lad out—the color of his money's good, any road."

"Thank you!" Essa put one of the sceattas in the old man's age-knotted hand. The man winked, as if he were assisting Essa in some youthful prank. *I wish it were a game,* Essa thought, trying to picture what life had been like before Egric's gold ring slid down his finger, so cold against his skin. He glanced down at Fenrir.

"My dog must come as well."

They stared at him, then at Fenrir.

"She's half the size of a dray horse!" They all laughed again, shaking their heads, so he held out another gold sceatta and they shrugged. "All right," said the white-haired man. "I wouldn't part a lad from his dog. Bring her in, then."

Essa helped carry one of the skiffs to the water, and he had to stop to take off his boots and tie the straps so they could hang over his shoulder with the leather saddlebag he'd taken from Grani. The fishermen jeered as he caught up with them, wading out up to his knees, the water shockingly cold against his legs. The old man gestured at him to climb into one of the boats; he did, wobbling like a child as another fisherman stepped nimbly in over the side.

"Sit thee down, lad — if we're to take tha, we don't want to drown tha!" said the fisherman, a thick-necked, freckled man with an amber bead hanging from his left earlobe. He laughed loudly, and Essa sat on a bench before the mast, drawing Fenrir close to him till she lay down in the bottom of the boat, flattening herself against the side. He felt useless and awkward, watching the fishermen as they drew long, narrow oars from beneath the benches and fitted them to the sides of the boat. They sat down, the old man in front of Essa, the younger behind, and dug their oars into the water without a splash, in long, graceful movements. The skiff leaped forward in the water, following the other boat. A feeling of freedom unfolded in Essa as he listened to the waves foaming around the prow.

He would be home soon.

"What about the sail?" he said, staring at the bunched-up cloth lashed against the mast. The wind suddenly seemed to get up; his hair whipped into his eyes. Long cowhide ropes hung down from the cross mast, flapping in the breeze; he had to keep ducking out of their way.

Amber-earring laughed again. "Where's the wind, lad?" he said. "Sail's no use 'less the wind's behind us. And we're gan across it, so it's the oars for us."

"Lord, he's an inlander, all right," said the old man. He turned, glancing suspiciously at Essa over his shoulder. "Thought tha said tha was Egric's man? He's no inlander."

"I'm not from his hall. He came to mine and took me." *What does it matter?* he thought. *You're happy enough with the gold.* He felt the other coins, heavy in his belt bag.

The old man said something, but Amber-earring cut him off. "Trader, ho!" he shouted, and Essa turned to stare where he pointed. Off to the east, something came into view on the lightening horizon. The fishermen turned the boat to face it, dipping their oars deep on one side and lifting them clear out of the water on the other so the skiff's nose swung around.

Essa stood up, clutching the mast, hardly noticing the skiff wobbling beneath him or hearing the fishermen telling him to sit down, for he was naught but a useless inlander. The dark thing on the horizon grew bigger: a long, lean shape, low in the water, huge sail billowing out in front. Dawn was breaking: back in the great hall at Ad Gefrin,

Godsrule would soon know he was gone. He whispered a prayer, sending it to the horse goddess, to Jesus Christ, and to Eostre, goddess of the dawn, because it would be her moon on the rise when this one died, begging all three to save Roe, the old man, and the Fox from Godsrule's rage if they were ever found out.

"She's running with the wind, lad," said Amber-earring. "'Less she changes, tha'll be in Gipswick in four days, and then it's only a day or so's walk to Bedricsworth, if tha doesn't dawdle around, getting girls in trouble." He laughed again, slapping his hand down hard on the bench. Then both fishermen started hailing, and Essa shouted with them, yelling for his life.

Four days. Three nights. Four days and three nights, and he would be with Egric, back by the side of his lord. Back by the side of his mother.

From Northumbria to East Anglia

ESSA spent days sitting up on the prow with Fenrir curled up beneath him: she was just as tired as he was. Boots off, he dangled his legs over the side, gazing at their long shadow on the green water moving fast below, his whole body singing, thrilled, when the boat cut across a large set of waves and his feet were splashed with cold water. Dazed, leaning back against a barrel of salted cheese stacked as ballast, he watched the endless movement of the sea. Dark patches would appear on the surface, wrinkled with choppy waves, and when the boat reached these places, she leaped forward, her square sail billowing and tugging the boat through the water.

The traders gave him a fishing line to hold, and he sat waiting for the twitch at the end of the line, heedless of the sun marching through the sky above him. They were going too fast for mackerel, and it was early in the year for them, but a few times each day he caught one and broke its back, whispering a silent apology to the fish's quick, silvery soul as its red gills cracked open.

Every now and then, one of the four traders would call to him in their strange, crackling tongue and gesture for him to grab a rope or hold the rudder steady for a moment while the steersman took a piss over the edge. They smiled and were friendly enough, especially at the sight of his gold sceattas. They pressed dried figs on him, and flat, stale bread, and wine. One of the traders was hardly older than Essa, and he cooked the fish over a fire lit in an iron bowl wedged in the stern.

Essa wondered how Wulf fared now, riding back to his father as if evil spirits were on his tail. They would have to change horses at every village they found. Anwen would be sorry to lose her mare.

And what's to stop them from buying passage in a trader boat? They might be a day's sail behind him, but they could land at the coast north of Wolf Folk territory and miss out riding through enemy marches. Wulf was clever. He would find a way to get back to his father quickly.

And when he did, Penda would ride out.

If he hasn't already. The words played in Essa's mind over and over again, until they drowned all other thought. When he slept, he saw the village burning.

In the end, the journey took six days. By the time the traders put him ashore at Gipswick, the moon had died.

They landed on the dawn tide, after rowing up the long,

silver elbow of the River Orwell. Essa had taken an oar, and his back and shoulders were hot with pulling against the water. The traders had laughed at him every time he missed a stroke, but he barely heard. He was home, back in the land of the Wolf Folk.

The harbor in the bend of the river was peppered with trader boats, quiet in the thin, silvery light of early morning. When they got to the waterfront where the riverbank was fortified with a wall of slime-blackened woven wattle, the youngest of the traders leaped out and tied the bowline to an iron ring set into the earth. Essa scrambled out and took the stern line thrown to him. Following the trader boy's pointed finger, Essa kneeled and tied it to another iron ring a few paces apart from the first. Standing and stretching, he saw a small hall nestling below a rising sweep of heath land, surrounded by outbuildings and a couple of long store sheds. He heard goats calling and a tinny clang as someone dropped a pot. The sound of people, of ordinary life, was strange after being cast out on the whispering sea with men he could not talk to.

Fenrir jumped out after him, walking stiff-legged, then leaned forward on her front paws, stretching out her back, easing her cramped limbs. Essa helped unload sacks heavy with amber collected from the frozen beaches of the north, bales of fine sheepskin, and the barrels of salted cheese. He bade the dark-skinned traders farewell and stood watching them, waving as they rowed out against a tide in flood. The women who had come to trade were loading the sacks and barrels onto a cart while their ass stood waiting, flicking its tail at a fly. Overhead, thick white clouds scudded across the sky. They were arguing about one of the sacks, but Essa was not listening, although the familiar accent was like tasting honey after eating nothing but bitter roots.

He was back. He was in Wolf Folk territory.

His throat tight with misgiving, he lifted a sack of knotted amber and turned to the two women on the jetty. "Hey." He loaded the sack onto their cart, the amber pieces clinking together musically as he wedged it next to the barrel of cheese. "What's the news from the border?" They turned to glance at him: one looked but a few years older than Essa, the other older still, as though she could be her mother. They both had round, freckled faces and thick fair hair hanging over their shoulders in fat braids. They were just a couple of Gipswick traders who knew nothing of kings and spying and betrayal.

He half wanted this moment of not knowing to last forever.

"I must get on my way. Bedricsworth. What's the news from the border?" He held up his ring finger. "I'm Egric the Atheling's man." He felt a thrill of danger — as if they would know he was in fact wearing Wulf's ring, Mercian gold — and would have him dragged off to their lord, a proven traitor to the Wolf Folk.

The older woman raised an eyebrow. "You are, are you? Well, he's at Bedricsworth — and the only news from the border is that there's no news. My man and our young lad have been sitting it out for days, waiting for the word. Not right, is it? They could've stayed at home longer, instead of—"

"For the Lady's sake, Ma, do you just tell him!" The young girl rolled her eyes, grinning at her mother. She reached out a hand and played with Fenrir's ears. "She's always going on! Lovely hound you've got here. She's a real beauty, aren't you, girl? Look, if you want to know, Egric put out the call to muster near on two weeks back, but they're all waiting by the abbey till he gets Seobert out to fight. And he won't."

There was still a chance.

"On account of being a Christian!" said the older woman darkly. "I always said they'd be trouble. And Penda won't wait forever! If they don't do something, those Mercians'll be lording it over everyone, emptying our barns to feed their greedy armies and taking their pick of the young girls. They'll be having us eat dogs' heads and newborn babies! They're like monsters. I don't—"

But Essa wasn't listening. Grabbing her daughter's arm, he said, "What's the quickest way to Bedricsworth?"

"More than half a day's walk," said the girl, round-eyed. "Sun at your right shoulder."

Then he ran.

He slowed to a walk, ran again, Fenrir beside him, slowed again, ran. Now he was so close, it felt as if an unseen hand had him by the tunic and was dragging him along. He could not stop. He could only go on. He was spent; he hadn't slept properly since the bothy. His sword slapped at his left leg as he ran, and he was so hungry that his stomach was gripped by a solid, dull ache. But he could not stop.

He heard Bedricsworth long before he saw it. Passing through a wood, scattering old pine needles as he ran, a low, rumbling hum grew louder and louder: voices, many voices. The thick white smoke of campfires misted the sky above the woods, and he could smell the sour stink of men sweating out their fear. Egric had mustered an army.

The pine trees began to thin out. He loped with long strides through the last of the trees, and that was when he saw the first of them. More men than ants in a nest, as far as the eye could see, all gathered in the fields surrounding a jumble of buildings he could just make out in the distance. Some were slumped around the embers of last night's campfire, talking, others playing knucklestones. Horses stood in groups, cropping the grass. Men lay sleeping; some wandered around in tense little groups, while others just sat by themselves, sharpening swords that had hung for years on the wall, without a taste of blood. Many were Essa's age, boys really, and a few even younger. Walking past a group sitting by a gray-embered fire, he heard one of them say, "What's the use, anyway? Our own king won't even fight along with us. We've not got a chance."

He saw an old man fletching an arrow, feathers scattered on the ground beside him as his bent fingers shook and struggled with the arrow shaft. He saw a fair-haired boy running by with a parcel wrapped in an old tunic. They had mustered everyone.

This was it — Egric's army.

Essa had tried to stop this, and he had failed. Soon, Wulf would be back in his father's compound with the west secured, and Penda would strike. Essa smiled grimly to himself — the west was not so tight as Penda thought. He tried not to listen to the small voice that whispered that it was the Mercian people who would suffer, not Penda himself: Mercian women and children who would flee as the Magonsæte attacked their homes.

All Essa could do now was fight.

He broke into a sprint, Fenrir at his side, ignoring the shouts of anger as he knocked over a cup, barged into someone's shoulder, and scattered the embers of a fire. There were guards at the gate. He bent low to catch his breath, sucking in great gasps, pushing the sweat-soaked hair from his face.

"Come a long way, have you?" asked the younger guard sarcastically. "There's no hurry, my friend. Seobert's still not coming out, and there's not a man who'll fight without him."

The older guard, a man with long, graying hair and a string of glass beads around his neck, said, "Shut your mouth, Frica — where've you come from, boy? Is there news from the border? Has the Mad Dog attacked?"

Essa shook his head. "I've not come from the border. I'm Egric's man."

He held up his right hand so they could see the ring and said, "Is he here?"

They nodded and stepped back to allow him in.

"Has he been here long?" Essa asked, taking deep breaths, heart pounding.

He could feel a thick stream of sweat running down his spine, pooling in the small of his back, soaking through his tunic. His hair was sodden, sticking to the back of his neck.

The guards looked at him mistrustfully.

"Nearly a whole month — but should you not know that, if you're his man?" said the older one.

"Come to that, I've not seen you before," said Frica.

"I'm from the Wixna," Essa said. "He sent me away to do something, and I —"

"All right, all right. Save your excuses for Egric, I should!" said the guard with the glass beads, and they both laughed.

"Do you take my dog for a bit?" Essa said. He was desperate for Fenrir not to be there when he first saw Egric — the last thing he needed now was the hound leaping to his defense. "I know it's not your task, but she's come a long way, and she's hungry, and —"

The older guard raised his eyebrows, sighing. "Go on, then — Frica, take the wretched hound to the stables, and get the boy there to feed her."

Essa knelt down beside Fenrir, resting his face against her neck. *Thank you. I can't ever repay you for this, my honey.* She whined, licking his hand.

"Let's get on with it, then. I haven't got all day to be looking after your cursed dog." The younger guard looked at Essa resentfully as he led Fenrir away across the yard, but Essa hardly noticed.

It was time to face his lord. It was time to see Elfgift.

The courtyard was quiet and still. It was another world, far away from the sweating, noisy throng of men outside. The shadows of fear in their eyes did not matter here: this was God's hall. The hot trickles of sweat gliding down his back grew cool, touching him like icy fingers.

Off to his right he could see gardens: rows of winter greens and leeks tucked into the dark earth, beyond them an orchard of apple trees, pale blossoms sprinkled among new spring leaves. He could smell rosemary, and it reminded him of Anwen: there was an herb patch somewhere, maybe beyond the apple trees. The faint sounds of clinking pottery drifted across the garden, and someone was humming a tune. They were baking bread; he could smell the hot, sweet warmth of it. Spittle pooled in his mouth.

The god house reared up before him, huge, silent, with images from Christ's life carved into the high oaken walls. Off to the side were more halls, two large, one smaller, and Essa guessed Seobert's god people must live there. A woman in a gray dress hurried across the far end of the courtyard and went into the big god house by a side door. The sound of her sandals slapping the wooden floorboards receded. Then the singing started. High, clear notes rang out, rising and falling. It was a language he did not understand—

what was it called? Latin, that was it: they were singing vespers — the early evening prayer, like they did at the great god house down in Kent. He could not move; the music froze him where he stood, because it meant that everyone here was in the god house, singing vespers.

Egric. King Seobert.

And Elfgift.

Now. He had to do it now.

The god house was full: crowded with men and women — most were standing, only a few cripples and girls heavy with child sat on the low ledges at the foot of the walls. All were dressed in black, brown, white — plain colors, with no ornament. Some of the women had covered their heads with linen veils. He had never seen that before — it must be a new fashion. Why was he thinking of women's clothes at a time like this? Where was Egric? He searched, peering over the heads of the crowd, looking for his lord: the wide, bearlike shoulders, the fair hair. He remembered Egric when he first saw him, riding toward the village like the leader of the Wild Hunt, besmattered with gold. It was hard to believe that was in Sun-cake month, when winter still gripped the earth, and now it was nearly Eostre month.

The priest at the altar said something in Latin; the crowd answered. *Why do they do that*, he thought, *when no one understands?* People were turning to look at him now.

More people turned. The god man fell silent, stared straight at him, and said, "Yes, my child? Would you like to join us?" He smiled. "Jesus Christ welcomes all."

244

"Dear God," someone said. "My eyes are serving me a trick."

Essa looked up. It was Egric, coming toward him. The crowd parted to let him by, and Essa sank to his knees. Weakness overtook his body and he rested his forehead on the floor. He felt rough hands on his shoulders, raising him up.

"Essa, for God's sake," said Egric. "What—" He broke off, laughing. "You've got a tale to tell me, boy!"

Essa stared straight into his pale, oyster-shell eyes. "I'm not the only one," he said.

Egric helped him up, turning to the god man, smiling at the crowd, saying, "My most loyal retainer! We'd given him up for dead."

A babble of noise broke out, the god man held up his hand for silence, but no one listened. Egric's grip tightened around his arm, and they were outside, blinking in the bright light of the courtyard. Egric's face changed once they were alone: his mouth a thin, angry line.

"Where have you been?"

Essa opened his mouth and shut it again, not knowing where to start. He swallowed: it felt as if there were a ball of wool stuck in his throat; he could not get the words out. "Powys," he said. "But Lark told you that, didn't she?"

"The stupid girl should have come and fetched one of us—not just let you go. She should have been whipped. And we've all heard the gossip from the west—that you and Penda's brat left Caer Elfan with Eiludd's daughter in the middle of the night, without the girl's chaperone—"

"It was the morning, not the middle of the night. And they were married by then; she didn't *need* a chaperone."

"With her brothers and half her father's men chasing you. A trader heard it, and the news will be all over the country by now, that kind of hot talk. They'll be singing about it in every hall from Kernow to Dál Riada. Not the kind of thing I like my men to be doing. Where in the name of God have you been since?"

"Ad Gefrin."

For a moment, he thought Egric was going to hit him, but he did not. He was staring over Essa's shoulder at someone who had just come out of the god house.

"You have been where?" said Cai. He was standing in the doorway. Breathless, Essa stood staring at him for a moment, unable to believe what he was seeing. Then he leaped forward, his face burning with rage. "You liar!" He lunged at Cai, and the two of them went slamming into the wall of the god house. *"You lied to me! Where is she?"*

He felt hands on his shoulders, Egric trying to pull him away, but he twisted out of his grip, shoving his father hard against the wall. Cai's eyes were black and impassive, drawing him in so he could not look away.

"Hush, cub." Cai's voice was calm; he gripped Essa's wrists and lowered his hands. Essa found he could not move his arms. Cai's eyes were sucking him in, twin pools of dark light. "Where have you been?"

"I thought you were dead. Wulf said they'd killed you."

He drew in a deep breath. His legs were weak; all he wanted to do was sit down.

Cai smiled. "They'll have to be quicker than that to catch me. I was halfway here by the time they knew I was gone. Tell me, where have you been?"

"Ad Gefrin. I've been to Ad Gefrin. *Where is she?*" His voice rose to a yell.

Egric pulled him away from Cai, saying calmly, "Come, do not speak to your father like that. No man of mine acts with such discourtesy."

Essa turned and shouted in his face, "Shut your mouth! You don't know what you're talking about!"

Egric's eyes went dark gray, like cold stones at the bottom of a river. "Cai, this brat of yours —"

"You've just been using me like everyone else," said Essa, heart pounding. Penda wanted him dead, so did Godsrule, and now he had added a third royal enemy to his list. He did not care. "You thought I'd be useful, didn't you? Thought you'd get the house of Ad Gefrin in your bag if you had me. Well, it's no good. I went up there, and Godsrule won't help. He's a gutless fool, and he's scared stiff of Penda."

Cai and Egric looked at each other. Cai laughed sharply. "You did what?"

But Essa did not answer, because someone was coming out of the garden, walking toward them, holding a basket of greens: a tall woman with red hair hanging bright around her shoulders, falling to her waist like tongues of

247

flame. He saw her face: high, curved cheekbones, arched eyebrows, her long gray eyes, the same shape as his but a different color. She smiled at Cai and Egric, saying, "I've missed vespers, haven't I? And all for picking greens — what a fool I am!" Then she saw Essa, and a strange stillness spread across her features so that her beautiful, elf-shining face looked like a mask.

They had both lied to him. What they had done was unforgivable.

Essa stepped back: if one of them touched him, he would not be able to bear it.

His fingers closed around the handle of his sword. "You stay away from me," he said to Cai, voice shaking. "And keep her away from me too."

"Essa, Essa, we only did it to keep you safe, " said Cai, reaching out to lay a hand on his arm. "Do you think I wanted to live away from your mother? Do you think she wanted to leave you? There was no choice."

"Oh, dear God," said the woman. Her hands started to shake, and she dropped the basket. Dark green leaves spilled out over the packed-earth courtyard. Essa felt something inside him snap. He drew the Silver Serpent; the blade sang through the air. Elfgift suddenly stepped toward him; it was as if she hadn't even seen the sword.

"My love, no." Cai pulled her back. "Essa!" He sounded quite calm, but Essa had seen that look in his eyes before.

The sword handle seemed to burn his hand, and he threw her to the ground, just as he'd done in the hall at home all those years before, when he first realized Cai had left him there for good. The Silver Serpent was a beautiful weapon; she had no equal, but she was poisoned.

"It's all lies, isn't it?" he said. "No king gave her to you, she's *her* sword, isn't she? Well, you can have her back, and I hope you both choke."

"Aesc!" Egric said. "They're trying to explain. Why do you not try listening? Hild would be disappointed in you."

"She's a lying bitch as well."

That was when Egric hit him. He heard Elfgift cry out as he stumbled backward, falling awkwardly, knocking his elbow so hard that a jagged line of pain ran up his arm.

He heard his father say, "For the love of Christ, Egric." Then he felt hands gripping his arms, dragging him to his knees. Both Cai and Egric held him; he could not fight them both. He was too tired now to fight anyone. He looked down and saw dark spots of blood staining the dusty ground. He could feel it running from his nose, into his mouth, dripping off his chin. *Another bloody nose*, he thought, suddenly feeling removed from it all, as if he were outside his body and watching himself.

"Take him out of my sight," Egric said, his voice tight with rage. "Before I have to kill him. I will not have anyone speaking of Hild like that." He went back into the god house, and Essa was left kneeling, hands cupping the blood that dripped from his nose and mouth.

So there it was. Egric and Hild were lovers. What was their story? he wondered. A thwarted marriage? Hild sent

249

out to marry the chief of the Wixna, while Egric had to take some other princess, one from another clan?

Then Cai hauled him to his feet, speaking to him in British, the words harsh and vicious. "You are like a dog that pisses everywhere — you cannot restrain yourself. How can you behave like this before your mother? How can you say such foul things? You're filth."

He hates me because I forced them apart. Suddenly, Essa was ashamed of the misery he'd felt when Wulf told him Cai was dead. *Why should I care about him, if he doesn't care about me?* So he spat blood on the ground at Cai's feet and said, "At least I'm not a liar."

"You just don't know when to stop, do you?"

Then, at last, Elfgift spoke. "Cai, please. Can you not see how weary he is? And he's right. We did lie to him. He's every right to hate us." Her voice was calm and measured. Essa was surprised and a little relieved. There was one person amid all this madness who had kept hold of her senses.

He still could not look at her, though, could not bear to see his face reflected so clearly in hers. He stared at the dusty greens lying on the ground. He dared not speak: he was afraid of what might come out of his mouth.

Cai swore. "Egric's right," he said. "You need to cool your temper, and so do I. Come." And Essa followed him across the courtyard, leaving Elfgift standing alone, the Silver Serpent lying in the dust at her feet as she watched them go.

24

Bedricsworth

be awoke in a tangle of blankets, the narrow
chamber in darkness. He was starving hungry; his
stomach felt hollow, like a dried-out nut. He put
a hand up to his face and touched blood encrusted under
his nose, down his chin, smeared across his cheek. It hurt;
everything ached. Sitting up, he wrapped the blankets
around his shoulders and pulled back the shutters. Outside,
the sun was westering, setting the apple trees on fire with a
golden light, their pale blossoms bobbing and swaying in
the breeze. The sounds of Egric's army settling down for the
night drifted across the fields: the crackling of fires, a horse
nickering, a low hum of voices. Someone was playing a
pipe. He wished he was outside with them, instead of
trapped in this lonely god house. He had never been in a
chamber by himself before, let alone locked up in one.
Even at Ad Gefrin there had been the hounds — and Fenrir.
But here there was no one.

His throat ached with thirst, but the wooden cup in the corner was empty. Then he remembered the key clicking in the lock as Cai left. Back home, no one had ever asked Ariulf's father to make a key or a lock. What would have been the use? There was nothing worth locking up and no chamber to shut people in. Cai was a fool to have locked him up, anyway. He could just as easily get out through the window if he wished. He was about to try when the key scraped in the lock again. He leaned back against the wall. He hated to admit it, but he was not looking forward to facing Cai again, nor Egric. *I'm not scared of them,* he thought. But he was. He waited for the door to open. It did not. Someone knocked. *Not Cai, then — surely not Egric.*

"Come in," he said.

It was Elfgift. "Are you sure?" she asked. She stood in the doorway, holding a tray with a tallow candle in a clay dish on it, a cup, and a bowl covered with a cloth.

He nodded. She came in, a tall, slender shape in the flickering shadows, and sat on the end of the bed, setting her tray down on the floor. As she went to sit down, he noticed she wore the Silver Serpent buckled to her belt. Lit up by the sun slanting in through the window, her hair looked as if it were burning.

As though she couldn't keep still, Elfgift leaned down and picked up the cup, offering it to him. "Drink this; it will calm you. And you must be thirsty."

He took it silently, gulping the spicy warm wine.

"Your face is all over blood — shall I clean it?"

Essa shrugged. He still could not quite bring himself to speak to her, could not believe that it was really his mother here in this room with him.

"Come sit by me, then." Elfgift lifted the bowl of water and dipped the cloth. It smelled of lavender, and he thought of Lark, and wished she were here. Elfgift cleaned the blood away, gently dabbing the cloth, her touch light on the sorest parts, her long, freckled fingers cool and quick.

"I know what you must think of us," she said. "Especially me. Do you see why we did it?"

Essa did know why: in his mind's eye, he saw King Godsrule's face, lined with almost fifteen years of hatred, and the man he had killed in the beech coppice. He sat there, frozen, unable to tear his eyes away from her.

"You never would have been safe here, or anywhere near me," Elfgift said quietly. Her voice held just a trace of the Northumbrian accent. "Godsrule would have hunted me to the ends of the earth to find you. When you were only a baby, he sent a man down here in the guise of a convert, and he smothered the kitchen girl's child, thinking it was you. And that's why we did what we did — that's why Cai had to take you away. I'm sorry — it seemed kinder to tell you I was dead. Essa, when it all happened, I was only the same age as you are now."

Essa stared down at the floor. It was Godsrule he should be angry with. But he knew he would never forgive Cai; it was Cai who had lied to him, Cai who had left him,

Cai who had said those dreadful things outside in the courtyard. *You're filth.*

He heard the familiar hiss of the Silver Serpent being pulled free of her scabbard. Elfgift sat holding her, the sharp, shining point touching the floor, the hilt resting in her lap.

"Edwin had her forged for me," she said. "Years ago now. I was meant to marry someone else, and she was part of my dowry. He was a Pictish chief twice my age, whom I'd never met — it was all for tribal reasons, you see. I think Edwin guessed I'd leave with you; he knew I'd not let Godsrule hurt tha. And so one day, he called me to him and gave me the Silver Serpent. He'd taken it from my dowry box, the dowry I was to take to the Pict, and gave her to me. *Keep thaself safe, my dear*, he said. *Tha and the child.* So that's what I tried to do. Now do you take her back, Essa? So I know you're safe?"

"Yes," Essa said. "I'll take her." And he stood up while she buckled the sword belt around his waist. It was good to feel the familiar weight resting against his hip again. The Silver Serpent was his once more.

Elfgift folded the bloodied cloth and placed it back on the tray. "Now it's time to eat. Would you like to come? You need not."

"I'll come," Essa said, his voice coming out in a hoarse whisper.

He followed Elfgift down the corridor, his legs burning after the long run that morning. She led him through a wide doorway into a hall full of men and women eating at long tables. The rich smell of fish stew and fresh bread made his stomach clench with hunger. A large crucifix hung on the far wall between two brightly woven wall hangings. It was strangely peaceful — there were only a few children, and they were sitting quietly. Huge windows with the shutters flung open let in the last of the evening light, and the walls were lit with torches in iron sconces that cast long, flickering shadows over the people gathered on the benches. Most of them were eating in silence, others having quiet conversations. Some looked up and smiled when they saw Elfgift walk by with Essa, and he wondered how many of them knew his story.

"In here." Elfgift smiled, and pulled back a heavy wool curtain. In the chamber beyond, Cai and Egric sat at a table, deep in talk with two men Essa had not seen before: the younger had the same bearlike frame as Egric, only his hair was darker, his face clever and shrewd.

But it was the older man who drew Essa's gaze; he was tall, spare-boned, with large, calm eyes. His hair was shaven close to his scalp, just a dark shadow. For a moment, Essa could not stop looking at him: the man seemed to give off a deep sense of peace, of power, as if there were a light inside him, glowing.

Cai glanced up, outwardly calm, but Essa knew that he was still angry with him; he could almost feel it crackling in the air. Egric, on the other hand, looked as though he had forgotten the whole thing; he barely even looked away from talking as they came in. Essa knew what he must do and, loathing every moment, walked around to the other side of the table and knelt before Cai and Egric.

"I am sorry," he said, staring down at the floor. There was a greasy mark under the table where someone had dropped a piece of meat. He could feel everyone's eyes on him. He had to clench the muscles in his belly to stop it from rumbling. *Come on, come on, let's get this finished.* Then, at last, Egric clapped him on the shoulder, and he sat up, eyes cast down. "It's all right," said Egric. "I'm glad you've the spirit to beg my pardon. Not many would, after a crack like that." He turned to his companions, laughing. "Essa had a little falling out with his father and me just now. But let's say no more about it, shall we?"

Essa looked up at Cai, who nodded briefly and then turned back to his talking. Elfgift went over to the table and started pouring wine into cups.

"Seobert, my lord, this is my son," she said. Elfgift turned toward the younger man. "And this, Essa, is Anno, Egric's cousin. You've been on a long journey to get here, have you not, Essa?"

The older man got to his feet just as Essa was about to kneel again. His eyes flickered over Essa's face, taking in the bruises and the raw cut where Egric's ring had scraped his cheek. He smiled kindly. "There is no need for that," he said. "All are equal in the eyes of God. Come sit by me — tell me of your journey."

So he took his place on the bench between Seobert and Egric, and Elfgift spooned steaming fish stew into their bowls. Egric broke the bread and passed it around. Essa stirred a clump of steamed greens around in his stew, his hunger gone. He was trying not to look at Cai; his heart beat faster whenever he did. Essa felt as if the silence were pressing the air from his lungs. The torches cracked and flickered on the walls.

"So, Essa," said Egric. "Are you going to tell us how you ended up at Ad Gefrin? I'm curious. After all"—he laughed"—I only sent you out for a night, and you've been gone nearly two months. What happened?"

Essa told them the whole tale, from the moment he'd left the fortress with Wulf right up to his landing in Gipswick that morning. When he had finished, Egric and Anno were staring at him in awe, the king gazing at the candle flame. Elfgift's face was stiff with horror; Cai's expression flat, giving nothing away.

"Why did he not kill you at once?" Elfgift said. "He had men following your father and you for years. And yet you walked straight into his hall, and he did nothing?"

Essa stared down at his stew. Was that really true? All those years, moving from place to place, they had been running from Godsrule's men? And once, that summer afternoon in the beech coppice, one of them had found him.

"He said he would have killed me," he told Elfgift. "But he had lost so many men, he thought I might be useful after all. Yet I think he would kill me if he saw me again. Or he'd try to."

Elfgift smiled and suddenly looked very young. "Why?" she said. "What did you do? Godsrule always was easy to bait."

Essa shrugged. Now was not the time to tell them all that he had struck the High King, his own uncle, in the face.

"More to the point," said Egric. "Why did you see fit to ride up to Northumbria in the first place, when your duty was to come here, to me?"

Essa stared down at the table again. "We thought it would be better to go to Godsrule and see if he would send a message to Penda, ordering him not to attack. But when we got there, he would not. And I thought it might garner you some time."

Egric's cousin Anno was laughing, his shoulders shaking. "I like that," he said. "Just leave it to the children."

"I wouldn't want to be Wulf if Penda ever finds out what you did," said Egric. "He'll kill him. He has courage, that boy."

Essa shrugged. Now the dream he had shared with Wulf and Anwen seemed like a foolish game. That morning in the gully, he had been sure that anything was possible. Why had they even thought they could change the tide? No one could stop this war.

"I think you were all brave," said Elfgift quietly. "And lucky to escape alive. There aren't many can outwit my brother."

"So does this mean he's in line for the throne at Ad

Gefrin?" said Anno, looking at Cai and Egric as if Essa weren't even there.

"Yes," Essa said, angry. "What's it to you?"

Anno laughed. "Temper!" He turned to Egric and Cai. "What I mean is, you should get him married off. He's useful."

"No!" said Elfgift.

Cai was smiling. He said to Essa in British, "If you don't stop acting like a boorish fool, I'll flay you alive." He switched languages: "There's plenty of time to think of that later."

Essa felt heat flash to his face and stood up. All he wanted to do was get out of that place, away from Cai. He was about to leave, and answer for it later, when Seobert spoke. "I am humbled by you, Essa," he said in his quiet, calm voice. "I shall ride out with my men, and may God forgive us all."

Everyone stared at him, stunned. Essa felt a surge of hope, his anger forgotten.

"Egric, Anno — at dawn, rally the men and make sure all are fully armed," said Seobert. "I will ride out with you, and we shall see if they'll flock to my banner still. Essa, you shall ride with us too. We leave the following morning. And let us hope we reach the border before Penda's son. It'll be a bloody battle."

The Wolf Folk had unsheathed their claws at last.

To the border

SSA was awake before dawn, out in the stables. He was meant to be collecting a horse, but instead he found Fenrir curled up near some of the other dogs in one of the stalls by the door. He squatted down beside her, scratching her behind the ear till she woke up. With one eye open, she licked his hand. They sat there for a moment, Fenrir nudging at Essa's fingers with her nose. He remembered that day, long ago, when he had sat in the stables in the village with Meadowsweet, and Fenrir was just a puppy, so new in the world that birthing fluid still clung to her fur. Meadowsweet had known then that he was sorrowing, aching inside. And now Fenrir knew that soon they would be leaving each other.

I wish I could take you when we go. But you've come far enough with me, my honey. I can't take you to this fight. You'll just have to wait here for me till I come back.

She whined softly, licking his fingers again. She knew.

"Oi, is it you wants a horse?" Essa looked up and saw a skinny boy only about eight summers old, leaning over the stall gate. "That your hound?" he said. "She's a lovely one. Wish I had a dog like that."

Essa smiled. "Will you look after her for me while I'm at the fight? You can take her to catch a hare, if you like."

The boy nodded eagerly, staring at him in awe. "We'll catch a hare all right! She's a beauty. Do you come with me, then, and we'll find you a mount."

He was given a chestnut mare, a beautiful creature with a nice long step, and went out into the yard to wait for the others.

They rode out behind Seobert: Egric, Anno, and Essa. Anno gave Essa a quick glance up and down as he rode up, looking riled to find him there. All the way across the yard and out of the gate, Essa had a tight feeling in his chest, wondering what would happen if the men simply paid no heed to Seobert. What if the will to fight had drained out of them after weeks of waiting for his word? Seobert's face was calm, peaceful, but Egric and Anno sat stiffly in the saddle, hardly exchanging a word or a look. Essa's chestnut mare was tense beneath him. He leaned forward, rubbing gently in circles behind her ears till he felt her steady. *It's all right, my sweet.*

The air was thick with woodsmoke seeping from banked-down campfires, and trails of white mist hung low above the grass in the field. The few men he could see walking about at this time looked as if they were floating above ground like spirits.

Nobody will notice us, Essa thought. *Egric will blow the horn, and everyone will just ignore it. It's too late: we're too late. They won't fight—they've given up.*

But, in the end, Egric did not even need to blow the horn. They were only just into the first camping field when, suddenly, men came walking toward them out of the mist.

"Hey, what's to do?" someone shouted. "It's barely dawn—"

But then they saw Seobert, their king, riding among them. More men came, then more. There was no shouting, no yelling; Essa could not even tell how they all knew Seobert was there. But all the same, they came. Soon, they were surrounded by an ever-growing crowd of men, all silent: men with swords, men with daggers, men with bows on their backs, men with nothing but the scythe from the barn wall, who would be the first to fall but did not care now that their king was riding out with them. Soon Essa would be home—back in the village. His longing for Lark ached in his belly, and he knew then that if he came through this battle, he was going to swing her up into the saddle and they would ride away together.

And then someone began to cheer, and the fields around Bedricsworth god house came alive with the sound of it: a great, ragged burst of noise. They were riding to meet Penda, all the way from the coast to the western edge of Wolf Folk land.

They were going to fight.

* * *

The race back across the marshes took two whole days. Essa forced himself to concentrate on the ride so he didn't have to think of anything else. His thighs ached after so many days out of the saddle, his share of water was meager, and the food was almost as bad as he and Wulf had eaten on their great journey. He never wanted to see dried fish again. He had heard stories of armies sweeping across the land, gasping to drink the blood of their enemies as they bore down on them like flocks of dragons. The stories did not tell the half of it. They never spoke of the boredom, the waiting. But he had not ridden with so many men before — the pounding of the horses' hooves was like the beating of a great war drum, and it stirred his heart.

Gradually, the land grew more and more familiar — he began to recognize particular stands of trees, places where the marshes thinned out or spread into shallow, weed-filled ponds. Soon he could see the great earthwork stretching across the horizon, the one Cai had shown to Essa when they first arrived at the village: the Wolf Folk's westernmost border. Behind it was the village — he could not see it yet, but it was there: the hall, the smithy shed, the orchard, the grain mounds, the hounds asleep under the ash tree. He could see it all so clearly in his mind's eye it was almost as if he were really there. *I'm going home*, Essa thought. He felt tears start and hoped anyone watching would think it was only the wind making his eyes water.

After all this time, he was nearly home.

*   *   *

The men with the fastest horses reached the Wolf Folk's western defenses in the afternoon of the second day. Close up, the wall was huge, a massive bank covered in patchy grass. Essa left the chestnut mare and crawled to the top, keeping low down so he could not be seen.

Lying on his belly in the grass, he saw the green earthen village walls, coiling round the hall like a sleeping dragon. Smoke from the big fire in the hall streaked the sky with gray. And he wished more than anything that he were there with Cole and even Red at his side—and Lark. *Don't let me die before seeing Lark.*

Figures as small as ants moved about on top of the walls, and his stomach knotted—it could be Lark he was watching or, if the village were already taken, Mercian soldiers. He squinted at the horizon, watching for campfire smoke, clouds of kicked-up dust, anything that might give away the presence of the Mercian army. But there were only the great, flat marshlands and the village, and then the woods in the distance.

He ran back down and found Egric and Cai leaning against the grassy wall, talking fightcraft with some of Egric's other ring bearers. These men smirked at Essa: everyone had heard the story of his mad cross-country chase with Wulf, but he could see they were also suspicious of him. Cai did not even look at him.

"Essa, why are you in such a hurry?" said Egric. "Do you save your strength. You'll need it."

"My lord, someone should ride out to the Wixna and tell them we are here."

Egric laughed. "You, I suppose."

"I must go to the village, my lord, please!"

"Got a girl in there or something?" said one of Egric's men. The others laughed, making lewd jokes.

Essa looked desperately at Egric.

"Essa, if someone goes over there and the place has already been sacked, which it could have been, all we'll do is let the Mercians know we're here — they're sure enough hiding back in the woods. It's not worth it. I would give a lot to go myself, but I cannot. We ride out at dawn, so save your strength for something useful."

Essa looked at his father. Hild was in the village: Cai's foster sister. Surely he would go?

Cai stared at him impassively; Essa turned away. It was as if a wall had grown between the two of them — a thing woven of elf magic, like something out of a song. Even if they won the battle, Cai was a stranger now: a man who had loved just one person in all his life and cared nothing for anyone but Elfgift. Essa remembered seeing Cai bid her farewell. They had stood in the courtyard at Bedricsworth, locked together, her head on his shoulder, her hair spilling like fire down her back, as if they were the only two people in the world and everyone else was in the way.

Essa wished he could tell his father that he understood. He longed more than anything to hold Lark so. Even if it was the last time he ever saw her and he was riding to his death, then once would have been enough.

To pass the time, one of Egric's older men set up a target,

marking a cross on a willow tree with hare's blood. These men had fought many battles — some of them had even fought on the banks of the River Idle all those years before, when Redwald put King Edwin on the Northumbrian throne and when old Onela White-beard lost his right arm.

"I was younger that day than you are now, lad," said one gray-haired man with a long beard that hung down his chest in two braids. He clapped Essa cheerfully on the shoulder. "And half as good a shot, too. You'll be telling your grandchildren all about the day we kicked Penda and his Mercian dogs back west where they belong."

Essa knew they were trying to make him feel better, but the old man should have been at home, warming his bones by the fire. He should not have been sitting in the middle of a bog waiting to ride to his certain death. Essa smiled, but he could barely look the man in the eye. It was his fault they were here. His fault for not persuading Godsrule to send riders to Mercia forbidding Penda to fight and, failing that, to send fighting men to Seobert's aid. He had failed.

He collected his arrows and went to sit alone by a willow growing almost out of the side of the great wall. There was nothing to do now but wait for night to fall — and with dawn would come the fight.

He leaned back against the ridged bark, listening to the wind singing through long, trailing branches until night fell. He was in a strange space between sleep and wakefulness: he heard someone call his name — it might have been Cai — but could not make his lips form a reply. He saw bats darting from tree to tree. He was cold and wrapped his heavy cloak tighter around his shoulders, trying to seal all the gaps, but the wind's cool fingers still found a way through, chilling him to the bone. When he moved, he could feel the scab on his right-hand side pulling against his skin. He remembered Anwen bending over him in the bothy, spreading the wound with honey.

In the weak moonlight, Essa stared down at the ring on his finger: Wulf's ring. Mercian gold. *We tried so hard*, he thought, *but here we all are anyway—the Wolf Folk on one side of the border, the Mercians on the other, and the village stuck in the middle. The new moon of Eostre is on the rise, but we'll never see her fullness. We're all going to die.*

He could not let it happen.

Everything seemed so clear then: the men of the Wolf Folk had come too far for this; for weeks they had waited, despairing, as the king they loved refused to lead them into battle. Now that Seobert had finally come, riding out at the head of his clan as they tore across the marshes, they could not just sit here waiting till the Mercians chose to attack. He could not just do nothing while the village and all the people he cared for sat helplessly trapped between two armies.

He had to act—and almost at the same moment as he realized this, he felt the twist deep in his belly and a flash of joy as he flew free of his body, higher and higher, up into the night sky.

Where am I going?

He caught the sense of an owl, swooping low above the

marshes, and knew it had seen a water vole twitching down in the roots of a willow, but he did not become the owl; he went higher and higher till he could see the flatlands spreading out below him.

What am I?

There was the long line of the Wolf Folk's wall stretching out like a grass snake basking in the sun. To the east, the marshes gave way to the rolling marches of East Anglia, and then the vast, glittering sea: the path of his grandfathers, of Elfgift's people.

He was the silver serpent, the dragon, keeper of the night sky.

Higher and higher he went, swooping along on warm shelves of air, slipping through water-beaded skeins of cloud. To the west of the Wolf Folk's border, there was Wixna-land and the village, a drift of smoke rising from the roof of the hall. There was light in the smithy. The orchards were dark, Long Acre empty—the cattle had all been herded in with the goats and sheep; he could just make them out, dark shapes all clustered at one end of the corral by the stable.

The Wixna fields and meadows gave way to the woods, and beyond that to another flat expanse of glittering marshland. There, he could see it now: Penda's camp, a dark hump, and the pale cluster of tents. He remembered the saltwater tang rising gently off the old sailcloth, and the stink of the skins. Beyond the camp, the forest stretched west to the plains of the Magonsæte and the gates of Powys.

Essa remembered the British boy and his sister, and the vow he had made to himself. One way or another, he would find a way to stop Penda.

Well, if he could not stop him, he could at least give the Wolf Folk a fighting chance.

And there they were, the Mercian army, waiting hidden in the trees, just as Egric had guessed. Though he could see keenly even from a great height, he flew lower.

It was like climbing down into the grain mound at the end of summer, when almost a whole year had passed since the last harvest. In the lamplight, you'd scoop barley into your bucket and, stirring it around, see a maggot. Then another. Then the whole contents of the bucket would seem to shift as one, crawling with maggots.

The forest was full of men, seething with armed fighters. The sight of them was terrifying. Like the Wolf Folk, they had lit no fires, but Essa could just see them moving quietly among the trees. For a moment, it seemed the forest itself was shifting, moving east, like waves lapping a beach on an incoming tide. It looked as though there were almost as many men as there were trees.

He felt a thrill of cold fear.

The race was over. He had won it by a breath, getting to Bedricsworth just in time, but now Wulf was back — he must be — and the Mercians were coming. They were coming, and Egric's men were sleeping.

With a jolt, Essa sat up straight, the bark of the willow tree digging into his back. He was on his feet in a moment, running to the thicket of crabbed hawthorns in the lee of the wall where he had last seen Egric and his father. Blood pounded in his ears as he picked his way through the maze of sleeping bodies. Some men were not even trying to sleep but sat together in small groups, talking in low voices; others sat alone. He passed Seobert, kneeling with a large group of men who had flocked around him and were very quietly chanting the Lord's Prayer over and over again. When he heard that, he felt quite wild with fear for a moment, because he knew then that everyone was afraid of dying, and because their king was more like a god man than a war leader. It would take more than a few prayers to defeat an army so huge that it made their own look like a hunting party.

When he found his father and Egric, they were still awake, playing knucklestones with Anno and a couple of Egric's younger ring bearers — Essa recognized Frica, the boy who had been guarding the gate at Bedricsworth. He stared at them all for a moment, stunned. How could they be playing *knucklestones* now? Everyone looked up as he approached, and he felt the words fly out of his mouth before he had time to stop them.

"Egric, my lord, the Mercians are coming!" He knew he sounded afraid, and he felt his face grow hot with shame. Some of the younger men laughed.

"We know *that*," Frica muttered. "We're not sitting in this cursed bog for fun, are we?"

"Silence," said Egric sharply. "Essa, how do you know

this? I've men on top of the wall watching, and they've seen nothing."

"Well, no," Essa said. "They're in the woods, we couldn't see them from here, but—"

"How do you know, then?" said Egric. "I *told* you not to ride to the village, Essa—"

"I didn't, I—I just know they're coming. You must believe me."

Cai laid down his stones then and stared at Essa.

Anno and most of the younger men were laughing now. "I think the lad's had a night terror," said Anno. "Get back to sleep, boy; you'll give everyone the shakes—"

"Be quiet, Anno," said Cai. He turned to Essa and spoke in British. "Do not speak of it to the men, because they are all Christians, but did you leave your body to know this?"

Essa nodded, glancing at Egric, who was staring at Cai in disbelief.

"Listen to him, Egric," Cai said. "It does not matter how he knows it. Essa, what did you see?"

Essa was so shocked to hear Cai speaking out for him that it took him a moment to reply. "Men, all in the forest," he said at last. "More men than there are leaves on that willow tree. On all those trees. And they're coming this way."

"But it's the middle of the night," Anno said quickly. "They won't make their move till dawn. That's if Essa isn't just dreaming."

"He is not," said Cai. "Take my word for it." Anno looked

ready to laugh again, and so did the younger men, but then a look passed between him and Cai, and Anno turned to the younger ones and said, "Do you stow your talk and listen."

Egric's eyes narrowed. "But Essa, did you not say Penda would hold his hand till Wulf returned with Eiludd Powys's daughter? How long is it since you left Ad Gefrin? Eight nights? Surely they can't have ridden down in that time — and, Lord knows, it's hard to change horses in Elmet and Lindsay. It's mostly British there, and they move about like smoke."

"Mostly, but not all," Cai said. "Wulf's done that journey more than a few times — he knows where to go. And if Essa came down the coast with a trader boat, what was to stop Wulf from doing the same? If Essa says the army's on the move, I counsel you to listen. Wulf's back under Penda's wing, and he's got Powys's daughter with him — Penda's about to ride out, Egric, mark my words." He caught Egric's eye. They looked at each other for a moment, then Egric nodded slowly.

"There's nothing to say Penda won't attack before dawn," Egric said. "It's a fool's trick unless you want to break the legs of half your horses, but they must know we're here, and they will want to take us by surprise. They must gather in their shield walls first, though — and with so many men, it won't be a quick task. Essa, I'll only ask you one last time: are you sure?"

"Yes," he said, heart pounding, wishing it were not true.

His spirit animal had shown him, though, and he could not change that.

"Shall we make our shield wall, too, my lord?" said one of the younger men.

Egric laughed. "No," he said. "We're going to ride like berserkers across the marsh and spear the bastards full of holes before they know what's hit them — and hope we don't lose half our horses in doing it."

Word spread quickly through the camp.

"It's nothing more than an ambush," said the old man Essa had been shooting targets with the night before. "Egric's breaking all the fight rules. What's he thinking of, to have no shield wall, and nothing more than a crazy ride across the marsh?"

Essa said nothing. Egric was right: they had no choice but to catch Penda's battle hordes unawares. The men fell quiet as Egric walked by, and he clapped Essa on the shoulder, saying softly, "Do you ride by me, Aesc, since were it not for you, Seobert would still be praying to God."

"Me?" Essa said. "It's not my place, lord. I should be marching behind with the other boys."

Egric smiled. "You still have not learned to follow my word, have you, Aesc, son of Cai? If I wanted you on foot with Frica and the others, I should tell you so. But since I do not, do you take up a shield and ride with me and your father."

At least I'll be able to see the Mercians coming, Essa thought.

Quickly and quietly, the men got to their feet, rousing their companions from sleep, shrugging their shoulders up and down to keep out the cold and loosen cramped limbs.

Leather pouches of boiled woad-flower paste were passed from man to man. The paste was itchy where it dried in stripes on Essa's face, but when dawn finally came it would mark him out as Wolf Folk, and he would not be killed by his own side. *If I get as far as that,* he thought, and then had to busy himself with fitting the saddle on the chestnut mare. Everyone was doing something—tightening sword belts, mounting up, licking the feathered flight of their first arrow so that it would slice through the air straight and true. Someone handed Essa a drink, but the honey wine tasted sour, and he could not swallow it.

He took his place beside Egric, hefting the shield across his back. The chestnut flinched as she felt it brush her withers, and he leaned forward and whispered, "Calm, my honey, calm," till she stood quietly.

"Here, take these." Cai was standing beside Melyor, and she nuzzled at his ear as he passed Essa three throwing spears, making sure the chestnut saw them. Cai patted the mare's neck and spoke to her in British, saying, "There, my swift one. See, the cub is holding spears, so do not panic when you see them fly."

Essa clutched the throwing spears, fingering the leather straps that marked the balance points. Cai looked up at him, and Essa thought he saw the briefest hint of a smile, but the next moment his father had turned away and was mounting up, taking a shield passed to him by the boy Frica.

Frica raised an eyebrow as he walked past Essa to take his orders from Egric.

"Not out the back with the rest of Egric's boys, chucking stones till you drop, then?" he said quietly. "I thought not. Well, doubtless you'll bleed just as hard when Penda's men get you."

"Don't fear; I'm sure I will," Essa replied, and stared straight ahead at the earth wall, set on looking unafraid till Frica had gone, at least. He pictured Wulf riding in the front line, too, wearing the Mercian boar crest beside his father. Would they see each other? Would he have to fight Wulf?

Essa had expected Seobert or Egric to make a blood-stirring speech, like kings did in songs, but everyone had been ordered to keep quiet, and there was no rousing battle cry. Seobert was alone just a few steps ahead, astride his royal white mare. He carried nothing but a pale holly staff, and Essa could hear Egric trying to persuade him to bear a weapon.

"We're outnumbered by hordes, and you carry nothing but a staff, like one of our old spirit men," Egric hissed. "It's pure folly. You'll be killed, and once the men see that, the battle's as good as lost. Seobert, my lord, for God's sake, if Penda wins this, it's the end of the Wolf Folk. Carry a spear!"

Seobert turned his horse around to face the men. He had nothing but the holly staff, not even a shield. He would not last the first charge.

"If God is on our side," he said, "Penda will be defeated, and the Wolf Folk shall ride home in victory."

Essa turned to his father. "What are we going to do? He will be the first to die." His face was sore where the blue paint had dried in thick stripes across his cheeks. He wanted to scrape it all off, but knew he could not.

Cai shrugged. "It takes more than one king to win or lose a battle."

But Essa was not so sure. He had seen the change in the men; he remembered them sitting disconsolately by their campfires when he had first arrived at Bedricsworth, and the cheering when Seobert had ridden out among them.

This was their only chance, and the king was riding out with nothing but a bough of holly.

When the order came, he hardly heard it, and it was only when the chestnut mare panicked and twisted beneath him that he saw that everyone was moving. He felt a jolt of fear: he had to keep his wits sharp and clear; Eostre's slender new moon was behind a cloud, and he could hardly see to ride. If he made a mistake now and the chestnut put her foot in a hole, he'd be dead, trampled by those coming from behind.

He leaned forward, laying his hand on the chestnut's neck to soothe her, and started riding properly, steering with his thighs, so she felt he was in charge, that she was safe with him. He knew he should be afraid, but somehow he was not. It was thrilling to be riding at the head of all these men, at the side of Seobert and Egric and his father. He could just see the king, a length ahead of everyone else, his dark cloak streaming out behind him, the pale holly branch held high.

The air rang with the sound of horses' hooves pounding the earth, splashing marsh water, spraying great showers of mud. *We must look like an army of ghosts*, Essa thought, *riding silently through the night with no horn blowing, no harsh battle cries rising like crow song.* The wind rushed at him, whipping his hair around his head; his hands were frozen, but after a while he did not notice even that.

They rode past the village, and he saw people standing on the walls, leaning over the fence, watching the ghost army thundering by. They passed so quickly he could not tell who was there, but he hoped they'd seen him, so that everyone knew he was safe. He felt ashamed that he had gone to Powys without saying good-bye to Hild. He knew how worried she must be, and he wished she could see him now, riding into battle beside Cai and Egric.

The wood shore was getting closer and closer. Then, suddenly, Essa saw men riding toward him — a ragged group of Mercian soldiers. And now that it was finally happening, he could hardly believe it.

It was time.

Steering with his knees, he gripped the shield handle with his left hand, holding the throwing spears in place with his thumb. He had only three, and no boy to come running up and pass him a stabbing spear, as Frica would do for Egric. Suddenly, the pearly gray sky was dark with arrows and stones as the Wolf Folk bowmen and boys with slingshots let their missiles fly and the Mercians returned the gift. Ahead of Essa, Seobert rode on and on, the God King of the Wolf Folk. Arrow after arrow flew down, and spear after spear, and men dropped back like dead moths shaken out of a winter tunic. But Seobert was never hit, either by a stray Wolf Folk arrow or the hard iron tip of a Mercian spear. It seemed as if he had been touched by God, that he was saved, protected in some way, for he rode so fast that none of the Mercians could get near him.

Suddenly, the man next to Essa was gone. Gasping, he turned back, saw a body mashed into the grass, a horse running loose through the charging men. *We're only a few compared with the Mercians,* he thought. *And that's one down already.* He looked around for Cai and Egric but could not see them. He couldn't even see Seobert now, either—just Mercians thundering toward him. Then, suddenly, they were in among the trees, and it took all the skill he had to ride a path through them.

Somewhere, he heard voices shouting and heard Egric yell, "Watch out for the shield wall—we shall put them in fear of their Maker yet!"

Through the rain of arrows, stones, and spears, Essa saw a hard-packed wall of men edging out from the wood shore, their shields round and pale in the thin light. He wished he was marching with comrades on all sides, but he had only the chestnut mare for company. He could not see Cai anywhere.

"Ride on! Ride on!" Egric's voice rang out again, and

Essa joined the throng of Wolf Folk horsemen thundering by the Mercian shield wall, screaming and jabbing at the air with their spears. But the Mercians came on without stopping, and the storm of arrows from behind them thickened. The air rang with the cries of the dying. Was it true what they said, that a dead man in a shield wall would not even fall, so close did they march?

Then, out of nowhere, a Mercian on horseback charged toward Essa with a spear. The pointed head shot past, missing him by a finger's width. Hardly thinking, he snatched the shaft out of the air and threw the spear back with all his strength. He just caught a glimpse of the horseman's twisted face before he fell in a shower of blood. Mercian yellow paint across his cheeks made him look catlike — and he had a brown birthmark in the shape of a bean on his forehead. His wide-open eyes were green, flecked with amber lights. Essa knew dawn must have broken, because he could see the first person he had killed.

He looked around again for Cai, but all he saw were the flailing limbs and screaming faces of strangers. The hot stink of fresh blood never left him, and he felt it drying on his face with the blue paint: the blood of strangers.

Essa thanked God the chestnut had been trained so well. She was like a rock beneath him and moved at the slightest touch — he hardly had to think. It was as if they were one creature. It was the next best thing to riding Melyor. But where was she? Melyor and Cai — he hadn't seen them for a long while.

Gasping for breath, he looked around and saw that he was surrounded by men with yellow faces.

The village. He must get to the village. Letting out a fierce yell, he turned the chestnut and set her through the trees, letting fly his ashen spears one by one. A Mercian throwing spear crashed to the ground just beside him, and he felt a jolt of pain in his left shoulder, but he would get to the village; nothing could stop him.

Suddenly, he was out of the trees, and he could see the village gate. He saw with horror that the gate had been breached — a dark hole yawned in the wall where it had once been, and everywhere he looked, he could see men with yellow faces. He dug his heels into the chestnut's sides. The horse raised her head and gave an unearthly scream, bucking so hard that Essa could barely keep to his saddle as he set her at the village wall.

My good girl, my honey — you can do this for me, I know you can.

He had to get in there. They turned, spattering mud and grass, and Essa leaned low over the chestnut's neck as she galloped up and over the village wall, scattering the men cutting and hacking at each other in the courtyard. The familiarity of the place was a shock.

Was that Red he could see by the weaving shed, his face twisted with rage, shoving a spear into someone's guts? Essa screamed out his name, but when he next looked, Red was gone. He saw no other face he knew — were they all dead? His stomach clenched. His sleeve was sticking to his arm, and he felt dizzy. He couldn't hold on. He jerked his feet out of the stirrups and rolled out of the way just as the chestnut lurched sideways and fell over, kicking up a cloud of dust. Where was his shield? The cross strap must have broken. A spear protruded from the side of her neck, dark and black like a long claw. One of her back legs lay bent at a grotesque angle, broken.

I'm sorry.

Essa just had time to see the fear in his horse's eyes before he drew the Silver Serpent and plunged her into the flesh next to the spear. Blood spurted up into his face. He choked with a rush of tears that mingled with the congealing blood and turned around just in time to rip the sword from the horse's neck and plunge it into the guts of a man who was running toward him with a double-headed ax. Essa did not remember his face, but he would never forget the fear in the eyes of his horse as she lay dying. Where was everyone?

He scrambled toward the gate and had to run over the broken door, torn from its hinges and pushed inside by the Mercians. His fingers were numb. The wooden planks bucked and cracked beneath his feet before he hit the ground again and felt himself hauled backward by an arm around his neck, choking him.

So this was dying. He saw a flash of polished iron and whipped the knife from the scabbard at his belt. He still had the bone-handled knife—Wulf's knife. Strange how cold his left hand felt—he could hardly grip the handle—

and the arm too except at the top, just under his shoulder, where it felt as if he had leaned against a scalding pan drawn out of the fire. He went to plunge the knife backward, into the soft parts of whoever had him by the neck, when a hand closed around his wrist. He was pushed around to face Red, who let him go, breathing heavily as he stepped back. One eye was blackened and swollen, and his face was redder than ever, beaded with sweat.

"Essa!" They threw their arms around each other, holding on so tight that Essa could barely breathe.

"Where is everyone?" He stared around but could see only strangers.

"In the weaving shed and — Essa, quick! Cole's just been hit."

They ran across the courtyard, cutting and thrusting as they went, whirling and running as if they were in some strange dance. There was blood everywhere. Essa could hardly see, but he caught up with Red just as Cole came running out of the weaving shed with his cloak on fire. Essa barely knew him; his face was knotted with rage and agony. Essa tore the cloak from Cole's shoulders and threw it to the ground. Flames leaped up around his legs as he stamped out the fire.

"Cole, Cole!" His voice did not sound like his own.

"Essa!" When they hugged, Essa came away soaked in Cole's blood. "They're torching it!" Cole shouted. "Most of the women are in there with the children, and someone's just torched the thatch. Quick!"

"Where's Lark?" Hope leaped in Essa's chest — maybe she was in there, and he could save her.

"Don't know. She was up on the wall with Ariulf and the other archers — haven't seen her for ages —"

The weaving-shed door burst open, belching flame. Cole fell down beside him, and Essa went to kneel at his side, but Red grabbed the back of his tunic. "It's no use; he's dead — he took a sword in the belly."

Blinded by tears and smoke, Essa followed Red into the weaving shed. The great looms were burning as they leaned against the wooden walls, half-finished cloth in flames. He heard screaming and saw women and children huddled up on the platform where they stored raw wool in sacks. Suddenly, Red was no longer beside him — someone up on the platform screamed Essa's name, and he whirled around to find a Mercian swinging a blood-soaked sword. His hand flashed to the knife at his belt and it flew from his fingers, like a deadly silver bird. The Mercian fell, howling, the knife sticking from his right eye. Then Red was on his feet again, a long cut behind his ear spilling blood down his neck. He reached up to take a child passed down to him from the platform. Essa, understanding, turned and fought at Red's back as the women ran out the side door, brandishing knives and swords, hurrying the children out toward the grain mounds. He could still see Cole lying in the doorway, his silvery-pale hair soaked in blood, his head twisted at an odd angle. A deep, animal rage filled Essa's body, and a red mist clouded his sight. Someone ran at him — he killed the man instantly, his sword arm moving so fast that the blade blurred before his eyes. The Silver Serpent was thirsty, and he let her drink.

He could hear the women and children screaming from outside and knew someone must have seen them making for the orchard. Flames leaped around his feet and he ran through them, feeling nothing, out into the courtyard. The women were shrieking, their faces twisted with fear and fury, shielding the children with their bodies as they fended off the yellow-faced Mercian soldiers, some stabbing at them with long spears, others throwing knives, stones, even an old shoe. Essa leaped forward, hacking and slashing.

"Essa, behind you!" screamed Starling, and he turned, blinded by flying mud as a Mercian on horseback thundered across the yard, dark hair flying out beneath a boar-crested helmet.

"Fall back, for the Lady's sake," said the rider to the warriors. "They're just women and brats!"

It was Wulf. Essa lowered his sword. Wulf pushed back his helmet. They stared at each other a moment, then Wulf looked away.

"Fall back," he said again. "The Wolves are retreating. Follow them, and get out of here."

And then he was gone, riding through the gateway and away.

Essa glanced back over his shoulders — Starling and the other women were running toward the grain mounds, hurrying the children before them. "Essa, come on!"

shouted Starling. "Come with us! We can get out by the orchard!"

But where was Hild? Where was Lark? He heard himself say, "No—do you run, Starling. I'll watch your back."

The courtyard was still seething with yellow-faced men on horseback—most of them were following Wulf, but not all. Three were riding toward Essa, two swinging axes, one a sword. And then he caught a flash of white-blond hair—a girl scrambling up the wall to escape two more horsemen riding toward her, laughing and jeering. She was about to be crushed beneath the horses' hooves. *Lark*.

Time seemed to slow down. The three men were nearly upon him—his sword arm was heavy; he could not lift it—it was like being trapped in a bad dream. Then he saw what he had to do—the Mercians might want to kill him, but their horses did not care whether he lived or died.

He felt the tug in the pit of his stomach and wondered if he had died without feeling it and that was why his spirit was leaving his body. But he knew he would not be so lucky. He closed his eyes. If he died here, it wouldn't be a painless journey to the Land of Mist, it would be—

And then Essa knew how it felt to have a creature riding on his back, to be surrounded by screaming men and sharp, biting metal.

He was not just one horse but many. Penda's horse folk had not forgotten the days when their kind ran free in herds across wide grassy plains, before they were taught to carry these little two-legged beasts.

Run free again. Run free.

Essa sank to his knees and looked up just in time to see an ax swing past his head—but then the Mercian dropped it, screaming a curse as his horse reared up on her back legs. Almost as one creature, every horse in the village bucked and thundered toward the gate, heedless of the men riding them.

And then they were gone. When he turned to look, so had Starling and the children. They had escaped. *Thank God,* he told himself wearily, feeling hot tears spring to his eyes. *Thank God.*

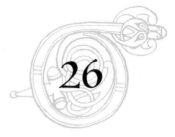

26

WHEN Essa woke, his back and neck and the backs of his legs were boiling hot, the rest of him cold. He sat up, aching all over, and saw it was because he was lying just yards from the burning remains of the weaving hall. He watched for a moment. The roof had fallen in, and a thick black column of smoke stained the sky. It was Cole's funeral pyre. *Cole, Cole.* He could not believe Cole was dead. It could not be true. Where was Red? Had he escaped with Starling and the others? And what about Hild and Ariulf?

And Lark . . .

The light had changed. He got to his feet, loosely gripping the handle of his sword. The courtyard was nearly empty now, but he could still hear screaming, metal clashing on metal. The battle had moved on, the village left behind. Broken bodies littered the ground; sightless eyes stared up at the sky. It was a beautiful day: a clear, unblemished blue spring sky arching over the world.

He found Egric and Hild lying under the ash tree like a pair of lovers, his body curled around hers, his arms crossed protectively across her chest. Essa's heart ached at the sight of her; he knelt down beside them just to make sure, but her eyes were wide open and a trickle of blood had set as it seeped from the corner of her mouth.

No, Essa. This won't do, will it? He remembered her wrapping a shawl around his shoulders, getting up and following her toward the stables. She had been his true mother, and she was dead. He stared down at the ring on his middle finger — Wulf's ring, but Egric's had been there first. His hands were smeared with blood, but the gold band still shone, fire of the sea. He was a free man now. He need not wear anyone's ring.

He got to his feet, going from corpse to corpse, looking for faces he knew, wondering if this would make it all seem more real.

He found his father by the forge, lying in the shadow cast by the open door. He could see the ruin within, where Mercians and Wolf Folk alike had raided it for every last weapon, every last piece of pig iron that could be used to smash a man's brains out.

Cai lay on his side. Essa sat on the floor next to him and saw that his father was still breathing, gasping for breath. His tunic was soaked in blood.

"*Elfgift.*" The word came out in a whisper, the sigh of wind moving through trees.

"No, it's me. It's Essa."

"*Hold me, Elfgift.*" Cai turned his face toward him. His eyes were wide and glowing with a feverish light. The blood on the front of his tunic was nearly black, and Essa knew he would die, because it was heart blood. Cai spoke in their own language, and it sounded like water falling over rocks. He was heavier than Essa expected but hardly made a sound as Essa lifted his father's head and shoulders, letting them rest in his lap. He leaned back against the forge door and felt the wood warm against his back. He stared across the courtyard at the smoke and ash billowing from the roof of the weaving shed.

"*Elfgift, I tried to keep—*"

Essa looked down. The fierce brightness in Cai's eyes was dimming. His hand moved, reaching for something.

"*Elfgift.*"

Essa half expected to look up and see her standing there, but of course she was not. Instead he let Cai's fingers close around his hand.

It took Cai a long time to die, longer than Essa had expected, after Cole had gone so quickly. He leaned against the forge door watching the weaving hall burn to the ground as the sun sank lower and lower until it rested above the horizon, a fat, orange ball. Cole was in there, burning too. At last Cai's chest stopped moving, and his body lay still across Essa's lap. He did not move even then. His left arm was still numb, and Cai was heavy. It was too hard. He was tired. Everywhere he looked, there were broken bodies lying like woollen dolls dropped by children. Something reminded him of the autumn. It was the smell of blood that rose above the village when they slaughtered animals to salt their meat for winter. He thought for a moment that he might be sick, but in the end nothing came up but a choking cough. A moving shadow brought relief from the fading heat, and he closed his eyes. It would be good to sleep again now. He had not slept at all last night, leaning against that tree, waiting for morning.

"Essa, do you wake up. Don't close your eyes." Her face was blackened with soot, smudged with tears, and there was a long, purple bruise on her jaw. Dirty white-blond hair had stuck to her forehead, matted with dried blood. She was holding something in the crook of one arm — it looked like a bundle of cloth. She lifted a dusty wooden cup to his lips, and he saw tooled leather archer's braces strapped to her forearms. So Lark had been fighting too, like a shield maiden in one of the old songs.

"Cole's dead," Essa said, and looked down at Cai, lying still in his lap. Tears spilled down his face, dripping off his chin.

"I know," Lark said. "I know. Granfer and Ma, too." She sounded strangely calm, and he knew that, like him, she did not really believe it had happened.

How could Onela be dead? Essa remembered the old man sitting with him in the stables, guarding him from an angry ghost. He was so kind, and he had lived so long. It did not seem fair his life should have been snatched away by a Mercian spear.

He took the cup and swallowed, but most of the water dribbled down his chin. He let it trickle coolly down his neck, into his tunic, down his belly. He threw the cup to the side and reached for Lark, pulling her close. Cai's sightless eyes looked up at their embrace. Her hair smelled not of lavender, but of sweat and blood.

The bundle in her arms seemed to twitch, but he hardly noticed. They broke apart; she shifted the parcel of cloth so that it rested on her hip, then helped him move Cai so that he lay on the ground. Essa stood up, his arm tight around her shoulders. The bundle moved again.

"Lark, what is it? What are you holding?"

She stared at him for a moment, shocked, as if she had forgotten about it. "Oh!" She folded back a corner of the bloodstained cloth.

It was a child. Lark was holding a baby—no more than a few weeks old, and fast asleep.

Essa stared at her, not understanding. Lark, standing right next to him after all this time longing for her, and she was holding a baby.

"She's all I found," Lark whispered. "The only one left."

They stood gazing down at the baby as one of her tiny hands made a fist. Essa felt cold with horror that Lark had found no one else alive, but at the same time happy that this small creature had survived. He tried to cast his mind back to the village before he'd left. Which of the girls had been with child? He couldn't remember. Not Starling again? No. Who else?

"She's Hild's," Lark whispered at last. "Essa . . ."

He reached down and gently nudged the cloth away from the child's face with a fingertip. Her mouth worked quietly as she slept. Her eyelids were like the wings of a pale butterfly newly hatched, laced with a tracing of delicate blue veins.

"Hild and Egric," he said.

Lark nodded, smiling. "I don't know how you didn't see it," she said. "Six months gone she was, when you left. All the women knew, but it's funny, when Hild told the men, some of them hadn't guessed. I've never seen Ariulf look so shocked. She'd been trying to tell you."

"Six months gone," Essa repeated, staring down at the child.

"She came early, almost a whole moon early, and we didn't think she'd live, but she did," Lark said. "Hild wanted to show her to you when you got back."

"Only I didn't come back."

"But you did. You did."

"Where is everyone?" said Essa at last. "They're not all—"

She shook her head. "Most of them got out. We were up on the wall this morning, and we saw you all riding past, so we hid the children and the old ones in the weaving shed. Apart from Granfer. He wouldn't hide—he said if he had to go, he'd rather it was a fight that took him than a fever. We couldn't get out, you see, because the Mercians were all in the woods. But once we saw them all ride out, we decided to make a run for it and get away from here till they'd gone. We nearly didn't make it, see, but then one of the Mercians told them all to get gone, and then all their horses just went berserk. I've never seen anything like it — they all just ran mad, and nobody could do anything with them. It was as if they were all cursed. They're all away now."

Despite everything, Essa felt a tug of happiness. They were safe; most of them were safe. It hadn't all been for nothing. "What about Red?" he said, his voice cracking. "And Ariulf?"

Lark nodded. "They got out too, but they were here till the end. Ariulf tried to force me to go with them, but I cut away and came back. And I found her." She looked down at the bundle. "They'd hid her in the linen trunk but she was crying, and I heard. Thought you might be in here somewhere, too."

Essa took her hand. "You're a fool," he said. "Ariulf shouldn't've let you come back."

She shrugged. "He had no choice. Your father wouldn't leave, either, so I knew you were here. He said he'd not go without you."

Essa looked down at him and knelt one last time at Cai's side. If you looked past the blood, he could have just been sleeping. He looked so young.

They walked hand in hand around the village but found only corpses.

"We must get away," Essa said finally. "There's no one here we can help. The Mercians'll come back, and they'll kill you and me too if they find us."

"But how are we going to—" Lark stopped, gesturing around at their ruined home, at the still-smoldering thatch of the smithy, at the blackened timbers of the weaving hall, at the dead. "We've got to bury them properly."

"How can we? Lark, we must go! The Mercians'll come back through here when they've—" How far were Penda's men going to get? he wondered. Would they fight their way to the coast, as Penda had promised? Would there be anything of the Wolf Folk left? He had to get back to Bedricsworth. He owed Elfgift the news of Cai's death. He reached out, drew Lark close. "The Mercians'll come back. They'll bury everyone properly. They've got to clear the place up, or it'll be no use to them."

He hoped they were all together, the dead: his father, Hild, Onela, Egric, Cole. There were so many of them. He hoped they were going to the same place, not having to leave each other behind as they had left the living, with the Christians going to heaven or hell, and everyone else to the Hall of Warriors. *It's all the same place*, he told himself. *It's all the same.* But even so, it would be a long journey through the Land of Mist, across the great expanses of the night, and it would be better to go with friends.

Then Lark said quietly, "We're never coming back, are we?" The baby was wailing now, and Essa just stood there for a moment, his arm around Lark's shoulders, not knowing what to say, how to comfort either of them. She was right: her brother was dead, her mother, her grandfather. Hild. How could they stay now? What was there to stay for? Most of the others were all right — Red, Starling, Ariulf, Helith — they would live to rebuild the village, but Essa knew he could not do it with them.

Life would not be so different here — the boys of the Wixna would wear Penda's rings now, that was all, and they would fight for him instead of the Wolf Folk when the time came. But Essa's place with the Wixna had died with Hild. He was no longer the boy who had left the village that night, sneaking across the marshes to Penda's camp on Egric's orders. He was an atheling of the house of Ad Gefrin, and there was no need to follow orders anymore.

Lark's eyes were dry, but she was shaking like someone with the palsy. He held out a hand smeared with blood, Cai's blood, and saw that he was shaking too; he could not keep his fingers still. It would have been easier if she were crying, wailing like the baby. Did she know about him? he wondered. Did she know the truth — that Elfgift would be waiting at Bedricsworth?

Lark shifted the bundle in her arms, "Shhh," she said. "Shhh." She turned to Essa. "Where are we going?"

Essa hesitated. Did she know? "We should find the others first," he said. "Let them know we're safe." He paused, not knowing how he'd bear it if she'd known all along, too. "And after that, we'll go to my mother."

But Lark just stared at him. "*What?* But your mother's—Essa, what are you talking about?"

She had not known, then. Relief coursed through him. It was just Hild, and she'd kept his secret all these years. He wished he could see her one last time. He wished he were nine years old again, sitting in the stable with her, watching Meadowsweet feed the new pups.

"Listen," he said, "and I'll tell you."

They found a horse in the orchard, standing with one leg dangling free of the ground, broken. Essa had to kill it. Lark burst into tears then, as if the dying horse were worse than anything else they'd seen. Essa remembered killing his own horse, and how that still seemed more real, more dreadful than any of the other things he had done that day.

Then they heard a horse whickering from behind the grain mounds. It was Melyor, calm the moment she saw him. She came walking out toward them, the saddle hanging loose from her side.

"Melyor," said Essa. He pulled Lark to his side, holding her tight. "Oh, Melyor." He remembered finding Melyor's stall empty that morning, long ago, wondering if he would ever see her again. The baby stopped crying, and in the sudden quiet, Lark smiled. "You're bleeding all over me," she said. "Your shoulder."

But Essa did not hear. Not letting go of her hand, he went and shifted the saddle so it sat true on Melyor's back. Lark tightened the straps, and he handed her up into the saddle as she carefully cradled the child, Hild's little daughter. Once they were safe, he got up behind them.

It was time to go. Time to leave, go to Elfgift. There was so much he had to tell her. He leaned forward, breathing in the scent of Lark's hair, drinking in the warmth of her body as she sat before him, holding the sleeping baby close to her breast.

He was free again now, as he had been with Cai when he was a child. There was nothing but the sky above them.

The earth was theirs.

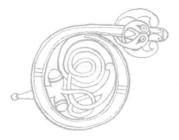

Historical note

BRITAIN as we know it would be almost unrecognizable to Essa: there were no such places as England, Scotland, Northern Ireland, and Wales, just a collection of much smaller warring tribes or kingdoms. There is endless argument about the people who lived there—had all the native British been killed or pushed into the western hills by invading Anglo-Saxon tribes from mainland Europe, or was there a more gradual settlement? To this day, no one knows for sure, but I think there was probably a mixture of invasion and more peaceful immigration. Maybe it depended on what the harvest had been like and how much food there was to go around. Today, at such a great distance from Britain as it was then, it is hard to know precisely what happened and when, and so I have had to make a few guesses about the exact years in which Cai might have left Essa with the Wixna, and when Mercia marched on the Wolf Clan.

In the year AD 731, about a hundred years after *Bloodline* is set, a monk named Bede finished writing the first-ever history of the English, a sign that the tribes in part of Britain were starting to see themselves as one kingdom, united by Christianity. Bede describes how King Penda's Mercian warriors attacked East Anglia, whose king rode into battle armed only with his faith in God. It's worth remembering, though, that there were gaps in Bede's knowledge, so we can't trust everything he says—and history is always colored by the opinions of the person writing it. Penda is not the only character in *Bloodline* to have made his way into recorded history—others did, too, although a few names have been changed. Some Anglo-Saxon names seem to have had literal meanings, and so I have translated a handful of them (badly, no doubt!) into modern English. Elfgift, from Ælfgifu, is an example, and hopefully these translations help to create a sense of what Essa's world was like.

When the last Roman legions left Britain in about AD 410, most people were Christian, but because the incoming Angles, Saxons, Jutes, and other tribes could not write about what they believed in, we don't know much about how they saw the world. The names of a few gods and goddesses survive in the days of the week—Tiw's Day, Woden's Day, Thor's Day, and Freyja's Day. It's likely that people whose lives were ruled by sun, rain, and harvest worshipped the earth itself, sure that the animals, trees, and streams around them were deeply connected to the spirit world: the realm of the elvish. Similar beliefs are still held in many corners of the world from Russia to the Amazon, where spirit men and women are known as shamans. Many of these ancient traditions lived on in Britain long after Christianity had taken hold again — Essa has his serpent spirit guide, and until relatively recently people believed that the witch had her familiar: an animal spirit in the shape of a cat or perhaps a bird who would do her bidding.

There are places in Essa's story that still exist, much changed, to this day. The once-great hall at Ad Gefrin is long gone, but if you visit Northumbria and hike to the top of Yeavering Bell, you'll look out on the hills patrolled by Godsway and his brother the Fox. Bedricsworth monastery is now buried under the cathedral town of Bury St. Edmunds, and there must have been many small tribes like the Wixna who had the bad luck to find themselves settled in a kind of no-man's-land between bigger, warring clans like the Mercians and the Wolf Folk. (The East Anglian royal family were known as the "wuffings," which is believed to translate as something like "little wolves.")

A lot has changed, but out in the countryside you might find a place where the sound of the highway has faded and there are no houses in view, no electricity poles, no cars — a place where the grass is long and the sky is high and wide above you. These places are rare and getting harder to find, but it's here that we're closest to the past.

Acknowledgments

MY GRATEFUL thanks to all at Felicity Bryan and Walker, especially Catherine Clarke, Denise Johnstone-Burt, Chris Kloet, Ellen Holgate, and Claire Elliot; to Dr. David Hill and Helen Caffrey for their historical expertise; to Clare Purcell for sharing her horse knowledge with me; and to Sam and Karen Llewellyn for their encouragement. I would also like to thank Kim Siddorn, for his excellent advice about Anglo-Saxon fight craft, and Jeanne Feasey, who suggested the historical bit was best. *Bloodline* would have been very different were it not for a truly brilliant work of British history by Rowland Parker, *The Common Stream*, which showed me how much the story of the island has been shaped by people who left barely anything behind but the changes wrought on the land by their spades. Needless to say, though, any mistakes are entirely my own fault. Thanks are due as well to my erstwhile colleagues — particularly Marion, Elv, and Amanda — for all their support, and to Willie, James, Mart, and Sophie for putting up with me the rest of the time.